THE CONVOY COMMODORE

The CONVOY COMMODORE

Philip McCutchan

St. Martin's Press
New York

Library of Congress Cataloging in Publication Data

McCutchan, Philip, 1920–
    The convoy commodore.

    1. World War, 1939–1945—Fiction.   2. Great
Britain—History, Naval—20th century—Fiction.
I. Title.
PR6063.A167C6 1987   823'.914   86-24833
ISBN 0-312-00116-9
First published in Great Britain by George Weidenfeld & Nicolson
Limited.

10 9 8 7 6 5 4 3 2

THE CONVOY COMMODORE

ONE

The weather was cold, very unseasonable for early August, but the North Atlantic was as ever unpredictable. The Commodore, on the bridge of the former Mediterranean-Australia liner *Ardara*, wore his bridge coat, the shoulder-straps carrying the thick gold bar surmounted by the crossed-triangle 'curl' of the Royal Naval Reserve, hands clasped behind a broad back as he scanned the convoy, watching the ships astern and on either beam. They formed a great spread of bottoms mainly in ballast out of UK ports for a troop and war materials pick-up in Halifax, Nova Scotia, currently on the starboard leg of the zig-zag and some of them having trouble with their station-keeping.

The Commodore glanced aside as the *Ardara's* master, Captain Arthur Hampton, joined him at the bridge screen. 'Damn big target,' he remarked.

'It is, sir. We've been lucky – so far.'

Mason Kemp grinned. 'Don't tempt fate! Homeward bound . . . that's when it's more likely to come, when we're laden. I doubt if we'll be having much luck then, somehow. That's the way things go.'

Hampton nodded and turned away from the Commodore to pace his wide bridge wing. This OB convoy, which would turn into an HX convoy on the homeward route from Halifax, was the biggest ocean lift in terms both of ship numbers and the size of many individual ships that he had so far sailed in – no less than five liners, average 23,000 tons displacement apiece, liners that in pre-war days had sailed to Australia and South Africa, India and South America and the Far East; four deep-

1

draught tankers of around 17,000 tons which would detach once the convoy was past 40 degrees west longitude to head for Galveston on the Gulf of Mexico to take on their potentially lethal liquid cargoes; a dozen sizeable dry-cargo vessels on hire contracts from such companies as the Port Line, Clan Line, Union Castle and British India, together with eighteen smaller ships, tramps in peacetime mostly, that would load to their marks in Halifax with all manner of humdrum cargoes that would help to sustain life in war-torn, besieged Britain. The Battle of the Atlantic had begun only three months before; none of the men who sailed beneath leaden skies this particular morning had any notion of how long that battle against U-boats and aircraft and surface raiders was destined to last, no idea of the scale of the sinkings that were to come.

They had all, or nearly all, been in action before; some of them in the last lot, the 1914–18 war, as well as since September 1939. It was little more than a year since the period of the phoney war had ended with the threat of invasion following Dunkirk, and then the airborne Battle of Britain, but the months of continual sea-keeping had taken their toll of men and men's endurance and they felt as though they had been at war for a decade. Peace forgotten, war had already become a way of life. Not for the merchant ships alone: the men of the warship escorts had done their share and more, the destroyers and corvettes, always too few in number and driven to the limit, bringing biting cold and wet and extreme discomfort to their ships' companies as so often in the winter storms they rode gigantic waves that could make life aboard even the *Queen Mary* into a time of desolation. The North Atlantic could be hell, far worse than the Bay of Biscay, worse than the Great Australian Bight where the storm roared straight up from the southern ice or the westerlies bellowed round the globe in the High South latitudes. And always there was the potential threat of the lurking U-boats of Grand-Admiral Dönitz and, when the ships were within their range, the Nazi air armadas, the reconnaissance Focke-Wulfs and the bombers.

The escort apart, the best defence of the convoys was the zig-zag. The point was always made by the officers of the Naval Control Service and it had been made this time at the convoy conference held before the bigger ships joining from the Clyde had left the Tail o' the Bank off Greenock. All masters of the Clyde contingent had attended, along with the Commodore of the convoy and the commanding officers of the naval escorts. So vital was the OB that additional escorts had been provided: four heavy cruisers and an old, slow, rusty battleship, a mixed blessing whose fifteen-inch guns might well be effective enough if the convoy should come under attack from a surface raider, a German pocket-battleship perhaps, but which the Commodore fancied would tend only to slow the convoy's advance into safer waters beyond forty west.

Commodore Mason Kemp lifted an eyebrow at Hampton as the latter's pacing brought him close again. 'I'm going below,' he said. He rasped at his chin, and yawned. He had been almost all night on the bridge as the ships from the Clyde, having made the rendezvous with those out of Liverpool, moved away from the Bloody Foreland at Ireland's north-western tip. 'Shave, if nothing else! You know the orders, Captain: I'm to be called immediately if anything happens. I'll be back in fifteen minutes in any case. Where's that assistant of mine?' He looked around, saw the RNVR lieutenant in the wheelhouse, and lifted his voice. 'Williams!'

A lanky figure emerged from the wheelhouse, clad in a duffel-coat, balaclava, thick woollen scarf and gloves. 'Here, sir.'

Commodore Mason Kemp grunted: there was a gleam of humour in his eye as he remarked, 'Warm life for some. Where's your normal sartorial elegance, Williams?'

'Sorry, sir –'

'Oh, don't apologize, it's not vital.' Kemp stretched. 'You can go below when I return to the bridge –' He broke off as a shout came from the signalman of the watch. 'What's that, MacCord?'

'Destroyer leader, sir, reports contact starboard. Submarine, sir.'

Kemp caught Hampton's eye. The long business of the convoy's defence had begun already. 'Sound action stations,' he said.

3

[ii]

On the outbreak of war nearly two years earlier Captain Kemp, as he had then been, had brought his ship along the English Channel from Brixham, where he had embarked the pilot, to the Downs and Tilbury, homeward bound from Sydney. Soon after the ship had berthed in the basin the chairman of the line had come aboard and had been taken to the master's day cabin. He said, 'We're going to lose you, John. I'm more than sorry, I need hardly say.'

'Lose me?'

'Yes. You're RNR. And this has come for you.' The chairman handed over a buff envelope marked ON HIS MAJESTY'S SERVICE, with the Admiralty crest embossed on the flap. It was addressed to Captain J. Mason Kemp, RD, RNR.

Kemp said, 'Not unexpected, Sir Edward. But what'll they do with a captain RNR? They won't give me one of their battle-wagons, I'll bet!' He held the envelope in the air, quizzically, as though keeping himself deliberately in suspense.

The chairman said, 'I understand the Admiralty's bringing in the convoy system – right from the start this time. Carrying on where they left off in '18.'

'Commodore of convoys?'

'That's my guess, John.'

Kemp slit the envelope, using an ivory paperknife from his desk. The guess had been a good one. That afternoon Commodore Kemp left the liner to report to the Admiralty and then to proceed on a fortnight's leave before taking up his war appointment. The liner was the *Ardara*. Leaving the ship with much nostalgia for a life that had come to a sudden end, it never occurred to the Commodore that within two years, after many convoys, he would once again be upon her bridge. He went home, home being an olde-worlde cottage in Meopham in Kent, and broke the news to his wife.

Mary Kemp was no more unexpectant than he himself had been; one didn't join the RNR and expect to be left to carry on one's peacetime ways in war. Expectant, and accepting of the lot of a seaman's wife, though with sadness for all the

4

exposure to danger there would be.

'Tripe,' Kemp said, and grinned. 'We're all in it together. If I'd been left in the *Ardara*, I wouldn't have been protected by different gold stripes, would I? Look on the bright side, Mary.'

'What bright side?'

He kissed her. 'More leave. The RN's good at that.' The Merchant Service wasn't: an Australian voyage, then a week or so at home, and back again to Australia, world without end. Kemp had been married almost twenty years, and if he added all his leaves up he reckoned he's seen his wife and children for a little less than two years in all. Young Harry, nineteen and likely to volunteer now for the navy, and Rufus, sixteen and currently with a few more days left of his summer holiday from Pangbourne, scarcely knew their father other than as a fleeting and somewhat autocratic stranger who reappeared at intervals. They had taken to calling him the Ancient Mariner, unflatteringly . . .

Mary said, 'All right then, the bright side.' She said it determinedly, then added, 'I don't know about Granny.'

'Oh yes, Granny. How is she?'

'Better than she thinks she is. You'd better go up and see her, John, otherwise –' She broke off. 'Started already. Go on up, do!'

A walking stick was being banged on the floor; flakes of ceiling came down. Commodore Kemp left the drawing-room and went up the twisty staircase down which Granny could never again walk, being bed-bound with all manner of disabilities, some of them real. Granny Marsden was in fact Kemp's grandmother and had been inherited when Kemp's mother had died. His mother had died young; Kemp had been devoted to her and had accepted the burden she had left. Granny Marsden at ninety-six was something of a miracle, if a tiresome one. Everlastingly expectant of death, she continued to survive, smoked like a dangerous chimney and drank two weakish whiskies every evening to help her sleep. She came of seafaring stock and in her childhood had sailed in the square-rigged ship commanded and owned by her father. She had been round Cape Horn to Chile and Australia not far off as many times as her grandson had taken the Suez Canal route to Sydney. She still had all her faculties and her hearing was as

5

sharp as her voice; her eyesight was more than equal to the task of watching out that the right quantity of whisky went into her tumbler.

She was propped up in bed by what looked like half a dozen pillows when Kemp entered the bedroom. 'Well, Johnny,' she said.

Kemp bent and kissed her on the marble-like forehead. 'Well yourself, Granny.' It always struck Kemp as slightly ridiculous that a middle-aged shipmaster should be in the position of addressing anybody as Granny. 'You look it, I must say.'

'Look what?'

'Well.'

She gave a snort. 'If you did but know. No one ever listens to me! I keep telling Mary –'

'Yes, I'm sure you do. She does her best.'

'If you call –'

'Now, now, Granny.' Kemp began to use his master's voice, not wishing to hear criticism of his wife. It had its effect: Granny Marsden knew when she was being told to watch it.

'Well,' she said grudgingly, 'it's nice to see you again, Johnny. What are they going to do with you?'

'Do with me? I –'

'There's a war on, so they tell me.' Kemp didn't realize how many times he was going to be told there was a war on over the coming years. 'That man Chamberlain, such an idiot. And as for Hitler!' Words seemed to fail her, for she didn't go on. 'They'll call you up, I suppose.'

He told her the facts. 'Second time round,' he said. He had served right through the last war in the RNR, in Q-ships and later in minelayers, and he'd been torpedoed twice and had to swim for it. 'War to end wars my foot!'

'Your great-grandfather always said –'

'Yes, I'm sure he did,' Kemp broke in quickly, for his great-grandfather had evidently said plenty; his sayings never ran out. He made his excuses and left the bedside; he would be up later to say goodnight if she wasn't asleep.

'Huh!' Granny Marsden said scornfully. 'How *anybody's* expected to sleep in this house I *don't* know!' Kemp knew that the reference was to Harry, who possessed a bagpipe chanter

6

and made hideous noises on it, though, out of respect for the wrath that would otherwise descend on his mother's head, not unduly late at night. Kemp's view was that within reason there were times when the old had to give way to the young with their lives before them and Harry, curiously perhaps, had talent in a musical direction, or so he insisted. He was currently employed by the BBC . . . but when he came home that evening he confirmed what Kemp had foreshadowed earlier: he intended going along to the naval recruiting office within the next few days and joining up as an ordinary seaman. In the middle of this announcement Rufus turned up: it now being officially wartime, he had put on his Pangbourne cadet's uniform and this brought a lump to Kemp's throat. So young . . . and God alone could tell how long the war was going to last. Rufus expressed the hope that it would last long enough for him to join in.

One way and another, the home wasn't going to be the same. Only Granny Marsden went on for ever.

[iii]

Two years on now, from Kemp's first wartime homecoming: Paul Williams, lieutenant RNVR, looked at himself in the mirror in his bedroom at home in Hounslow. He liked what he saw: the second wavy gold stripe had only recently been sewn on to his uniform by Gieves on the Hard in Portsmouth, turning a sub-lieutenant into a full-blown lieutenant, and it gave him added importance, the equivalent of a captain in the army to whom in fact, being of the Senior Service, he would rank senior. More importance, in his view, was given by his new appointment to the staff of a convoy Commodore – even though he understood it to be normally a sub-lieutenant's appointment. Never mind: no doubt an important convoy, a very large convoy, needed the extra rank. The personal staff would consist of himself and two signalmen, plus telegraphist ratings. The Commodore was to be an RNR with the Reserve Decoration, an oldie from the liners and probably with a constipated mind, but Lieutenant Williams could cope with that. So far in the war he hadn't coped too badly, he believed,

7

though his last 'flimsy' – the copy given all officers of their captains' personal and confidential reports – had made use of the expression self-assertive and bouncy. A previous one had indicated cockiness but both went only to show that senior RN officers were also constipated mentally. If he had been all that, he wouldn't have landed a staff job – which was how Williams thought of it.

He saluted himself in the mirror, smartly. Then he coloured as he recalled not so long ago overhearing a leading seaman in his last ship referring to him as being all wind and piss like the barber's cat. He had been mortified but had prudently turned a deaf ear. It wasn't the sort of comment you made a song and dance about to the extent of putting the man in the rattle and having the phrase repeated loud and clear at Captain's Defaulters. Anyway, wind and piss or not, it paid to be smartly turned out, since then you got noticed. Having saluted himself, the new lieutenant removed his cap and went downstairs, but not in time to hear the conversation between his father and mother. His mother had been fondly enthusing over her son's elevation and appointment.

'*Staff*,' she had said almost reverently. 'Isn't it splendid, Fred?'

'I don't know so much.' Williams' father didn't know the contents of the flimsies, but he would have been in some sympathy with the commanding officers. He knew his son pretty well.

'But *assistant commodore!*'

'Is that what he calls himself? I hadn't heard . . . and I wonder what the Commodore'll call him!' He filled in the blank for himself: 'Commodore's assistant, I reckon.' When Paul came in, his father heaved himself to his feet. He'd got his stint at Air Raid Precautions; he was on duty as a warden. Working in the City, chief clerk in a firm of insurance brokers, he often didn't get home till late but he was determined to do his bit to flatten out Adolf Hitler and teach the Nazis a lesson about ordinary Englishmen.

Three days later Lieutenant Williams left Hounslow and went north by train from Euston, speeded on his way by the air-raid syrens and then the falling bombs, bound for the naval office in Greenock's Albert Harbour to report to Commodore John Mason Kemp for the OB convoy.

Kemp and Hampton met at the convoy conference, duplicates of which were being held in the other assembly ports. Kemp and Hampton, both Mediterranean-Australia Line, were old friends; and two years earlier, when Kemp had been taken out of his command for war service, Captain Arthur Hampton had been appointed master in his place: Hampton had never bothered with the RNR and had thus been left in peace, if such was the word, in the liners, now converted as troopships and on loan to the government as hired transports in the official term. Kemp had been delighted to be told at the Admiralty that he was to hoist his broad pennant in the old *Ardara*.

'Just like old times, Arthur.' Hampton, some five years before, had been his staff captain in the *Aratapu*, which as it happened was another of the troopships in the OB convoy.

'Same but different, sir. No parties.'

'They won't be missed.' One of the bugbears of liner life had been the entertaining, the enforced giving of Captains' cocktail parties – the gin-palace aspect of the job – and the need to appear as often as his duty permitted at the Captain's table in the first-class dining-room where there were important passengers to be entertained with small talk, something John Mason Kemp was not good at and had had to force himself into. He would have been highly surprised had he known how popular he was with most of his passengers. One thing he did know: right through his career in the liners he had been the target of forward young women and some not so young: the liner atmosphere did funny things to women, especially once the ship had entered the Red Sea. It had been all right until he had met Mary and married her; after that the female attentions had to be fought off, the more so when he got his promotion to staff captain and then Captain in Command. Senior officers could not afford to be put in compromising situations.

Kemp was about to make a further remark to Hampton about the peacetime liners when the conference was called to order by a lieutenant-commander RNR. The conference, Kemp reflected, was to be a high-powered one: as the conversation died, the Chief of Staff to the Flag Officer in Charge entered the room. The Chief of Staff was a pompous-looking officer, rotund, two pisspots high in Kemp's seafaring terminology, wearing a gold-rimmed monocle and carrying, of all things, a beautifully turks'-headed telescope. There was a good deal of other brass around: the Rear-Admiral commanding the cruiser squadron, no less than five four-ring captains RN from the cruisers themselves and the solitary battleship of the escort, each of them accompanied by his navigating officer. The remainder were a mix of commanders and lieutenant-commanders plus a number of lieutenants, mostly RNR or RNVR, from the smaller escort vessels – the corvettes – and the masters of the merchant ships.

The Naval Control Service officer was concise: time was not for wasting. As they all knew, the OB convoy route was normally south through the Irish Sea, the last pick-up being the ships out of Liverpool Bay. This time, they were going north about, taking their departure from the Bloody Foreland. Why? The answer lay in the intelligence reports. Some German cyphers had been broken and it was known that there was to be a concentration of U-boats lying in wait off the exit from St George's Channel. So the Germans were to be fooled: no convoy would steam into their periscopes this time. Instead, the U-boats would come under heavy depth-charge attack from Western Approaches command. The lieutenant-commander went on to give the precise route to be followed clear of the British Isles and beyond the range of the German bombers. He stressed the importance of the convoy even though the ships were in ballast. Bottoms were valuable even without cargoes, and the cargoes and Canadian troops that would be picked up in Halifax were very badly needed. As for the escort, the corvettes would break off for return to base at 19 degrees west longitude. The remainder, the destroyers, the heavy cruisers and the old battleship, would, exceptionally, remain with the convoy right through to Halifax to form part of the homeward escort which would if necessary be joined nearer home waters by a fleet aircraft-carrier being held in readiness in the Clyde. The destroyers would re-fuel as necessary from one of the tankers, a Royal Fleet Auxiliary tanker which would be carrying sufficient oil fuel for replenishment. The RFA would break off with the other tankers for the Gulf of Mexico, escorted by destroyers of the Royal Canadian Navy, which would leave Halifax for the rendezvous.

Afterwards Kemp remarked to Hampton that he had the feeling something hadn't been said. Hampton shrugged. 'They always keep their cards close to their chests when there's –'

'When there's something else. That's what I meant. Apart from the sheer size, the convoy's not all that unusual. Why fall over themselves to provide an escort all the way when they're always so short of escorts? There's *got* to be some other factor.'

'I dare say we'll be told in due course,' Hampton said.

They made their way along the dockside at Albert Harbour, stepping over the usual clutter of any dock – coils of wire and rope, broken packing cases and the like – closely attended by Lieutenant Williams who was efficiently looking out for the drifter detailed to take the officers back to their ships in the stream. Kemp thought his assistant looked like an impatient bird, peering about for its nest. Back in London words had been uttered in the Queen Anne's Gate office of the Naval Assistant to the Second Sea Lord, known in brief as NA2SL, the officer responsible for appointments. Naturally, the confidential nature of Williams' flimsies had been respected; but the navy had ways of conveying information by facial gestures, waved hands and a minimum of words. Commodore Kemp had hoisted in that his new assistant walked with God, but was otherwise reliable and efficient enough. Williams needed to be sat on now and again, and Kemp was regarded at the Admiralty as someone who would sit hard when necessary.

'Training exercise?' he'd asked with a grin.

'You could put it that way, Commodore. Yes. Make something of him – what?'

Moving through Albert Harbour to the drifter, Kemp reflected on these words of wisdom. So far his contact with Williams had been of the briefest, a hurried introduction just before the convoy conference, but already he'd got the idea that his assistant was summing him up as a kind of blimp, a relic of the last war, and that he, the assistant, was going to

11

find it a bit of a strain keeping the boss up to the mark. Well, time would tell; Kemp wasn't the man to make pre-judgments. He had asked Williams a question that he knew the answer to already: was this his first experience of the merchant-ship side of convoys? It was; but Williams had served in the escorts, which should be of some help. Kemp had had, in the past, RNVR lieutenants who had never hitherto moved off their backsides in shore jobs, not as officers anyway: they'd done their sea-time as ratings and then promptly shifted out of discomfort and forgotten all they'd learned. Kemp had refrained from saying what Williams would learn for himself soon enough: that his job wasn't going to be so much that of assistant commodore, which his manner suggested he believed, or flag lieutenant, as of a kind of tea boy and general-purpose dogsbody.

Meanwhile Williams identified the duty drifter, not a hard task since so many officers were making for it, and reported the fact with a flourish and a salute.

'Well done, Williams,' Kemp said, keeping his face straight. Williams didn't seem aware of any irony. They embarked and proceeded out of the harbour. As senior officer present, Kemp was accorded the privacy, honour and fug of the wheelhouse where he did his best to interpret the Scots tongue of the skipper, a gnarled fisherman from Caledonia's wilder north-eastern shores. Kemp gathered that the skipper regretted his patriotism in making his drifter and himself and crew available to the English, like so many other skippers, for the duration when he could be making a damn sight more money by sticking to the fishing. Kemp saw that he was homesick: to the skipper, Clydeside was the south.

[v]

Leading Signalman Mouncey, together with his number two, Signalman MacCord, had already taken up his quarters aboard the Commodore's ship and was having his customary grumble about this, that and the other whilst waiting for the Commodore to come aboard. Their quarters, for one thing: a bloody great liner with hundreds of single-berth cabins and staterooms and they'd been shoved in a carved-up former nobs' suite on A deck together with the naval guns' crews, the gunnery rates who manned the two six-inch, one for'ard and one aft, that made up the *Ardara*'s main defence and despite the strengthening would likely split the ship asunder if fired. Signal ratings, Mouncey said, didn't expect to be berthed with common seamen gunners.

'Handy for the bridge,' MacCord said. It didn't sound like that, MacCord being very Scots, and Mouncey had to ask for a repeat.

Mouncey said, 'Bollocks. Plenty of other spaces just as handy. Just some sod being awkward. When I was in the . . .' He went on and on, moaning about better ships and better billets. MacCord listened philosophically, letting the killick drip himself out. Even a tap must eventually empty the reservoir. After a while Mouncey, a small, dark man with a repaired hare lip and the screwed-up eyes that spoke of many a long year gazing through a telescope at flag hoists and Aldis lamps and the big signalling projectors, came back from the past and peered into the future.

'That there RNR. Commodore Kemp.'

'What about him, killick?'

'Looks all right. Spoke to me decent, almost as if I was yuman. I've 'eard 'e used to be in this ship – must be funny, coming back like with a bloody great thick stripe on 'is cuff.' Mouncey sniffed and wiped the back of a horny hand across the end of his nose. 'That wavy bloke gives me the bloody creeps, though. The lootenant – Williams.'

'Looked all right to me, killick –'

Mouncey jeered. 'Call yourself a bunting tosser! Blind as a bat, you are. Tarted-up little ponce. Stuck up as a pr –'

MacCord never heard the rest of it. Mouncey was interrupted by the broadcaster coming on suddenly, almost in his ear. A voice said, 'Leading Signalman on the bridge. Leading Signalman on the bridge, immediately.'

That meant the Commodore of the convoy was aboard. Mouncey went up the ladders at the double. On arrival he got a bollocking from the Commodore's assistant, which didn't please him: he should have been on the bridge waiting for the Commodore, Williams said, not skulking below. Mouncey

13

didn't answer back, you didn't answer officers unless you liked being put in the rattle, but he fizzed and muttered like a bomb. For his part, Lieutenant Williams didn't like that. He said something hasty, about dumb insolence. Mouncey's mouth fell open in astonishment. Daft young bleeder . . .

A moment later Kemp called Williams across for a quiet word. 'Laid yourself open, haven't you?'

'Sir?'

'Dumb insolence went out of the crime sheet years ago – as you must surely know.'

'Sorry, sir. Heat of the moment –'

'Well, don't let us have any more such moments, Williams. You did right to utter a reprimand, but don't overdo it. I like a happy signal staff. Understood?'

Williams, red-faced, said, 'Yes, sir. If I might explain, Mouncey strikes me as a –'

'All right, Williams, that's all.' Kemp turned away, walked with Captain Hampton to the port bridge wing. Signals were passing between the King's Harbour Master and the battleship, and between KHM and the senior officer of the close escort. The moment of departure had come. Five minutes later the great concourse of shipping was on the move, the battleship and the cruisers going ahead to be followed by the Commodore and the other ships in convoy, with the destroyers and smaller escorts bringing up the rear, proceeding in line ahead; the ships would remain in single column until the waters of the Clyde opened out beyond the Cumbraes, widening into the firth between Holy Island and Ardrossan so that the convoy could begin to move into its ocean formation. On the bridge of the *Ardara* Kemp stared ahead through binoculars, towards the anti-submarine boom strung across from Cloch Point to Dunoon, a strange stirring agitating his mind. This, he believed for no real reason beyond a hunch that he avoided thinking of as psychic, was going to be no easy convoy.

TWO

Signalman MacCord reported again: 'Lost contact, sir.'

'Thank you, MacCord. Scared off by the depth-charges.'

'Likely, sir. No apparent damage to the bastards, sir.'

Kemp nodded. That was convoy work: attack, draw off, come again. Alarms that were not false, but led to no result. A lot of it was boredom and fatigue, but you could never let up, never drop your guard, never allow yourself to miss the smallest feather of water that would indicate a watching periscope. Hampton, as the morning wore on into afternoon and the convoy left Ireland well behind, had a feeling of deteriorating weather: the wind was increasing from the south-west and heavy cloud was extending. White horses were forming on the water and soon there would be spindrift. That was good: the U-boat packs didn't attack when the weather was bad and if the wind strengthened to gale force, and stayed with them beyond the range of the hunter packs, then they would have a good chance of getting through unscathed. And before long they would be coming to the limit of the Nazi aircraft range, the bombers anyway.

Not the recce boys, the FW Condors. So far, by some stroke of sheer luck, nothing had appeared in the sky, but the convoy was not yet in the clear.

[ii]

Every convoy had its arse-end Charlie, the ship that couldn't keep up the speed and fell everlastingly astern to become the

15

bête noire of the Commodore and even more so of Captain(D) in the destroyer flotilla leader, whose job it was to detach one of his escorts for the job of chivvying. This time, arse-end Charlie was the ss *Stephen Starr*, one of the smaller steamers whose official maximum speed was said to be a fraction over the mean speed of the convoy which had therefore allowed her inclusion in what was a semi-fast convoy insofar as the outward run was concerned. The *Stephen Starr*, along with all the other smaller ships, was due to detach in Halifax and return at a later date with a slow convoy, while the Commodore and the troopships and armaments carriers formed a fast HX convoy for home waters.

But for now the OB convoy was saddled with her. Her master, Captain Peter Redgrave, saw the impatient signalling, saw one of the destroyers turning out of formation on the starboard beam and bearing down on him with a big bone in her teeth. As the destroyer passed along the steamer's side a loud-hailer boomed irritation across the water.

'What's it this time, Captain?'

'Trouble in my engine-room,' Redgrave called back.

'What sort of trouble?'

Redgrave set his teeth. 'Worn-out bloody machinery, that's what! If it's not one thing it's another. My chief engineer's doing his best.'

'He'd better do it fast,' the destroyer Captain said. 'Much longer and you'll be astern of the corvettes.'

The destroyer turned away, making back at speed for its position in protection of the main body of the convoy. Captain Redgrave thought: astern of the whole God-damn escort, right out on a limb! NCSO at Liverpool, where the *Stephen Starr* had sailed from, had put it very plainly: stragglers would have to lump it. The speed of the convoy would not be reduced and escorts couldn't be spared, not unless one of the big ships happened to become a straggler, which wasn't likely. Redgrave knew his ship was expendable, a casualty that could be accepted. Had it not been for the war and the need to keep as many ships as possible at sea, she would have gone to the breaker's yard long since. As it was, just so long as she could stay afloat without becoming an inconvenience, she could carry cargoes around the world and help to keep Britain fed.

16

Redgrave was well aware of the facts: neither the poor old *Stephen Starr* nor any of the other former tramps of uncertain years would have formed part of this convoy if it hadn't suited the Trade Division of the Admiralty to shove them in, tag them along with the big stuff and thus save on escorts. It was insane, and it was probably murder.

But didn't they all know there was a war on?

Redgrave knew, all right. Not just because he had sailed the war-torn seas right from the start. Because his home had been in Liverpool, or Birkenhead to be precise. In peacetime Liverpool had been his home port and he had sailed out of it for more than twenty years as second mate, mate and master. He had bought his house on a mortgage at the time he'd met his wife. When Clare had said she wouldn't marry unless he started buying a house, he had been in full agreement. That was – what? – ten years ago, just under. The house hadn't been much to start with, but it had become a little palace in those years, the happy years before Hitler had mucked everything up. Clare had done wonders with decorations and he'd spent almost all his leaves with a paint brush in his hand. A lot of hard-earned money had gone into it as well, and what with that and three children in due course, Redgrave had never had so much as twopence to scratch his own bottom with. But he hadn't minded that; though a seafarer, he was a home-lover and the mere thought of home, the satisfaction of owning his own place, had been his mainstay during days of boredom on the bridge, taking cargoes around the world from Liverpool to Sydney, Sydney to Japan, Japan to San Francisco and virtually anywhere else you cared to name.

And what had been the end result?

Extinction. Back in May the Luftwaffe had come to Liverpool in an attempt to put the city and docks out of commission. The result had been terrible but Redgrave's house had been all right. Then a sneaky raid had taken place, nothing very big, only a fortnight before Redgrave had sailed on the present run to Halifax, and this time his house had taken a direct hit in his absence on a coastal convoy. There had been nothing left when he'd come home, nothing but a heap of rubble. Somewhere underneath it all had been Clare and the children. He'd been told it was impossible to get them out. Maybe

17

they'd got the bodies out by now; if so, he didn't know. He didn't much want to. Probably they hadn't; too much else to do – and if they had, then presumably he would have been told.

Since then there had been nothing left but the sea, and the *Stephen Starr*. There was something very personal about the ship now: Clare and the children had come aboard whenever he was in Liverpool and he had the memories of them all about him, in his cabin, in the saloon, on the decks.

And now he was being a nuisance to the escort and the Commodore. Light signals were being flashed from the *Ardara*, admonitory messages similar to the amplified words of the destroyer captain, messages warning him that he would soon be on his own. The Commodore wished him luck and added his regrets. Redgrave knew the regrets were sincere; no seafarer liked the idea of leaving men to the mercy of the sea and the enemy, and Commodore Mason Kemp was RNR, had been a merchant shipmaster himself and would thus have an intimate understanding.

Redgrave sighed and moved to the engine-room voice-pipe.

'Chief? Bridge here. What's the score?'

'Heap of old iron.' The voice came hollowly up the pipe, and sourly. Mr Hankins, chief engineer, knew he could never get through to the deck officers, they were blind and deaf when it came to machinery and always expected miracles – like now.

Redgrave asked, 'Can you get just half a knot more out of her?'

'No, I can't. She's flat out now . . . too many worn bearings. Too many other things. It's hell down here. Talk about the Dustbin Line!'

Redgrave snapped the cover shut and stood back, looked across the increasing sea towards the other ships, steaming solid and in station, lifting and falling to the mounting waves. His thoughts were bitter – not as regards Hankins, for the chief was obviously doing his best since, to take the lowest viewpoint, his life was as much at risk as anyone else's – but about shipowners, peacetime shipowners who had let things slide, kept the repair bills down and let ships deteriorate in times that were admittedly not prosperous. The years of depression couldn't be shrugged aside, of course; but too many tramp owners had sent men to sea in coffin ships, uncaring so long as their own personal living standards were not affected. The rot for such old-timers as the *Stephen Starr* had set in and they were virtually beyond refitting, but the country needed them now and they still went to sea . . .

Captain Redgrave sent a final signal to the Commodore and Captain(D): Regret cannot maintain station and must drop astern.

[iii]

'*Stephen Starr* dropping out, sir.'

'Thank you, Williams. Make another signal: Our thoughts and hopes are with you.'

'Aye, aye, sir. Mouncey?'

'Yessir?'

'Signal to the *Stephen Starr* . . .'

Kemp, his back turned to what he preferred not to see, heard his assistant pass the message to the leading signalman. There was something in Williams' tone that suggested he found the words smug. Well, perhaps they were, but they were not meant to be. The *Stephen Starr*'s master would understand that, better than Williams could ever hope to. Mason Kemp's jaw was out-thrust, his face set hard and grim. His whole instinct urged him to turn his ship to stand by the drop-out himself, but that was manifestly not to be done, and as regards detachment of an escort the orders had been clear, unequivocal.

Williams, however, had something to say on the point.

'Commodore, sir –'

'Yes, what is it, Williams?'

The RNVR lieutenant gave a cough. 'Escorts, sir. I know the orders, but –'

'So do I. They stand – to my regret.'

'Yes, sir. But as Commodore –'

'I'm aware of my duties as Commodore.'

'Of course, sir.' Williams was at least dogged. 'But you have an option, sir. The officer on the spot and all that?'

'I have no option, Williams. If I had, I'd use it.'

'But –'

Kemp turned, sharply, angrily, caught a sight of the *Stephen*

19

Starr already well behind the convoy. He shifted his gaze to Williams' face, stared him in the eye. 'That's all, Williams. No more to be said. Except this: orders are to be obeyed and you're learning your first lesson in the conduct of a convoy. I am the *convoy* Commodore – I don't command the escort. Remember that.'

Kemp turned away again. Hampton had gone below now and the liner's bridge was in the charge of Hampton's chief officer, Marcus Whitehead. When Mason Kemp had served in the line, Whitehead had been a senior second officer. Now he caught the Commodore's eye and said, 'I'm sorry, sir. I know how you feel.'

'Thank you, Whitehead.'

Whitehead had overheard the remarks offered by Williams. He said sourly, 'Saturday-afternoon sailors . . .'

'No criticism, Whitehead. He's spoken his mind. That showed guts.'

'I suppose so, sir.'

Kemp didn't say anything further. He was thinking about Redgrave, the story of whose recent loss had permeated even the Clyde conference. A hard-luck story, so close to sailing. Redgrave could have got out of this convoy; even in wartime there was such a thing as compassionate leave, but apparently he'd preferred to sail. Redgrave, of course, wasn't the only one who'd lost everything to Hitler and there were going to be hundreds of thousands more such sufferers before the war was won. Redgrave was one of those who was going to ensure that it was. Standing four-square on the *Ardara*'s bridge Kemp found himself wondering if Redgrave would find death came easy if the *Stephen Starr* should fall victim to the Nazis. As for himself, he knew that if enemy bombs destroyed his own family he would find no more joy in living but would hang on in the hopes of driving a few nails into Hitler's bloody coffin. Probably Redgrave felt the same way.

[iv]

Below decks, far below in the working alleyways beneath the passenger accommodation – passenger accommodation now

20

converted to troop decks much used as such over the last eighteen months and now ready for the reception of the Canadians – Mr Portway, second steward, was in his cabin, an inboard compartment with no outlet to the fresh air other than by way of the forced-draught trunking. Mr Portway, the stewards mustered and detailed for the day's work by this time, was making up his overtime bill for eventual presentation to the purser. War or no war, the routine of a liner went on notwithstanding, if in a less glamorous way. Troops were passengers of a sort, and the first-class saloon, officers for the use of, was still a somewhat superior place and with an air of distinction, though Mr Portway had found that some so-called officers were not quite what would have worn stars and crowns in pre-war days. Some of them didn't know how to treat stewards – chucked their weight around and were rude and dismissive. Once, Mr Portway had been first-class head waiter in the *Aramac* on the Australian run. The passengers had been ladies and gentlemen then; they treated you decently and also they tipped well. Often on arrival in Sydney Mr Portway's pockets had bulged with five-pound notes, and in those days five nicker was five nicker and bought a lot. Of course he didn't keep it all himself: like the table waiters, he passed some of it on to the pantry and galley. The waiters did it because if they didn't, then they would get rotten pantry service and passengers kept waiting didn't tip well.

Mr Portway did it for similar reasons: the galley was the primary producer as it were, and their chagrin would reflect upon the head waiter.

Somewhat the same with the overtime. Overtime was in the second steward's gift and a lot went down, in fact, that had never been worked at all. Mr Portway knew that the stewards called him a fat-arsed bastard who put most of the overtime down to his blue-eyed boys but he wasn't worried by that. No one ever liked second stewards, and he knew that the best way to get efficiency was to encourage the good hands and then, when the message penetrated, add some of the improvers to the overtime bill. It worked. Other things worked too: the chief steward was accustomed to receiving a bonus at the end of each voyage based to some extent upon the muster of crockery when back in Tilbury. One of the lowest of the low categories aboard a liner was that of dishwasher, a lazy lot and inclined to chuck huge quantities of dirty china into the hogwash via the gash chutes rather than wash it up. That cost the Line money and it was cheaper to grease the palm of chief stewards – not only cheaper, it also meant that the passengers didn't have to go without plates, since a lot could go overboard between Tilbury and Sydney. The next stage in the game, of course, was for the chief steward to farm out his bonus so that next voyage he didn't lose the lot.

Wheels within wheels, all of them turning over very nicely, even in wartime. You didn't often come across a penniless chief or second steward. Mr Portway, the overtime totted up, pushed himself back from his desk, reached into a drawer, and brought out a bottle of whisky and a glass.

He was pouring out his tot when the balloon went up. Or anyway, the alarm rattlers sounded. Bloody Jerries around, evidently. Mr Portway put the bottle back in its safe stowage and lumbered to his feet. In action – or defence stations, in the case of a virtually unarmed troop transport – Mr Portway had a place to go to, in charge of the stewards' fire parties. He put on speed, shouldering his way through a rush of men, eager to get higher up in the ship before the bridge shut the watertight doors.

[v]

Captain Hampton was on the bridge again within thirty seconds of the alarm being sounded, and found the Commodore staring into the sky astern, using his binoculars.

'Aircraft report, Hampton. Picked up by the rearguard.'

'How many, sir?' Hampton brought up his own glasses as the close-range weapons' crews doubled up the ladder to man the machine-guns in the bridge wings.

'They think just one. So far unidentified. I'm thinking of the *Stephen Starr*.'

'Yes indeed. But it's very likely a recce Condor.'

Kemp nodded. 'Could be, at this range. But some of the Condors have cannon, Hampton. All the *Stephen Starr*'s got is

22

Oerlikons and a 3-pounder.'

Kemp said no more; they all listened for the sound of aircraft engines. Kemp swept a glance around the convoy, still keeping good station, the ships large and small steaming in apparent unconcern through the increasing waves. The warships of the escort were at action stations, their ack-ack armament trained on the reported bearing. Two destroyers had turned, following upon signalling by light between them and Captain(D) in the flotilla leader. Hampton said, 'It looks as if they're going back to stand by the *Stephen Starr.*'

'Let's hope so.' In such circumstances, so long as the straggler was still close enough, the orders could be ignored. The two destroyers were now making back at speed, throwing up great swathes of North Atlantic from their bows, the White Ensigns nearly rigid in the wind. They were joined by a corvette, already astern of the convoy. The cruisers and the rest of the destroyers maintained their station as close escort, and astern of the centre column the old 'R'-class battleship came on ponderously, like some huge, camouflaged block of flats, surrounded by foam as the sea surged along her anti-torpedo bulges.

A report came from the battleship a few moments later, flashed by light, the all-round masthead lamp, addressed to all ships. Leading Signalman Mouncey reported, 'One aircraft, sir, Condor, bearing green one-seven-oh.'

The binoculars swung. 'Recce,' Kemp said. 'Got it!' They could hear the engine beat now. Hampton picked it up: it was at a distance, and high, but he believed it was losing height. That could be to come down on the straggler, arse-end Charlie. Hampton glanced at the Commodore: Kemp was thinking the same. There was a haggard look in his eyes, as though, foolishly, he was blaming himself. As the convoy moved onward, the sharp crack of anti-aircraft gunfire was heard. Puffs of smoke appeared in the sky. Lieutenant Williams, still wrapped in wool, was alongside Kemp, giving what he considered a useful commentary.

'High but losing height, sir –'

'I've seen that.'

'Gunfire, sir, heavy. But having no effect.'

23

'Ditto.'

Williams gaped. 'Sir?'

'I mean I've seen that too. We can all see it. Save your breath.' Williams looked put out. 'You're not covering cricket for the BBC,' Kemp added with a grin. He watched out astern. The Focke-Wulf had come a good deal lower, obviously over its target, and the fire from the destroyers was hairy to say the least, going nowhere near the aircraft. A moment later there was something else to worry about: Captain(D) reported a contact. His Asdic had picked up an echo. Leading Signalman Mouncey read off the lamp.

'Submarine bearing red three-oh, sir!'

Already the escorts on the port beam of the convoy were swinging round.

THREE

The attention of the bridge staff was now on the coming underwater attack – coming, unless the speeding destroyers could intercept and frustrate. Mr Portway was supervising the laying out of the fire hoses along the alleyways that in peacetime had seen nothing more lethal than the involuntarily-ejected contents of passengers' stomachs in bad weather. That, and at other times the smartly-dressed ladies and gentlemen, or the inevitable cabin-crawlers, mostly east of Suez, in pursuit of sex. There was none of that now, it was in the past for both passengers and crew: no women aboard beyond the two nursing sisters, officers for the use of. Not that Mr Portway cared. There never had been much opportunity for a fat, middle-aged second steward whose only hunting ground had in any case been the tourist end of the ship: second stewards were not permitted the freedom of the first class other than on duty, and the tourist end was never quite the same. Their morals were different, they weren't so forthcoming, even to the brassbound ship's officers who had the run of the whole ship including the first class . . . and anyway Mr Portway had his own arrangements made at either end of the run and in some of the ports – if ever there was the time *en route*. Mabel in Grays, near Tilbury – Mrs Portway was frigid and lived in Thurrock – Daphne in Melbourne; Lou in Sydney, down by the Cross and desperate for it: she wasn't too good-looking, it had to be admitted, and it was a case of any port in a storm for both of them, but Mr Portway got by and it didn't cost him anything beyond the odd meal in a café. While he carried out his defence duties his mind roved ahead of the

25

convoy's track to Halifax. They would be in port the best part of a week, or so he believed, and with luck he might get fixed up fast. Mr Portway hadn't been in Halifax before so had no organized up-homers.

When a broadcast throughout the ship from the bridge told him there was now a U-boat in the offing as well as an FW, he forgot about his sex life. The bowels of a liner was a poor sort of place to be if a torpedo should hit.

[ii]

From the bridge of the *Ardara*, in the lead of the centre column behind the extended escort, they could only watch, wait and pray. A troopship had no part in submarine attack other than to be attacked. All she could do was to take appropriate avoiding action at the right time, which could only be when the torpedo's trail was seen approaching. Under certain circumstances the convoy could be ordered to scatter so as to diffuse the target. But scattering was never something you did other than as an extreme measure. Ships of all sizes, of all speeds and with varying manoeuvrability, could be an awesome sight when scattering. This way and that, a disorganized rabble in effect, with collisions being avoided by a hair's-breadth or not avoided at all. And afterwards they had to be shepherded back into formation again, a job that could take a very long time and cause oil fuel problems to the escorts, who had only a certain range at the best of times.

Captain(D) was signalling again: only the one contact so far.

'Thank God for that,' Kemp said heavily. He and all the bridge personnel were watching the bearing where the U-boat had been reported. In the breaking waves the periscope would be almost impossible to pick out; it would be raised only just far enough and just long enough to give the U-boat captain a sight of his target. In a flat sea the feather of spray should be visible if the lookouts were alert, but not now. They were watching the bearing when the destroyers reached the point of attack and Kemp saw the depth-charges ejecting from the throwers and being dropped from the racks, but it was a little late. Without warning a loud explosion came from half-way

26

down the port column of the convoy and a flash appeared over the port bow of a former Clan Line cargo vessel and she began to dip by the head.

Williams consulted a list which he had ready in his hand. '*Clan MacWishart*, sir. Captain J. R. Rawlings, master –'

'Thank you, Williams.'

'P. V. Dunhill, chief engineer.'

Kemp nodded, his attention on the damaged ship and on the huge spouts of water coming up from the explosion of the depth-charges on the port beam. Hampton glanced at Williams, still scanning his list. Captain Hampton had an urge to ask the RNVR lieutenant for the name of the ship's cat but knew this wasn't the moment. More explosions came from the attack area, now drawing astern as the convoy continued on its course. The *Clan MacWishart* had slowed and her stern had swung out to starboard. She was causing confusion to the next astern and the next abeam to starboard, but not for long.

'She's going,' Kemp said suddenly.

She was, and quickly. The bow went down, the sea could be seen climbing the fo'c'sle towards the island superstructure, the stern rose high in the air, the screw still spinning, and there was a rush of steam from somewhere aft, and then she was gone, a steel finger lifting to the sky and then going down with a rush.

Kemp said, 'Mouncey?'

'Yessir?'

'Make to the *Clan MacWishart*'s next astern, you may ease engines to pick up survivors.'

'Aye, aye, sir.' Mouncey got busy with his Aldis lamp. While the signal was being made the lamps were busy between Captain(D) and the attacking destroyers, and soon after the message came for Kemp. Commodore from Captain(D): Got the bugger.

Kemp rubbed at his eyes and blinked: getting old, he thought, binoculars were becoming a strain. He said, 'Well, one for one.' He didn't add that it was also one up for the convoy in a sense: a U-boat was a more valuable kill than the *Clan MacWishart* since if it had lived, that U-boat would no doubt have sunk a good many more cargo vessels in the future. That was the way to look at it, though the survivors wouldn't be looking at it like that. Kemp watched as the *Clan MacWishart's* next astern slowed right down, put out nets and cast heaving lines attached to lifebuoys. Like anglers from a pier, Kemp thought. Unlike the majority of lines cast from piers, however, these made their catches. When the report came in for the Commodore it indicated twenty-three survivors out of a complement of thirty-two, none of them injured. Kemp remembered the *Stephen Starr*. He asked, 'Any word of the straggler?'

Williams said, 'Detached escorts rejoining now, sir.'

Kemp turned to look aft. The two destroyers and the corvette were coming up fast, the corvette taking up her station astern and the destroyers weaving through the convoy to their own positions, a lamp flashing as they came. Mouncey read it off for Kemp's benefit. The FW Condor had got away but before turning for home had come down to strafe the decks of the *Stephen Starr*, killing the semi-trained merchant guns' crews manning the ship's pathetic armament, sweeping the bridge and colandering the helmsman – the actual signal was a good deal briefer but that was the picture Kemp received. The master had a flesh wound; medical assistance had been offered but refused. The ship herself was sound. She was carrying on for Halifax. Or staggering on.

Kemp said, 'You know what the Scots' toast is, Hampton?'

Hampton raised an eyebrow. 'Which one?'

'The one that goes: here's tae us, there's nane like us. Boastful . . . but why not? I feel the same way. Master mariners, Hampton – *all* mariners, come to that. We've lost too many men like Captain Redgrave.'

The convoy moved on; there was no further attack. Defence stations were fallen out but Kemp made a warning signal to the convoy masters, even though they probably didn't need it. The Condor, he said, would already have reported their position and their anonymity as it were was gone. Any number of U-boats could be in the area and could be moving in to attack. Extra vigilance and alert lookouts were the order of the day.

Deep down in the ship, Mr Portway was seeing the fire hoses returned to their normal reel stowages. This done and some of the watertight doors opened up, he returned to his

28

cabin and his bottle of whisky and after a couple of measures he returned to his ponderings on sex. He didn't know much about Canada or Canadians, still less about Nova Scotians in particular. Cold country, warm women – or not? All done up in fur, parkas and all, you wouldn't get a fair summary just by looking, no idea of the figure beneath. Mr Portway ticked off names on pudgy fingers: Mabel, Daphne, Lou, not to mention Mrs Portway and the *en route* popsies. Quite a lot to miss him if that Jerry U-boat had struck. But he'd always been lucky and he reckoned his luck would hold.

He put the bottle away again and went up top to the purser's office, clutching his overtime sheets.

[iii]

The night fell. There had been no further attack. With the ship's first officer and senior third officer on bridge watch, with Lieutenant Williams strutting from one wing to the other in the role of Commodore-of-the-Watch as he regarded it (though Kemp didn't), Kemp and Hampton took it easy for half an hour once dusk action stations had been fallen out. They went to Hampton's day-cabin and eased dead-weary limbs in comfortable chairs beneath shaded light behind the blanked-off square ports that looked out on the Captain's deck. Two years earlier this had been Kemp's cabin. On joining the *Ardara* as Commodore of the convoy he had been offered Hampton's accommodation. He had refused. He would not, he said, turn out the ship's master. He never did. So he had taken up the spare cabin and was comfortable enough – he was seldom able to use it in any case, for his place was mostly on the bridge when at sea. But, the day he had joined in the Clyde anchorage, he had been attacked by a strong nostalgia for his old quarters. He had made no less than five Australian voyages in the *Ardara* and there were many memories. Like Captain Redgrave aboard the *Stephen Starr* he had brought his family to his quarters on many occasions. Now, at sea in wartime, he could see Mary sitting in the chair he himself was sitting in, could see her pride in him, aboard his own ship with the four gold rings on either cuff, the brass hat

29

chucked into another chair. Very nearly the senior master of the company, in line one day for Commodore – of the Mediterranean-Australia Steam Navigation Company, not of a convoy. He could see the boys, having a whale of a time rushing about the decks, yarning with the bosun, old Frank Bush who was still, this day, aboard the ship, still bosun. The younger boy, coming up for Pangbourne, had been overawed the first time he'd visited his father's ship and had treated all the officers down to the junior fourth officer almost as God.

But it wasn't only the family: it was the different voyages too. Each one had been just that – different. Different problems, different passengers, different crew members. When Kemp thought of crew members he meant his officers and senior ratings rather than the rank-and-file, not from any sense of superiority but simply because inevitably in a ship carrying some six hundred crew he never met some of the categories other than on Captain's Rounds: the scullions, the dishwashers, the kitchen porters, the firemen and greasers in the engine-room. It had to be a case of the chef and second chef, the engine-room storekeeper and his number two, and so on. Even so . . . the master was always Father to his officers, as in the RN – just a handy sobriquet but it had always meant, to Kemp, much more than was intended, and he extended his fatherhood to every man in his crew, whether he knew them or not. He was always available to them through their heads of department and often without the benefit of the proper channels – he was never stuffy or stand-offish and frequently passed the time of day with ratings on deck or along the alleyways or on the bridge. They were all doing the same job in basis, taking a great ship half across the world, and each man did his job – for the most part – with pride. Each had to be accorded his own dignity in Mason Kemp's book. Many of them had been with the Line, even in the one ship, for years, and even now when trooping under war conditions and government charter so many of them were there still. But now that he was Commodore, they were no longer his responsibility or of his seafaring family. They were Hampton's, and thus in good hands.

Kemp and Hampton chatted, mainly of the old times. 'A bit of a change from the Indian Ocean,' Hampton said.

Kemp laughed. 'You can say that again.' He thought of the sunlit days, the first-class passengers around the swimming pool, or in the tavern bar at the after end of C Deck which abutted the pool, and men and women sitting around with long, iced gin-and-somethings, in their swimming gear, the young girls largely surrounded by off-watch ship's officers, though the latter usually contrived to look as though they were only duty-socializing if they saw that the Captain's eye was on them. The assistant pursers were the worst, Kemp remembered – they had more opportunity than the deck officers.

Hampton, seeming to sense Kemp's thoughts, said, 'A different world, sir.'

'It'll come back when this lot's over.'

'I doubt if it'll ever be quite the same again.'

'Don't be so pessimistic! The Indian Ocean'll still be the same, so will the romance – it's human nature, isn't it?' Kemp could remember back to when he'd been a junior officer, young enough to appreciate the possibilities raised by the deep-sea moonlight, the balmy night air, the slow, gentle roll of the ship, and the undoubted attractions of a brass-bound uniform – mess dress, for the ships of the company changed for dinner every night except in port or on the first night after departure. Bow tie, wing collar, starched white bum-freezer and shoulder-straps of rank. Kemp had in fact met his wife on board one of the company's ships, going out to Sydney with her mother to visit an aunt who'd emigrated years before. Mary had returned alone to UK by the homeward voyage: it had been one of those whirlwind romances associated with the sea, and it had been a success from the start. They'd married before the ship sailed again, and next voyage Kemp had brought his mother-in-law back. That had been the one snag: mother-in-law had had a flea in her ear on account of the whirlwind element, but it had stopped biting after a while. Now, looking back after many years, Kemp could understand. The young were thoughtless.

Kemp got to his feet. 'I'm going to take a look around, Captain. Coming up?'

'Yes, sir.'

'After that I'm turning in for a spell.' He repeated, from force of habit, the order that officers in wartime knew by heart.

31

'I'm to be called immediately if necessary.'

The two men climbed to the bridge. Looking aft and to either side, Kemp could see the shadowy shapes, large and small, beamy and slim, moving in their formation through the night, following the zig-zag pattern, each ship darkened and showing no steaming lights other than the shaded blue stern lights that were needed to assist station-keeping. The wind had increased again and was now blowing, by Kemp's estimate, a Force Six on the Beaufort Scale. The more wind the better, at any rate until they had passed beyond the likely U-boat range.

Kemp remained on the bridge for a while, went into the wheelhouse for a word with the Officer of the Watch and the quartermaster, then went below and turned in, having told Williams he too could get some sleep.

[iv]

Andrew Pemmel, purser, had a drink or two too many with his deputy purser and Sister Jacqueline Ord who, with the second nursing sister, was one of the only two females aboard the troopship. Obviously, they would be in much demand, at least until more nurses, army nurses, embarked with the troops. The nursing sisters were usually considered the hunting ground of the deck officers, though humankind being what it was this was not always strictly adhered to, and Pemmel had currently more than an eye for Jackie Ord. After a while he looked at his watch and said, 'Well, lads and lassies, the time has come: bed.'

His guests took the hint and left. Ten minutes later Miss Ord was back. Pemmel said, 'Good ol' Jackie.'

She gave him a look, a raking one. 'Not so much of the old. Or the good either, not tonight. I only came to say you've had too much. You don't need me, you need the surgeon.'

'That old has-been.'

'Which is what you are at this moment. And you know what I mean, Andy. Do I have to spell it out?'

'Shut up,' Pemmel said.

'All right. I'll leave you to your Scotch bottles.'

32

'You bloody bitch,' Pemmel said. He said it without any particular emotion. Jackie Ord left his cabin, her retreating footsteps overlaid by the sound of the forced-draught blowers. Pemmel went for his cupboard and poured another whisky, which he took fast and straight. Then he looked at himself in the full-length mirror behind the door of his wardrobe. Tall and slim yet, no stomach, he looked years younger than forty-five. Even his face . . . well, no, perhaps not. No lines or wrinkles certainly, but there was a puffiness and a nasty pallor behind the suntan and in the morning his eyes would look like pissholes in the snow. But drink was part and parcel of a purser's life: so much duty entertaining of passengers, and he had been too conscientious. It was too late now to kick the habit, he was more or less immersed. He knew the line would say a polite goodbye once the war was over and for now he was going to make hay.

Pemmel shrugged, had another whisky, and dropped fully dressed on to his bunk. In the morning he would feel like death warmed up.

[v]

The *Stephen Starr* was now many sea miles astern of the convoy, way out of the helpful reach of the escorts even if they had been permitted to turn back. Captain Redgrave carried no doctor: the Nazi bullet was still embedded in his right thigh and he was in a good deal of pain and general discomfort: the climb to and from the bridge was difficult to say the least, and he had given up the attempt and now sat permanently on a hard chair in the starboard wing of the bridge, a case of watch on stop on. Hardy, his chief officer, had done what he could with a knife supplied by the galley and sterilized, more or less, by a naked flame. The result had been horrible. The bandages were bloody but Redgrave believed the flow had stopped. The bullet seemed to have missed veins and arteries, which was something to be thankful for. He would make it into Halifax and hospital. As the painful hours passed, however, Redgrave began to regret his quick dismissal of the aid offered by the escorting destroyer that had turned back to the *Stephen Starr*'s assistance. That doctor could have made all the difference, but Redgrave hadn't wanted to be the cause of any ship hanging about in dangerous waters. Nor had he wanted to be yanked off the ship, which had been to say the least a possibility. The *Stephen Starr* had become home now; even back in Liverpool he would remain aboard all the time and then sail again, quite likely without setting foot ashore except on duty. There were those memories of the family . . . now he would guard them personally all the way across the North Atlantic wastes, come gale or sunshine and enemy attack.

His steward came to the bridge, bearing a can of water, a tin hand-basin, a flannel, bandages and some sort of white powder.

'What's all that, Flynn?'

'Bathe the wound, sir.' He pronounced it 'sorr'. Flynn was from County Galway in the west of Ireland, a good and loyal steward who had once been a soldier, a lance-corporal in the Connaught Rangers, a regiment disbanded in 1922 when the British had left and the Irish Free State had come into existence. 'Keep it nice and clean, sir.'

'It's clean enough. Mr Hardy did a good job.'

'Ach, maybe he did, sir. But it'll need attention. We don't want to lose you, sir.'

Redgrave managed a smile. 'In case you can't find the way across without me, no doubt.'

'Ach, that'll be it, sir.'

Redgrave knew it wasn't just that. Flynn looked after him like a nanny, anticipated his every whim with true devotion. Redgrave had lost count of the times he'd bailed Flynn out in the various ports of the world they'd visited. Flynn had been his steward in every ship he'd commanded and Redgrave knew his ingrained habit of drink. Once ashore, Flynn made for the nearest bar. His drink was either Guinness or whisky, usually both, but he was willing to drink the wine of the country when he couldn't get either. The results were often appalling. Redgrave paid the fine, argued the toss with the local police when they wanted to put Flynn in a cell, had even been known to make a metaphorical rude gesture at the Line and hold the ship in port when Flynn had been given an unavoidable week in gaol. Flynn was always grateful. There

34

was nothing he wouldn't do for the Captain.

'Have your way then, Flynn,' Redgrave said.

'Yes, sir. Hold still now – it'll hurt.' Redgrave felt a prize charlie: in the wheelhouse now, trousers down, shirt-tail flapping . . . deftly Flynn removed the bloodied bandage and got to work with the flannel soaked in salt water. It bit and stung, felt as though it must be doing some good. Redgrave could feel the bullet when Flynn pressed, however gently, a red-hot lump boring into his flesh. Flynn clicked his tongue.

'Now what?' Redgrave asked.

'It has an angry look, sir. Red and swollen. Maybe it's heat it needs.'

'What about a poultice?'

'Ach now, a poultice, sir, yes. I'd not be knowing how to make a poultice, sir.'

'You don't *make* a poultice, Flynn, you apply it. It's ready made. That's if there's any kaolin in the medical kit.'

'Kaolin, sir . . . no, there's not. I did happen to notice nothing called kaolin, sir –'

'It's great to be Irish, Flynn. Go and check through, just to be sure.'

'I'll do that, sir, I'll do that right away.'

'And if there's no kaolin, get some bread from the galley. Heat it.'

Flynn looked puzzled. 'Toast, sir, would it be?'

'Not toast. Hot bread. Crumbled, I fancy. Applied and bandaged.'

In truth Redgrave had no idea; nor had Flynn or anybody else aboard. Hardy had been unable even to find the statutory copy of *The Ship Captain's Medical Guide*, which should have been with the first-aid kit. Maybe the rats or cockroaches had eaten it. Redgrave felt as though rats were gnawing at his thigh as he waited for Flynn to prepare some sort of poultice. As he waited he thought of the convoy ahead – far ahead and steaming fast for Halifax. Those big liners . . . himself, he would have detested the life, detested passengers. He was dedicated to the carrying of inanimate cargoes, crates and bales and so forth without tongues to argue with, complain with, ask silly questions with. They could keep their passengers, Redgrave thought, but he could have done with a bit of the plush now, the sheer comfort below and the high bridges that didn't often get swept by spray or solid water. That, and the ship's surgeon. They were mostly a pissy-arsed bunch, but they did know more than Flynn with all his devotion.

The weather was worsening now. Nearly gale force already, and the spray was coming over, drenching the bridge wings, sounding like machine-gun fire on the wheelhouse screens and bulkheads. The ship was lurching heavily from time to time and water was cascading through one of the glass screens shattered by the FW's gunfire. Redgrave shivered, suddenly began feeling hot and cold by turns. Fever? If it was, there was nothing to be done about it except take aspirins. And whisky.

Flynn came back with a dirty-looking tin. He had found the kaolin after all and had sought help as to its administration. He brought a pad of pink stuff, lint. He was making his final preparations when the voice-pipe from the engine-room whined. The second officer, who had the watch, answered then spoke to Redgrave.

'Chief, sir. Wants to stop engines.'

'What for? Never mind, I'll have a word with him.' Redgrave hobbled across to the voice-pipe. All chief engineers were fairly impossible and Hankins rated high in impossibility: this was a fine time to stop engines, in worsening weather and with the glass falling so fast it was going to clang against the bottom. Redgrave knew that the closer enemy was no longer Hitler; it was the elements.

FOUR

Now it was another morning and a grey one. The sky and sea were bleak, the horizons close and seeming to merge with the sea itself. Mason Kemp went to the wheelhouse as soon as he woke, in his pyjamas and dressing-gown. He had found he couldn't sleep, had tossed and turned all night, woken right up at intervals, switched on his light and smoked cigarettes. He was thinking about the *Stephen Starr*: just one ship out of many that were his responsibility, but as important to him as any of the others. The ship was, of course, right out of contact: you didn't break wireless silence at sea in wartime. So Kemp had no notion of what was going on other than that the *Stephen Starr* had shaky engines and a wounded master. Redgrave had been a fool and a remiss one not to have taken advantage of the destroyer's surgeon lieutenant, but Kemp could understand what he knew would be the reasons behind the refusal. Masters stood by their commands. Redgrave had probably thought a lodged bullet not too serious, something not to make a fuss about – at the time anyway. During the previous afternoon Kemp had asked Hampton to send for the ship's surgeon so that he could pump him about lodged bullets, but the result had been unsatisfactory. The surgeon had never seen a lodged bullet and hadn't operated for more than a dozen years. God help passengers with appendicitis, Kemp had thought. He'd served with some first-class ships' surgeons in the Mediterranean-Australia Line; this particular medico was unknown to him until now, had apparently joined the Line from another shipping company just before the war – years ago he had been in general practice somewhere up in

Westmoreland, until his drink problem had eased him out of it, or so it was whispered according to Captain Hampton. Certainly he looked as though he might even clean his teeth in gin in preference to plain water . . .

The wheelhouse door opened and Lieutenant Williams came in.

Kemp turned. 'Morning, Williams.'

'Good morning, sir.' Williams was brisk, rubbing his hands together and smiling. The weather didn't seem to depress him – nice to be young, Kemp thought. 'Poor visibility, sir.'

'Yes, bloody awful. But some protection.'

'We're beyond the Nazis' range by now, sir, I imagine.'

'I wouldn't bank on it,' Kemp said. He reached into his dressing-gown pocket and brought out a silver cigarette-case: a wedding present from Mary and he was never without it. Opening it he handed it round. Williams and the Officer of the Watch, First Officer Wells, accepted. Williams flicked a lighter, always the attentive Commodore's assistant. 'Thank you, Williams.'

Kemp sucked the smoke in deep and blew out a grey-blue cloud. What men at sea would do without cigarettes . . . life savers, stopped you going round the bend, eased tensions, the first thing wounded men in both world wars asked for and were given. And they always kept up the supply to ships at sea, duty-free price sixpence for twenty, half a crown a hundred in sealed, airtight tins.

'Sea's increasing, sir,' Wells said. He looked up at the brass clock above the fore screen: ten minutes to eight bells and the reliefs were moving around the ship, on deck and in the engine-room, ready to take over and send weary officers and men below for breakfast. Wells was writing up the deck log at the end of his watch when the flagship of the cruiser escort began flashing a message to the Commodore.

[ii]

Purser Pemmel didn't feel at all well; it went beyond the expected hangover. He'd vomited and felt better, but only for a short time, after which he felt worse. He was shivering and

38

had a terrible headache and the cabin had spun in circles when he got up from his bunk to visit his bathroom. The symptoms were not unusual and it could be just a hangover but he didn't think it was. This time, there was an extra dimension. Approaching death?

Pemmel tried to pull himself together. It wasn't as bad as that, but there was something wrong. His mind reeled and he had weird thoughts, like visions almost, visions that receded and were replaced by a kind of blank blackness.

Pemmel was dead scared. There was a griping pain in his gut and his stomach felt bloated. When his steward came in with his early-morning tea Pemmel sent him for the doctor. The doctor took his time and came in looking like the wrath of God.

'Thank God you've come,' Pemmel said, looking at his watch.

The doctor sat beside the bunk. 'What seems to be the matter, Pemmel?'

'I'm bloody ill, Doc.'

"M-h'm.' The doctor reached out a shaking hand, holding a thermometer which he thrust beneath the purser's tongue. With the other he felt for the pulse. He was noncommittal as to the result of his investigations. 'What are the symptoms?'

Pemmel told him.

'A simple hangover, that's all.'

'No, it's more than that, Doc, I'm certain. Those queer visions . . . could it be DTS?'

The doctor shook his head. 'Oh, no, you're not a candidate for that. You'd have to be drunk consistently for something like three weeks, never let up, never *sober* up. You haven't reached that stage yet, have you?'

'Of course I haven't.'

'If I were you, I'd make sure I didn't.' The doctor caught the expression on Pemmel's face, the expression that said clearly: look who's talking. He didn't mind; there were few secrets at sea and he and Pemmel had shared many a gin session. There was little work for a doctor to do in all conscience, aboard a ship. He was really only there because the regulations said a doctor had to be carried – two doctors aboard the *Ardara* in fact, and he had an assistant not long out of Bart's, no experience to

39

speak of, mostly seasick, but as sober as a judge, fortunately. 'I do understand. You know that, don't you?'

'Yes.'

'There's not much I can do. I'll have a powder sent along from the surgery – that'll put you right. Better stay turned in for the rest of the day, perhaps – you haven't much to do till we reach Halifax. You can be spared.'

'Yes.'

The doctor looked at him quizzically, bloodshot eyes narrowed above a purple nose. 'You really should cut it down. Think of what can happen. Cirrhosis of the liver for one thing, very nasty indeed.'

Pemmel said, 'It's an occupational hazard.'

'Up to a point. I know what passengers can be like. But use some will power. You must have the strength of mind. You'd not have got a full purser's berth unless you had.'

'For God's sake,' Pemmel said, 'don't preach!'

'I'm trying to help. As I said, I understand. I'm looking for a reason.' The bloated face hung close, like an engorged moon, but the look was kindly, as was the intent. 'Tell me something: is it Sister Ord?'

Pemmel gave a start. 'What's Sister Ord got to do with it – or with you either? What are you suggesting?'

'I'm not suggesting anything. But you can't expect these things not to be talked about. I've been at sea long enough to know that. I'm not moralizing either – it's not my concern other than as a medicine man. It's between you and me. I'm still looking for that reason, old chap. If you'd like to – to unburden yourself –'

'Are you after Jackie too?' Pemmel asked angrily. 'Is that it?'

The doctor wasn't offended. 'Goodness, no! I'm past all that sort of thing, a long time past. Don't worry on that score. If you'd just like to talk, I'm very willing to listen.'

I'll bet you are, Pemmel thought, dirty old man. Vicarious sex . . . the doc was after the gory details, would listen to all revelations with flapping ears, after which he would see Jackie Ord through different, lascivious eyes. Pemmel said, 'Just bugger off, Doc. If you're not going to treat me, just bugger off.' The doctor shrugged, looked sad, got to his feet and left the cabin. A few minutes later Pemmel got up. He felt better,

40

quite suddenly, and no thanks to the quack. He believed it had been a mild case of panic and all he needed was a morning stiffener of brandy and ginger ale.

[iii]

The signal from cs29 – the abbreviation for the Rear-Admiral Commanding the 29th Cruiser Squadron – though sent openly by lamp, was in naval cypher. It carried the Most Secret prefix and in addition to the convoy Commodore it was addressed to the senior officer of the destroyer escort and the captain of the battleship. Aboard the *Ardara* Lieutenant Williams had the decyphering tables in the safe in his cabin. One of his action duties, if the *Ardara* should look like being sunk, was to take the codes and cyphers in lead-weighted bags to the open deck where he would throw them over the side – just in case. An abandoned ship could stay afloat after all, and could be searched. Now, with Leading Signalman Mouncey's numeral-filled naval message form safely in his pocket, he went to his cabin to begin what was going to be a long job of decyphering.

Mason Kemp paced the liner's bridge, out in the open wing, facing the gale, bracing himself against the roll and pitch of the ship beneath him, pondering on the unexpected cypher. That it must be important was obvious. Even so, Kemp thought it was carrying security to extremes not to use plain language between ships out at sea with no enemy present. No U-boat captain would come so close to the surface in this weather that he could read a signal through his periscope. Was there, could there be, a lack of trust in the merchant-ship masters or their officers? Scarcely; but there was a parallel thought insofar as ships could be torpedoed when the weather moderated, and survivors could be interrogated, and the Nazi methods were far from civilized. Admirals had to have a care. Kemp paced on, felt the wind and spray, and now the rain, stinging his face; he willed his assistant to make fast work of the decyphering.

But below in his cabin Lieutenant Williams was having difficulty and was smoking one cigarette after another and looking distracted. He had always found decyphering – or

41

encyphering come to that – a hard task and this time there appeared to be some corrupt groups since some of it wasn't making sense. The originator of the signal was the Admiralty, not unexpectedly, and that was about as far as Williams had got so far. It was probably the fault of Leading Signalman Mouncey in not taking down properly the repeat flashed by light. Williams got a little further and decyphered the words Prime Minister. There was an obvious importance and Williams wrestled on, trying not to let himself get rattled by his slowness.

[iv]

Away astern of the convoy, the main body of which was now beginning to approach the longitude of Cape Farewell at the southern tip of Greenland, though well to the south, the *Stephen Starr* lay with her engines stopped, heaving and rolling to the deep-sea swell and the waves brought up by the increasing wind. That wind was now at gale force. Captain Redgrave was still in the wheelhouse, the chair having been brought in from the bridge wing after Flynn had finished his first bathing and poulticing exercise, an exercise that had been repeated several times since. Redgrave was in considerable pain and the wound looked nasty. Flynn was a worried man, and cursed engineers under his breath but not so low that Redgrave didn't hear.

'The chief's doing his best, Flynn. Criticism doesn't help matters.'

'That's right, sir.'

The Irish were a weird lot, largely: there were two physical types of Irish, one lugubrious and dark and with a long upper lip, the other fresh-faced and merry, always smiling. There were two mental types as well, one argumentative, the other tending to agree with everything that was said. Physically Flynn was group one; mentally, group two. A tiresome group; Flynn, having agreed that what the Captain said was right, went on muttering as he fixed the fresh bandage.

Redgrave said, 'Put a sock in it, Flynn. Not the thigh, your mouth.'

Flynn grinned. 'Yes, sir. Sorry, sir. It's you I'm worried about, sir.'

'Then don't be. You've done your best. The rest is up to God.'

'And the chief engineer, sir.'

'Oh, get away with you, Flynn.'

Flynn departed; Redgrave stared through the rain and the spray-slashed glass of the fore screen. He had an idea the engines would never start again; they needed the assistance of the shore, of the shipyard. Worn out, past it, and, according to Hankins, not the right spares aboard, not the ones he needed for the job. Hankins had tried to explain to the bridge but neither the Captain nor any of the deck officers seemed to hoist in the technical details and he'd given up. The screw wasn't turning over and that was all they were interested in, and it was his job to make the repair before Hitler found them wallowing and helpless. With his second engineer he worked like a slave, covered in grease and muck, perspiring and feeling savage and wanting to take a crowbar and smash the whole show up. He was as conscious as anyone else aboard of the potential dangers of lying stopped on the convoy routes, though very likely by this time the gale had blown them away to the north of the track, somewhere up towards Greenland and the Denmark Strait.

The voice-pipe from the bridge whined and the second engineer answered, then called out to Hankins.

'Bridge, Chief. Skipper wants a word –' The second engineer broke off, swore as his feet slid from under him on the greasy steel deck. 'Bugger!'

'D'you mind?' Hankins asked coldly.

'Sorry, Chief.' Hankins was religious, a member of the Elim Tabernacle, and swearing and such was a sin. 'Such' included almost everything a seaman indulged in: fags, booze, women. The second engineer thought what a hell of a life the chief must have had, always in the company of sinners; but no doubt it meant he saved money.

Hankins was at the voice-pipe. 'Chief here. No progress yet, Captain.'

'As long as you're doing your best, Chief.'

'Of course I'm doing my best. And it doesn't help to keep

43

pushing.' Ill-temperedly, Hankins banged back the voice-pipe cover. At once he regretted it: the skipper was all right and he was said to be in pain. Nasty, that bullet wound. Hankins had half a mind to call the bridge and apologize, but he didn't. It might show weakness. He lurched across the engine-room from the starting platform, fast and slow by turns as the deck heaved beneath his feet, and fetched up hard against a big handwheel. Not a tall man, he banged his face against the metal. His lips worked: often he wished he wasn't a member of the Elim congregation. At times like this a good, hearty 'bugger' would have been an immense relief. But as it was he had no intention of messing up his chances with the Almighty, whom he might be about to meet face to face at any moment.

[v]

When Williams had finished his task he had brought the result to the bridge, post-haste, doubling up the ladders, his expression urgent. Saluting Mason Kemp, he passed over the transcript on a naval message form. He couldn't wait to impart the news in person. He almost gabbled it out. 'It's Mr Churchill, sir!'

The Commodore nodded. 'All right, Williams. Thank you.'

He read. The Admiralty's signal as summarized by cs29 was very informative: 'The Prime Minister is currently aboard *Prince of Wales* steaming to the south of the convoy en route for a meeting with President Roosevelt in Newfoundland waters. *Prince of Wales* is strongly escorted but intelligence reports indicate two German commerce raiders proceeding north from the South Atlantic. One is believed to be *Scharnhorst* the other a converted merchantman. I am ordered to detach with all escorts except two destroyers and steam towards the Germans to intercept. Commodore will assume command of remaining escorts. The priority is obvious and the situation most urgent.'

Without comment the Commodore handed the message to Hampton. He said, 'This won't be Winston's wish. Very likely he doesn't even know. He wouldn't leave a convoy without protection.'

'An *empty* convoy,' Hampton said.

44

Kemp gave a hard laugh. 'Not quite empty! Just add up all the crews, Captain. However, those are the orders. We just push on. No option!'

Williams said, 'We're moving into safer waters, sir. Beyond U-boat range.'

'We won't count too many chickens, Williams. And the information about Churchill is to be kept to the bridge.' Kemp moved away, paced the bridge wing as he had done so many times. To reduce the escort so drastically was an extreme measure whether or not the convoy was moving into safer waters; it was going to be bad for morale, would leave a very naked feeling as the warships turned to the south and steamed away. The little ships, the corvettes, had already withdrawn for home waters as indicated by NCSO in the Clyde, and even their departure had left a gap both in the defences and in the minds of the merchant crews who had watched them go. Soon the tankers would be detaching for the Gulf of Mexico – soon, but not yet. As this thought came to Kemp a light started flashing from cs29's signal bridge and Leading Signalman Mouncey banged the shutters of his signalling projector in acknowledgement. This time the signal was in plain language, and Mouncey read it out to the waiting officers.

'Commodore from cs29, sir. Tankers *British Light*, *British Lantern* and *British Leader* will accompany me for refuelling destroyers in suitable weather conditions and will then detach in accordance with previous orders.'

'Thank you, Mouncey. Williams –'

'Sir?'

'Make to the tankers: You are to detach with cs29 and then come under his orders.'

'Aye, aye, sir. Mouncey?'

'Yessir!'

Kemp listened to the rigmarole, the repetition to Mouncey of what he had just said to Williams. The RN was something of a marvel insofar as it found time to work at all amidst all the bull and flannel. All the niceties had to be observed, and that wasn't just as between Williams and the leading signalman. It was as between cs29 and himself. The Rear-Admiral could more expeditiously have made the signal direct to the tankers himself, but no, that would cut out the Commodore of the convoy, rip across his responsibilities. Sometimes Kemp thought he was just a messenger, a signal link between the escort and his merchant ships. Very largely that was so; but not any longer, not this time, not all the way in to Halifax.

In a few more minutes the convoy would be on its own and so would he, the Commodore. He would be in total command of thirty-four merchant ships plus two destroyers. They would succeed or fail, arrive in Nova Scotia or sink *en route*, depending upon his yet-to-be-proven ability to outwit any enemy that might be in the vicinity.

[vi]

Pemmel had gone along to the main office after all, but had skipped breakfast as he usually did, making do with a cup of strong black coffee to follow the brandy and ginger ale. He found his deputy purser in conference with the chief and second stewards. They all looked up as Pemmel entered. Mr Portway thought there was one thing about the purser: even when his eyes looked red in the whites he was always well turned out dresswise – he had his steward largely to thank for that, of course.

'Morning, sir,' the chief steward said.

'Good morning, Mr Sandys. Anything you want of me?'

'Not really, sir. Just a reminder: Captain's Rounds, 1100 hours.'

'God damn . . . what day of the week is it?'

It was the deputy purser who answered. 'Saturday, sir.'

'Ha!' Stupid of him to have asked. Captain's Rounds was always on Saturday. Pemmel banged his way into his private office, sat down and put his head in his hands. He felt ill again, his stomach heaving. He was losing his grip and hoped it wasn't becoming obvious. A knock came at his door and the second steward entered. Pemmel looked up.

'What is it, Mr Portway?'

'Permission to alter the last lot of overtime sheets, sir.'

'See the deputy purser. You know the drill.'

'Yes, sir. But Mr Lewis said to see you, sir, seeing as the sheets have gone through the Portage Bill.'

46

'Already?' The Portage Bill was the account of the crew's wages, overtime payments, allotments, fines, income tax and insurance deductions and so on. Even with no passengers aboard, there was still work for the purser's department to do. 'Someone's been conscientious, evidently. All right, Portway, tell Mr Lewis he can make the alteration.' He paused. 'What's it all about?'

Portway coughed. 'Dispute from some of the bedroom stewards, sir.'

'Dispute?'

'Bit of a moan, sir.'

'They haven't got enough overtime – even though the cabins are empty, and they haven't enough work even to fill the normal hours of duty?'

Mr Portway shuffled his feet. 'Well, sir. You know how it is, sir.'

'Yes, yes, I do. They have to keep their families in the style to which they've become accustomed – by way of unworked overtime. All right, Mr Portway, go ahead and work your ungodly fiddles only don't make it too obvious, eh?'

'Thank you very much, sir,' Mr Portway said, and backed out of the door obsequiously. Bedroom stewards were only bedroom stewards but when they banded together they could be a flaming nuisance to a second steward who liked peace and quiet – and good bonuses for himself. He looked at his watch: early yet, but he had things to see to, and if he spun them out he'd be right on time to bum a noggin off the chief steward at 1030. He went about his work, ponderously, carrying a sheaf of papers: you always looked busy when you carried a sheaf of papers and never mind what the subject matter happened to be. Sharp at 1030, which he knew from experience was the exact moment the chief steward relaxed on Saturday mornings with a bottle of beer before Captain's Rounds, Mr Portway knocked at the cabin door and went in, trying to look surprised at how well he had timed his arrival.

'Sorry to butt in, Chief –'

'Save your lying breath,' Sandys said amiably, 'and shove your arse in a chair.'

'Well, don't mind if I do. Thanks.'

'All ready for the skipper, are we?'

Portway nodded. 'All ready. Nice and easy when the ship's empty.'

'Still get accumulations of dust.'

Portway nodded and took a tankard of beer from the chief steward's hand. Dust. He knew captains, and he knew Captain Hampton in particular. Dust was his hobby and he knew instinctively where to look, where to draw his hand across the top of a steam pipe or similar and have it come away dirty. Then the rocket went right down the line: staff captain, chief officer, purser – if the dust was in the accommodation – chief steward, second steward. Mr Portway did his own bollocking afterwards until the actual miscreant was discovered and taught a thing or two. This time he'd been round all the accommodation twice, just to make sure. He was about to tell Mr Sandys this when the Tannoy came on, informatively, from the bridge.

'This is the Captain speaking. The naval escort is about to withdraw. There is no cause for any concern, the situation in regard to the convoy is in hand.'

That was all. The chief steward gazed blankly at Portway and said, 'Well, luv-a-duck, eh? What's all that in aid of?'

FIVE

If so many of the convoy crews were thinking in their quiet moments of home, of wives and girlfriends, parents and brothers and sisters, then an equal number of thoughts were winging out across the seas from the home front. Naturally, the tightest possible security screen had been thrown around the mission of HMS *Prince of Wales* and the fact of the vital meeting between Prime Minister and President. A handful of persons were in full possession of the facts; Mr Churchill had embarked in total secrecy and the *Prince of Wales*, Britain's newest and most powerful battleship, had slipped away into the dawn mists from Scapa Flow, as anonymously as was possible, carrying the hopes of a war-torn country across the seas to the New World.

Much secrecy: so the families knew nothing, had no knowledge that now their menfolk were being left unguarded. But no matter: they would have worried anyway, since they worried all the time when their minds were not otherwise occupied. One of them was Patricia Redgrave, Captain Redgrave's sister, a spinster of thirty-five who looked after her father, a widower. They lived in York, a house off the main road running into the city from Harrogate and Green Hammerton. Peter Redgrave filled Patricia's life: the father was tiresome, demanding, rude and unloved, and the fact of his continued existence had kept the daughter chained to spinsterhood. That, and nothing else: she was attractive enough to have married and she'd had her chances but she'd been loyal to her father, who was an invalid, and had never felt it fair to ask any husband to take him on.

The news from Liverpool earlier had been shattering: she had wept for Peter and prayed for him to come to York but beyond one quick visit he had not done so. Now she prayed for his safe return, knowing nothing of the current state of affairs aboard the *Stephen Starr*. She knew her father worried too, though he didn't say much. He was too preoccupied with his own state of ill-health, had too much to say on that subject to have speech for anything else. There were only so many hours in a day . . .

Mary Kemp worried too, down south in Meopham. John had a hard job to do, mentally and physically wearing, always at sea – but he'd been at sea all his working life. She believed he would come through the war: she had a strong belief in God and she knew her prayers were going to be answered, so her worries were more for John's day-to-day life than his safety and eventual homecoming.

In Thurrock in Essex Mrs Portway, as frigid as ever, had no idea that a girl called Mabel in Grays, not so far away, was worrying about her husband, although, when on Herbert Portway's last leave she'd been shopping with him in Grays, there had been a curious incident that had bothered her for a while and had then been forgotten: Herbert, not looking where he was going, had bumped stomachs with a fattish young lady outside the Co-op, quite an accident, but there had been some confusion, startled looks from both of them and the young lady's face very red, more as if they knew each other than reciprocal apologies between strangers over a bit of clumsiness. Had she but known it, that was Mabel. Mabel – a case of fat calling to fat perhaps, plus a certain mutual unattractiveness – was in love with Herbert Portway. They saw quite a lot of one another when his ship was in Tilbury: Mabel worked in Tilbury and it was comparatively easy for a second steward to find business ashore, comparatively easy for a second steward to find good excuses why he couldn't get home to a wife in Thurrock and by no means impossible for that second steward to bring a popsie aboard to his cabin in the bowels of the ship. A shade more difficult in wartime perhaps than it had been in peace, but not impossible. As for Mabel, she had no ties and could always take time off work on the ground of feeling seedy. It wasn't as though Herbert Portway

50

was continually on the scene.

Mabel was one of the worriers, whenever Mr Portway was at sea. She always feared the worse: he had come into her life some four years earlier, – she worked, as now in a laundry and Mr Portway had come ashore to negotiate for the laundering of the stewards' gear, or the gear of such as were not on leave, the liner's own laundry being temporarily out of commission due to a recalcitrant electric fault. It had been a case of love at first sight through the steamy mist of Mabel's working environment, at any rate on her part. To Mr Portway she was just another bit of fluff that might prove willing and did. He seldom thought about her when he wasn't with her, other than to hope to goodness she never got a bun in the oven and tried to pin it on him . . .

He wasn't thinking about her or any of the others now, as the *Ardara*'s staff captain made Rounds in the place of Captain Hampton who was otherwise occupied on the bridge as the warship escort withdrew to the south.

[ii]

The naked feeling had come. Commodore Kemp watched as more signals were made between cs29 and the rest of the escort. A flag hoist crept colourfully to the cruiser's starboard fore yardarm. Leading Signalman Mouncey trained a telescope on to it. Within the minute it was hauled down and Mouncey reported to the Commodore.

'Executive, sir.'

'Thank you, Mouncey.'

That was when the warships made their turn to port, increasing speed when they had done so. They steamed away through the gale, taking the three tankers with them. Kemp was lucky, he supposed, to be left with the RFA.

'Williams?'

'Sir?'

'Make to cs29: Good luck go with you all.'

Mouncey said suddenly, 'Rear-Admiral's signalling, sir.' He read it off. 'May God have mercy on us all.'

Williams asked, 'Do you still wish to make your signal, sir?'

51

'Yes,' Kemp said.

He looked around at the bridge personnel – Hampton, Williams, the two Officers of the Watch, Leading Signalman Mouncey, the ship's quartermaster and the bridge messengers and telegraphsmen. He looked out across the gale-torn sea at the accompanying ships plodding along for Halifax, all now wide open to attack. He felt very lonely. The two remaining destroyers steaming ahead of the convoy to port and starboard brought little feeling of security. There was a similar sense of loss throughout the ship: all personnel not on watch or caught up with Captain's Rounds were on deck, watching the inexplicable retreat of the heavy cruisers and the destroyers and the old battleship wallowing in the troughs and cutting through the wave crests to fling the tons of water back over her fo'c'sle to swill around the fifteen-inch turrets now moving to the defence of the Prime Minister. Not that anyone other than those on the *Ardara*'s bridge knew anything about that; Kemp's order had been strictly adhered to and no rumours had spread, no rumours, that was, that came anywhere near the facts. There was a similar situation aboard the rest of the ships of the convoy. Only the Commodore had been told; the masters and their crews were left to speculate. Aboard the *Ardara* there was a lot of speculation. To say that everyone was dazed would have been an understatement. It was unbelievable. Not unnaturally in the circumstances, the navy itself was taking the blame. A crowd of galley hands right aft on E deck, hanging over the guardrails of the open deck-space accorded the lower orders, were loud in their condemnation.

'Bloody yellow-bellies –'

'Pissin' off and leavin' us to it!'

The voice of common sense was there as well, insisting that there had to be a good reason, but it was shouted down. The only reason was the navy's own safety. The anti-navy sentiments took no time to reach the naval ratings who manned the ancient six-inch LA guns and the close-range weapons. Twelve DEMS – Defensively Equipped Merchant Ships – gunnery rates plus two leading seamen qualified as captains of the guns first class, with the assistance of some members of the *Ardara*'s own crew trained for the job by naval gunnery instructors. These latter mostly manned the ship's anti-aircraft armament, which

52

consisted of three Lewis guns and four 40-mm Bofors, mounted along the boat deck, plus two light machine-guns mounted in the bridge wings. The six-inch were manned only in action but there were always four ack-ack gunners on watch. In general charge was a petty officer with the non-substantive rating of gunlayer – PO Frapp, a pessimistic man, a pensioner of the Royal Fleet Reserve, three good-conduct badges, indigestion, and elderly to be still at sea. He had first seen service as a seaman boy before the 1914–18 war, back in the *Dreadnought* days.

A deputation waited on Petty Officer Frapp, complaining of hostility.

'I know, lads.' Frapp pushed his cap back and scratched at his head, grizzled grey in a fringe around a bald top. 'Only to be expected, I reckon. Me, I'm looking for a reason too. Could be anything.'

'Another convoy . . . under attack somewhere south?'

'No, that won't wash. Each escort to its own convoy, that's the flaming rule, lad. You don't shift things around like that, rob Peter to pay Paul.'

'There's going to be trouble, PO. Some of us . . . we're going to hit back if that bloody galley rabble don't shut their traps –'

Frapp shook a warning finger. 'Cool it. We don't want that sort of thing aboard. Tell you what. I'll go and see that Williams, see if he knows anything. Or Mouncey, maybe.'

[iii]

Frapp's journey to the bridge proved unnecessary. He was on his way when the Tannoy came on again – Kemp's voice, speaking to the crew with the formal permission of Captain Hampton. He confirmed: no reason to be alarmed. The escort was required elsewhere, in waters more liable to contain German forces, and the convoy was not expected to steam into any difficulties. A situation report had just been received from the Admiralty: there was nothing indicated on the plot, nothing between the convoy's position and Halifax. But as a precaution escorts would be leaving Halifax and were expected to rendezvous in forty-eight hours and take them over.

That, as Frapp said, was something. Things weren't so bad that they couldn't get worse, he said with a misguided attempt at humour. Anyway, Kemp's words had improved the atmosphere and the resentment against the navy simmered down. Then, just after the midday dinner, Frapp was sent for to go to the bridge.

He went up at once and reported to Lieutenant Williams. 'You wanted me, sir?'

'The Commodore.' Williams turned about, approached Kemp and saluted. 'Petty Officer Frapp, sir, reporting.'

Kemp came away from the bridge screen, returned Frapp's salute. 'Guns, Frapp.'

'Yessir?'

'As I said on the Tannoy, there's absolutely no cause for alarm. But we must be prepared for any emergency, naturally. I know you've been carrying out exercises on passage, but now I want gun-drill stepped up. Exercise action twice each watch – day and night. Get your guns' crews right on the top line – understood, Frapp?'

'Yessir.'

'And another thing: I want you to reorganize your watch and quarter bill. I want both the six-inch manned with skeleton crews from now until we make the rendezvous with the escorts out of Halifax. It'll no longer be good enough to have just the close-range weapons manned.'

'Aye, aye, sir,' Frapp said.

'If anything does happen, the convoy's going to be largely dependent on the naval guns' crews embarked aboard the merchant ships – that's obvious. The destroyers can't cover the whole convoy. All right, Frapp, thank you.'

When the PO had left the bridge, Kemp told off Williams to signal all ships that they were to bring their guns' crews to a similar state of readiness. By nightfall that day the weather had shown signs of moderating, returning to more seasonal conditions. The glass, which had started a slow rise, went up fast during the night and by dawn the sea had flattened considerably, with all the ships riding more steadily. Kemp, who had remained on the bridge throughout the night, remarked to Williams on the change.

'Not so good, in certain circumstances.'

'No, sir.' There was no need to spell it out: they both knew what better weather could bring. The convoy was not, in fact, wholly in the clear yet. Hitler had some very long-range U-boats; also, it was not impossible, as Kemp knew, for a German surface raider to steal down through the Denmark Strait past Greenland's eastern coastline and emerge into the North Atlantic to head for the convoy tracks. Not impossible, but perhaps not likely: in theory such a raider should encounter the armed merchant cruisers of the British Northern Patrol. The poor old AMCS . . . they might be sunk but at least they would make a report and the main battle units of the Home Fleet could then be sent out from Scapa and the Firth of Forth.

Kemp looked around: there was no one close enough to overhear. In a low voice he said to Williams, 'I wonder what this meeting's all about. Any ideas?'

'Not a clue, sir. At a guess, I'd say Mr Churchill's trying to prod the Americans into the war.'

'That's my idea too. A kind of grand alliance, reaching across the Atlantic. Well, I wish them luck!'

Williams nodded. 'Yes, sir, very much so. If the Yanks come in . . . well, it would make all the difference. I suppose they'd share the escort duties for one thing?'

'Yes. Just what we need. The poor bloody country's bleeding to death . . . and then there's their army, all those fresh troops. Not good for Hitler at all!' Kemp paused, lifted his binoculars and scanned the seas ahead and to either bow. Flattening out, but leaving the usual swell behind the departed gale. That sea still looked empty without the escort's protection. He said, 'D'you know, Williams, I've a feeling we're on the coat-tails of history – of history about to be made.'

'Perhaps we are, sir.'

Kemp looked at his assistant's somewhat blank face. 'Does that do anything to you, Williams?'

'Do anything, sir?'

Kemp gave a sigh. 'No. I see that it doesn't.'

'Well . . . not really, sir.'

'Pity.' Kemp had plenty of imagination; he believed young Williams hadn't any beyond his sense of self-importance and the dash he might cut with the girls when they reached

Halifax. There was something of a Brylcreem image about Lieutenant Williams, as though the creases in his uniform trousers were of more importance than the conduct of the convoy. He was always very well turned out beneath the layers of wet-weather gear and this morning, with the weather so fine, he was simply beautiful. Kemp turned away and went into the wheelhouse for a word with the watchkeepers, still thinking about history, which meant a lot to him. Twenty-odd years after the event, he was still glad he'd been present when the German High Seas Fleet had steamed under escort of Admiral Beatty to its final anchorage in the waters of Scapa Flow: that had been history, so had the act of scuttling when a whole navy had opened its seacocks and gone down to oblivion in the hour of its total defeat. Kemp, as a seaman, was glad enough that he hadn't witnessed *that* sad scene. There had certainly been no gloating from the British Fleet that day.

[iv]

Petty Officer Frapp had been allocated a cabin, all to himself, something he'd never been accorded before. In HM ships, you slept in a hammock unless you were the master-at-arms or managed to survive the rigours of the lower deck and the attentions of the enemy so far as to achieve the rank of warrant officer and above. Frapp really spread himself: it was almost like home. In peacetime some nob would have paid the earth for what he was getting for nothing, a nice single-berth cabin with a wash-basin on B deck . . . talk about posh! On the chest-of-drawers – much better than a ditty box or locker for stowing personal things – he had set up his family photographs. Doris and the kids, though they weren't kids any longer. Ron was twenty-one and already in the Andrew himself, if only as a leading writer in the Commodore's office in RNB Pompey. PO Frapp thought writers a smarmy bunch, not unlike that Williams the convoy had been lumbered with, thought a lot of themselves and filed their fingernails and had smarmed-down hair. Very uppish with common seamen, especially when the latter had any queries about their pay and allowances. They talked double-dutch mostly, baffled brains with bullshit and implied that you had no education. They treated even seaman petty officers as idiots and many a time Frapp had wanted nothing in the world so much as to take one of the pansy little sods by the scruff of the neck and kick his arse all the way across the parade ground from the Pay Office to the seamen's blocks and then stuff his face down a pan in the heads. It irked him continually that Ron was one of them.

The girl, Else, was all right. Risen in the world – married a pilot officer in the RAF! Not that Petty Officer Frapp had any more time for the RAF than for writers, they were such a scruffy and indisciplined shower and never around when wanted, but an officer was a catch. Pilot Officer Pinkney, when they had met, had told Frapp rather grandly that he needn't call him sir and had himself addressed Frapp as Dad, which Frapp liked – being called Dad by an officer was quite something. He had responded by calling Pilot Officer Pinkney son, after a bit of embarrassment and a tendency at first for the 's' sound to be followed by 'ir'.

Petty Officer Frapp, down from the upper deck to catch up on some sleep, looked at his watch, a pocket-watch he'd bought for five bob in Gibraltar years before when serving in a battleship of the Mediterranean Fleet, the flagship *Queen Elizabeth* no less. Just about now, Leading Signalman Mouncey would be coming off watch, his place on the bridge being taken by his side-kick, MacCord. The bunting tossers were berthed with the guns' crews, in a converted stateroom one deck up.

Frapp left his cabin and went up the stairs – real *stairs*, in a ship! – and hung about in the vicinity of Mouncey's accommodation, looking busy by shuffling a fistful of lists. Mr Portway wasn't the only one who knew the game.

Mouncey appeared. Frapp looked up. 'Oh – you, Bunts.'

'As ever was, PO.'

'Better up top, eh? Weather, I mean.'

'Yep.'

'Going to turn in?'

'You bet I am,' Mouncey said.

'Don't blame you, but . . . look, sleep comes better after a tot, right?' Frapp edged closer and gave Mouncey a wink. 'Not a word to anyone, Bunts, but I got a bottle of Scotch in my cabin.' Mr Portway, a power in the ship where the bar staff were concerned, had been co-operative. 'Care for a nip, would you, eh?'

'Don't mind if I do,' Mouncey said. 'Thanks a lot, PO.'

They went down and Frapp shut the door firmly, waved Mouncey to a chair and brought his bottle from the cupboard that in peacetime would have held only the bedroom utensil, which in fact was still there. There was a chink of china as Frapp removed the John Haig. In the meantime Mouncey had been studying the photographs.

'Nice-looking girl,' he said, flipping a thumb towards Else. 'Daughter, is she?'

'Married to an RAF officer.'

'You don't say! Cor.' Mouncey shifted target. 'That your missus, PO?'

'Yes.' The less said about Doris the better; she was pure vinegar and her tongue was busy acid, never still. Scraggy as a daddy-long-legs with it. Frapp, his back turned to Doris, poured two tots. They all missed the daily rum issue, the lack of which was the principal drawback of being in a liner rather than a warship.

'Cheerio,' Mouncey said. 'And thanks again.'

'Bottoms up. Don't mention it.' Frapp drank, folding his lips one over the other in appreciation. Then he approached the reason for his hospitality. 'Funny business, all this.'

'What, PO?'

'Withdrawing the escort like.'

'Yer.'

'Commodore doesn't go much on it, I'll bet.'

'No. 'E don't.'

Frapp coughed. 'I heard there was a signal . . .'

'That's right. Cypher. Officers only.'

'Course, yes. You wouldn't know what was in it, would you?'

'No.'

There was a short silence. The curtains over Frapp's scuttle swayed inwards to the *Ardara*'s roll: the swell was heavy still. Firing the six-inch from a ship with such a roll on her would be like trying to train and lay the turrets aboard one of the old County Class cruisers, the 10,000-ton three-funnellers with so much freeboard they rolled their guts out in a flat calm. Frapp

58

tried again, all his curiosity, his innate seaman's urge to pick up the latest buzz, consuming him.

'Dare say you may have heard something, Bunts,' he said. 'Being up there on the bridge, like?'

Mouncey shook his head. 'Not a thing. Not a bloody thing. Commodore, he don't say much.'

'Williams, though?'

'Likewise. Williams don't know he's born, half the time.'

'Not even a buzz?'

'Not even a buzz,' Mouncey said firmly, tongue in cheek. He'd heard all right – enough to have some idea at any rate. He'd heard Lieutenant Williams speak the name, Winston Churchill. That was about all in fact, apart from the Commodore's order that nothing was to be mentioned thereafter. Maybe Winnie had some special task for the escort, but if he had, then Mouncey didn't know what it was. And he wasn't going to open his trap about Churchill. If Frapp talked around the ship, which he would, the Commodore would know very well who to pin it on: himself, Leading Signalman Mouncey, who had no intention of risking his rate. He finished the second whisky and looked hopefully at his empty glass for another, but in vain.

'You can bugger off,' PO Frapp said sourly, having developed a sudden dislike for the sharp-faced little leading signalman, 'if you've got no bloody buzzes.'

Grinning, Mouncey left the cabin. 'Useless bloody article,' Frapp said as the door closed.

[v]

Williams had been with Kemp on the bridge for the latter part of the night and remained there when the Commodore went below for a wash and shave and a change of clothing. And breakfast, which Williams had already been down for. Wartime or not, the food was good. No rationing for those who ploughed the waves in merchantmen or warships. Williams had tucked into grapefruit, cornflakes with condensed milk, kipper, fried egg, bacon, sausages, hot rolls and marmalade and several cups of steaming coffee. Now he felt good as he paced the bridge, back and forth like Kemp, really feeling the assistant commodore and in charge of the convoy until Kemp returned. If anything should happen, it would be up to him to deal with it in the first instance and he rehearsed in his mind what he should do – not for the first time: it was the duty of an officer to think ahead, to visualize situations, use his imagination; and in that imagination Lieutenant Williams had dealt with all manner of emergencies. Fire below, the appearance of a periscope, sudden aircraft attack, the advent of a German pocket-battleship, man overboard, collision between ships of the convoy, some hiatus in the engine-room, defective steering for one reason or another, the sudden and unheralded impact of a torpedo. There was potentially any amount of drama at sea and Williams knew that his list of rehearsals could never be complete; it was always the unexpected, the unrehearsed, that tended to happen and then you were liable to be caught out. Nevertheless Williams went on dreaming, seeing himself as the saviour of the convoy, the one who had in fact thought out the unexpected in advance and had dealt with it, his sense of the dramatic and the heroic dimmed only a little by what would prove to be the fact: his immediate reaction would be to obey the Commodore's standing order: *If anything should happen, call me at once.* And in the meantime, the transport's Officer of the Watch, if not her master, would have acted.

After a while Williams' thoughts shifted elsewhere: they shifted homeward to Hounslow. He thought of his father, travelling daily to the City in a crowded District Line train, carrying his gas-mask dutifully – his father had always been dutiful. If anybody asked him to do anything, he did it, like sacrificing the iron railings in front of the house in aid of the war effort, fondly imagining they'd be turned into guns to blast off at Hitler. Williams believed that to be nothing more than a ploy, something dreamed up by Lord Beaverbrook, or Churchill himself, to make the man in the street, the civilian, feel he was doing his bit. His father had been angry when he'd suggested that on his last leave, telling him he shouldn't belittle what the civilians were doing. Look, his father had said, at the Home Guard and, come to that, the ARP wardens like himself. He'd got in such a state that Williams had banged out of the house, calling out to his mother that he would be back late, and had gone to the pictures and sat through Deanna Durbin.

He'd gone by himself, wishing he had a girl to take. He hadn't got a girlfriend and really he couldn't understand why. He'd tried hard enough but somehow things never seemed to click, or not for long. It wasn't as though he was a freak: he knew he looked smart in his uniform, top button always undone, handkerchief tucked into left sleeve, stiff collar, cap at a Beatty-ish angle, never a hair out of place. To think of some of the scruff girls went out with! But whenever he found a girl who seemed likely, he never had the right conversation. Perhaps it was too naval; even the odd Wren in Portsmouth or Greenock or wherever seemed to tire of naval slang and his yarns about old so-and-so and how tight he'd got last time in port. It always petered out, generally by way of a broken date followed by excuses, but once by more direct methods. A leading Wren called Judy, in Greenock.

She'd stopped suddenly one early evening, in the main street while they'd been on their way to the Naval Officers' Club for a drink.

She said impatiently, 'Oh, for God's sake, Paul!'

'What d'you mean?' He'd stared, blankly. He hadn't done anything that he was aware of.

'Stop looking at yourself, can't you?'

'I –'

'You haven't missed a shop window yet,' she said, really angry. 'Talk about Narcissus! Looking over your shoulder all the way along.'

He was hurt; his face flamed and he blurted it out. 'Oh, piss off, why don't you!'

Then she had slapped his face. There happened to be a naval patrol passing, trudging along the gutters wearing belts and gaiters, watching out for ratings who failed to salute officers. The seamen had grinned openly; Williams had been mortified. Of course, he could have run the girl in – a leading Wren, striking an officer, a Court Martial offence if ever there was one! Anyway, that was the last he'd seen of Judy. She had been fairly recent, not long before he'd got his present appointment as assistant commodore, and he wished she'd lasted. It was nice to have a girl at home to think about when

61

upon the lonely wastes of the sea. It wasn't the same, having only his parents to think about, the romance was absent.

But a time would come; Williams thought ahead to Halifax. Canadian girls might be more forthcoming, less inhibited and less formal than their English counterparts. After all, Canada had been a pioneering country with wagon trains, gold rushes, saloons and doxies. Some of that spirit must linger yet.

Williams was thinking un-naval thoughts when the escorting destroyer on the port bow of the convoy began flashing back towards the Commodore and was answered by Signalman MacCord, who reported to Lieutenant Williams.

'Contact, sir, bearing red two five!'

Williams went into the wheelhouse at the double and, wrenching back the voice-pipe cover to Kemp's cabin, called the Commodore to the bridge.

SIX

Aboard the *Stephen Starr* the engines were turning over again but Captain Redgrave's condition had worsened and Flynn was a worried man. The wound was an angry red and the flesh was very swollen and there was a lot of pus. Flynn began to worry about gangrene: could you get gangrene of the thigh? You probably could, and being high up made it the more serious. It wouldn't have far to go to reach the torso, which was something you couldn't very well chop off. Flynn consulted with the chief officer and the chief steward, out of the Captain's hearing – Redgrave was continuing to insist on remaining in the wheelhouse and was shivering most of the time like a castanet.

The chief steward reckoned he had a smattering of medical knowledge; it had been he who had advised Flynn over the preparation of kaolin. Now he confirmed Flynn's worst fears.

'Gangrene,' he said. 'Gangrene for sure. Only one cure.'

Flynn knew what that was. He looked up at the chief officer, his face crumpled with anxiety. Hardy said, 'We can't do that. Amputate, I mean. We could be wrong, and anyway we haven't the know-how.'

'No, sir, nor the anaesthetic.'

The chief steward said, 'There's always Scotch. That's how they did it in the sailing ships. Fill 'em up, uncorked bottle in the mouth.'

Hardy said, 'No, we can't possibly do it. It'd kill him.'

'He'll die if we don't, sir.'

'You really think so?'

'Yes, sir, I do.' The chief steward went on, 'I've seen gangrene before now. In the trenches, in the last lot – I was a pongo then, and never no more, that's why I came to sea the moment I got my demob back in '19. Gangrene took 'em off like flies if they didn't get back to the base surgeons fast. Which they didn't half the time.'

Hardy nodded, faced with a wicked decision – what to advise the Captain. And suppose he went unconscious? Then it wouldn't be a case of advice but of making up his own mind to it. Flynn was thinking of what they hadn't got aboard: scalpels. Or if they had once, they hadn't any more. Of course, the galley had knives and the chief steward could procure something, say one of the big cleavers used by the ship's butcher. Or maybe a nice slim carving knife . . . but that wouldn't go through a thigh bone, it would have to be a cleaver. Flynn shuddered. He made a suggestion even though he knew Mr Hardy would have thought of it already. He asked, 'How about sending a message, sir? Ask for assistance . . . or medical advice, sir, maybe?'

Hardy was definite. 'The Captain would never authorize breaking wireless silence. Nor could I.'

'But that Focke-Wulf, sir. They know we're here.'

'A while ago now – we've moved on, back into anonymity. We can't jeopardize that, Flynn. In any case, where would the assistance come from?'

There was no anwser to that; the convoy, presumably the nearest ships to them, wouldn't send a doctor back, not now. There was just a chance they might pick up a homeward-bound HX convoy but that was very slim, it would be like the needle-search in the haystack, since they had no idea of the sailings out of Halifax date-wise. Anyway, it would take too long. Flynn had an idea that if the chief officer didn't decide to operate mighty fast, then the Captain was going to join his wife and kids – and maybe he'd not be minding that at all.

[ii]

When Mason Kemp reached the *Ardara's* bridge the action alarm was sounding and the guns' crews were already doubling to their stations while down below Mr Portway once again supervised the running-out of the fire hoses. Kemp, through his binoculars, watched the escorting destroyer on the port bow of the convoy breaking off to make its attack on the reported bearing and a few minutes later felt the heavy thuds as the depth-charges exploded deep down. Spouts of water rose and the destroyer on the starboard bow raced across under full power to join in the attack, and there were more explosions. So far as Kemp could see there was no result: no patch of oil, no black, sinister bows or conning-tower emerging hurt, just nothing.

Then there was a shout from Williams. 'Port beam, sir! A periscope, I'm almost sure.'

Two seconds later confirmation came from Leading Signalman Mouncey. 'Torpedo trails, sir, port beam, two of 'em coming straight for us!'

Kemp saw them, between the two leading ships of the port column. He spoke to Captain Hampton, urgently. 'Turn towards, Captain –'

Hampton gave the order: 'Port twenty!'

Ponderously, the big transport swung to point her bows to the torpedo trail and give a smaller target. Hampton watched closely, ready to check the swing. Kemp said, 'Hoist the warning signal, Mouncey.'

'Going up now, sir.' Mouncey had the flags already bent on. A colourful hoist sped fast to the signal yardarm. Now it would be up to the individual ships to take their own avoiding action; Kemp held his breath, gripped the bridge rail until his knuckles stood out white. The trail of the tin fish was now plain to see, coming down on them to pass along their port side.

'I think we're in the clear, sir,' Hampton said.

'Yes. But some other poor bugger probably isn't.' Kemp waited in anguish. Astern of him now that he had turned, the ships of the convoy were moving on. The *Aratapu*, also of the Mediter-ranean-Australia Line, was one of those coming up to dead astern. Behind her was a 15,000-ton ammunition ship, fortun-ately with empty holds ready for Halifax. Farther out to the north were the one remaining tanker and a number of cargo vessels. The double explosion came within the next two minutes and Kemp swung round to see a sheet of flame and an outpouring of thick, black smoke from the 15,000-tonner. A few more seconds and another explosion came, from farther aft this time – the convoy was drawing ahead of the U-boat now. Kemp passed the word to Hampton to bring the *Ardara* back on her course, and as he did so he saw the escorts racing back along the convoy's flank, about to go into another attack.

Williams made his report to the Commodore. 'First casualty, sir, ss *Bellman*, master, Captain Harkness. Two torpedo hits. Second, ss *Cerberus*, Captain –'

'Yes, all right, Williams. Hampton, I'd like you to take her in and stand by the *Bellman*, if you please.'

'Aye, aye, sir. Boats away?'

Kemp nodded. 'She's going. And we can leave the U-boat to the escort. But keep way on – circle round.'

Hampton passed the orders. The staff captain and chief officer left the bridge at the rush and along the boat deck three nested boats were swung out on the davits and run on the falls to the waterline, their crews embarked at the davits. Slipped, they pulled away fast as the troopships circled, a rescue fleet making for the ammunition ship, which was well down fore and aft and settling in the water, an obvious loss, as was the *Cerberus* which was being attended by boats from another cargo vessel.

Two more gone . . . Kemp's face was sombre. There would be more casualties, more families back at home shattered. He watched as later the *Ardara*'s boats came back to be hooked on to the falls and hoisted to the embarkation deck. The moment they had been hooked on, Kemp had given the order to increase speed again. As the shivering survivors were lifted out Kemp heard screaming, a sustained high note of agony. He clenched his fists, fought to resist an urge to put his hands over his ears. He was thinking that the ship's doctor was going to be a busy man and hoped he'd be found sober enough to cope. Looking aft from the bridge wing he saw the doctor with his assistant, the recently qualified man from Bart's, bending over the injured men, then his attention was distracted by Lieutenant Williams.

'Message come from the radio room, sir. Another Admiralty cypher. Addressed Commodore, sir, prefix Most Urgent.'

'Very well, get on to it.'

'Aye, aye, sir.' Williams turned away and went at the rush down the ladder to the boat deck and his cabin, where he brought the naval cypher tables from the safe and got down to work. It was not a long signal like the previous one. From the bridge Mason Kemp watched as the torpedoed vessels disappeared in a swirl of sea, both of them abandoned just in time. The escorts

66

carried on with their attack. The convoy proceeded, the columns sorted out again. No collisions: that, Kemp thought, was something to be thankful for. He looked out towards the *Aratapu*, steaming majestically in her grey paint, and wondered how many years would have to pass before both she and the *Ardara* would be back in the company's colours of light blue hull with dark blue boot-topping, and brilliant white upperworks. Or whether indeed either of them would survive the war.

[iii]

The embarked survivors had been sorted out now. Those who were fit were allocated cabins by Purser Pemmel's staff and arrangements were made for them to be provided with dry clothing and a meal, plus hot drinks or brandy. One of the seriously injured was the master of the ammunition ship, who had been taken by the blast as he had leaned from his port bridge wing just at the moment one of the torpedoes had hit. There was little left of his face and the head injuries were bad. With the other wounded he was carried below to the sick bay. The ship's surgeon had never known the place filled up. In peacetime the casualties had been mainly seasick passengers and they hadn't needed the sick bay's facilities, or the hospital as it had been called then. There had been the occasional heart attack or stroke, and those had usually remained in their own staterooms, at any rate if they were travelling first class. The hospital's inhabitants when there were any had tended to be tourist class, the sharers of cabins, who paid less than the first class for the ship's medical facilities and surgeon's fees. And since the outbreak of war and the requisition by the government, the *Ardara* had been lucky in her convoys. She had sailed mainly south around the Cape of Good Hope for Australia, returning with Australian and New Zealand troops. Down there the threat had been principally from the German commerce raiders, surface ships that the *Ardara* and her consorts had mercifully not met.

So the doctor was unprepared mentally and was shaking like a leaf at the thought of his own inadequacy to cope. Just before the boats with the survivors had been hooked on to the falls, he had taken a stiffener and he knew the result was on his breath even though he had sucked a couple of peppermint tablets. Everyone else knew it too: peppermint on the doctor's breath had only the one meaning.

Sister Jackie Ord took him in hand. 'Dr Barnes can manage, Doctor.'

'Are you sure?'

'Yes. He's very competent.'

'If there's any difficulty . . .'

'He'll have your advice, Doctor, naturally.'

'Yes, well.' The surgeon dithered, hand pulling at his jaw. 'Frankly, you know, I don't feel too well. My stomach . . .' He laid a hand on it, and grimaced. He wove a path towards the lavatory, entered and locked himself in. Sister Ord reported to Dr Barnes and the junior sister that the boss was suffering the squitters due to pressure of events and would remain glued to the lavatory seat until the drama was over. At least he could do no harm there but was technically available.

Just before luncheon, the *Bellman*'s master died; soon after this two more of the survivors, men with widespread burns who had been among those screaming out in agony as they were embarked, also died. There was in fact nothing more that could have been done had he been present and *compos mentis*, but the doctor was seen to go to his cabin with tears running down his cheeks.

[iv]

Before the deaths had taken place Lieutenant Williams had reported to the Commodore with the plain-language version of the Admiralty's signal. It was stark enough. Interception of German wireless traffic and patient work by the cypher-crackers of the British intelligence services had produced some vital operational information: two large U-boat packs were in station across the track of the OB convoy, between their current position as estimated by the Admiralty and the coast of Nova Scotia.

'No orders, Williams. In the signal.'

'No, sir. Just the warning.'

'And no indication how far off the packs are.' Kemp's face was set hard. 'We're moving westwards of the meridian of Cape

Farewell now – this is totally unexpected so far west. And more than I'd ever have expected anyway, against a convoy in ballast!'

'Yes, sir.' Williams paused. 'It occurs to me, sir, they may have been moved into position ready to attack us homeward.'

'Unlikely. Time at sea, time submerged and all that . . . and they're at risk from our escort. The Asdics . . . they'd be giving the game away, surely?'

Williams said, 'They could lie doggo, down deep. Or they may not be right across the track. The Admiralty won't be that sure, sir. They could be well out to either side, north or south . . . just waiting.'

'Waiting for what, Williams?'

'Well, sir, our homeward run. Attack the HX.'

'Or something else.'

'Yes, sir. That did occur to me.'

Each avoided implication of the Prime Minister by name or office. Kemp turned away and began pacing the bridge, up and down on the strip of coconut matting. Always he thought better on the move; at the convoy conferences he was always restive, sitting on his bottom and listening to other men giving detailed instructions and assessments and so on. In a similar fashion to a piper who played best when on the march, Commodore Mason Kemp found that motion helped his decisions.

And this was a big one.

He saw three alternatives: one, he could hold his course and speed and rely on the escort and the zig-zag; two, he could order an alteration north or south and hope to elude the hunting packs, if the OB convoy was their target, but either choice could be the wrong one; three, he could turn the convoy and steam back on a reciprocal of his present course. That would keep them in the clear, at least as regards the reported threat ahead. But it didn't take Kemp many seconds to reject this alternative. It would be an act of cowardice and one that would be likely to upset the overall strategy of the North Atlantic and its intricate convoy system, the shuttle back and forth. And the U-boats, frustrated in their plans, might find that other target, Winston Churchill heading west aboard the *Prince of Wales* – if they didn't know about that already.

'Williams?'

'Yes, sir.' Lieutenant Williams, apprised not long after leaving the Clyde that his lord and master didn't like being followed up and down the bridge, had hung back in the port wing. Now he came forward, the dog given its bone.

'Pass the signal by lamp to the escorts.' The destroyers had broken off their attack some while earlier and had reported no luck. 'When they've acknowledged, make: Intend to maintain my course.'

'Aye, aye, sir. A word about full alertness, sir?'

Kemp snapped at his assistant. 'For God's sake, Williams, they don't need that!'

Williams, red-faced again, passed the word to Mouncey, who began clacking the big SP in the bridge wing. As the signals and acknowledgements were made, Kemp's mind was busy. His own belief was that the U-boats were after bigger game than an empty convoy, a point he had already made to Williams. True, they might, just might, be awaiting the homeward run with all the Canadian troops embarked, all the ammunition and guns, all the other war materials and supplies for the civilian population that was facing the possibility of starvation if the merchant fleet was too far decimated.

It might be that, or it might not.

Surely, Kemp thought, the biggest prize of war for Adolf Hitler would be the despatch of Winston Churchill. The mind boggled at what the result would be back home and overseas, in every part of the world where British and Allied troops were fighting, backs to the wall in a war that wasn't going all that well, when the BBC News bulletins and the world's press blew the shattering facts, HMS *Prince of Wales* sunk, Winston Churchill dead. They might try to hold the truth, anyway for a while. But it wouldn't be possible to keep up a pretence for any length of time. With that towering personality gone the facts would show in dither, in a lack of direction, in a terrible weakening of the war effort.

If necessary, the OB convoy must be the decoy.

SEVEN

Mason Kemp believed, had always believed, in keeping his ship's company informed of all matters affecting or likely to affect their welfare. This time it was their lives, and he gave them the facts whilst remaining silent as to the presence, not so far off by now probably, of the British Prime Minister and his entourage. He used the Tannoy and spoke of the information received that a large concentration of U-boats was somewhere ahead. There would be no interruption of the convoy's progress and every man was to be ready in his own sphere of action.

'Which means to be bloody sunk,' Petty Officer Frapp said, thinking of his museum-piece guns in action against a U-boat, a small enough target at the best of times. The convoy was wide open and they all knew it. The merchant ships would just have to steam on stoically, taking independent avoiding action as and when necessary, and hope for the best. There had been more signalling between the Commodore and the senior officer of the escort and when the visual signalling became heavy, Kemp, with the need for secrecy in mind, suggested that the senior officer lay alongside and be embarked by breeches buoy for a conference.

The senior officer concurred; and the destroyer turned sharply, heeling over to port to cross the columns with a big bone in her teeth and make her approach along the starboard side of the *Ardara*. When she was in position and the breeches buoy's gear ready, the two ships equalized their speed, maintaining way throughout, the ropes were sent across and the senior officer, one Commander Phillips, was hauled across the gap, legs protruding like those of a spider through the breeches part of the buoy,

71

hands holding fast to the ropes above his head, an undignified performance.

He was brought to the bridge, where he saluted the Commodore. Kemp walked with him to the port wing, where they conferred together with Captain Hampton and Lieutenant Williams.

Kemp spoke his thoughts about Mr Churchill. 'He's the first priority. Agreed?'

Phillips said, 'Yes, indeed he is, sir –'

'So my intention is to engage the attention of the U-boats. You understand?'

'A sacrifice?'

'Yes,' Kemp said directly.

'A big one.'

'A big reward, Commander. A big man. A vital one! In any case, I have no alternative. We are at sea, so are the U-boats.' Kemp returned to an earlier thought, the one that hadn't lasted. 'I can't turn the convoy back.'

'No, no, that's true, sir. And of course I take your point about the Prime Minister. But –'

'Then let's consider it settled, shall we?' Kemp said briskly. 'It's going to be up to you and your destroyers, I need hardly say – we're just the sitting ducks, but if some of the buggers can be brought to the surface, we have guns to fire at them. And sometimes a lot can be achieved by ramming, as we all know.'

Commander Phillips was sent back to his ship and as soon as he was aboard the destroyer moved away at speed to resume her position on the starboard bow of the convoy. The weather, unkindly enough, was improving all the time; apart from the swell, the sea was virtually flat as the sun began to go down the western sky. There was going to be a brilliant sunset, Kemp thought, blood-red amongst many other colours. Blood was on his mind: he was putting so many lives at risk. Just how many? Give or take a hundred or so, the convoy contained around three thousand souls. Churchill himself would not have considered his own life worth three thousand possible deaths, if the worst came to the worst – taking the most pessimistic view, that was. But this wasn't Churchill's decision and he wouldn't have been the best judge of his own value to the Allied war effort. Kemp fought down strange feelings that rose in him, feelings of acting God, taking Prime Ministerly decisions in a very wide interest. He must not think that way. He was just the convoy Commodore, doing his duty as he saw it. But his heart bled for the lives at risk.

Walking the bridge after the departure of Commander Phillips, Kemp looked aft along the boat deck and for an instant that seemed a lifetime he saw it as he had seen it in peacetime, as master of what had then been a luxury liner homeward bound from Sydney. Those nights in the Indian Ocean, the drifting music that used to come to him as he took a late-night turn up and down the master's deck below the bridge, the gentle hiss of water streaming away into a tumbling wake, the moon's beams slanting across the funnel and the lifeboats, touching the masts, bringing light and shadow across the first-class passengers, the gay evening dresses of the women, the dinner jackets of the men. The bridge watch changing at midnight, the off-going officer filling in the deck log and giving the course and speed to his relief, a similar changeover taking place at the wheel and down below in the engine-room, a never-ending routine at sea where the whole ship never slept all at once. In the passenger alleyways the cabin-crawling taking place, for passengers were human and never more so than when east of Suez . . . the night stewards patrolling in uniform blues even when the rest of the crew were in whites, blue tunics buttoned to the neck, brass buttons, men of special status, reliable and discreet. One of them had once been a colour-sergeant of the Royal Marines . . . where was he now? Still aboard, or recalled to Eastney Barracks and a draft to a warship? Most likely not the latter; he would have been too old.

In point of fact ex-Colour-Sergeant Crump was still aboard the *Ardara* in his peacetime capacity of night steward and had not yet found an opportunity of making his number again with the Commodore, or Captain Kemp as he thought of him still. Captain Kemp would remember him, he was sure, and wouldn't snub him when the occasion arose. There was no bull about Captain Kemp, no snobbery, he had always been man to man, and a man's man with it. Crump had a lot of time for Captain Kemp, as had almost everyone else; even those who had felt the weight of his tongue from time to time recognized that he was fair and that they'd asked for it. Crump as night came down to end that day moved on along the darkened alleyways, the alleyways lit at night by only the police lights. Coming out from a cross alleyway, Crump all but bumped into the ship's master-at-arms, prowling

73

in soft-soled shoes. Master-at-Arms Rockett, an ex-RN regulating petty officer also too old for recall, was a soft-soled-shoe sort of man and had a face to match, pale and lowering and with eyes that didn't meet another man's gaze. Big feet, the prerequisite for the navy's regulating branch, the ship's police – big feet, so it was said, that crushed cockroaches whilst on the snoop at night, hence their sobriquet of crusher.

'Well, Crump?'

'All well, Master.'

'Huh! Look down there, purser's alleyway.'

Crump turned and looked aft, just in time to see a nursing sister's uniform turn into the passage leading to Pemmel's quarters.

'Sister Ord,' MAA Rockett said with a sniff. 'That on again, is it?'

'Not my business to know that, Master,' Crump said.

'Oh yes, it is, you're the night steward on this section –'

'Not for snooping on the ship's officers I'm not. Not unless there's a complaint. Which there never has been. Anyway, Mr Pemmel, he's been sick, a day or two ago, had the doctor, so –'

'Sick my backside,' Rockett said with a short laugh like a bark. 'Pissed to the gills, is Pemmel, half the time. Think Miss Ord's taking his temperature, do you? Time you grew up, Crump.' He paused, said, 'So just watch it, all right?' and moved on, hands clasped behind his back, soft soles shuffling over the polished corticene. Crump shrugged, made a rude gesture towards the departing back, dismissed the 'just watch it' as a bit of bull designed to cover up the fact that Rockett didn't know quite how to disguise the irrelevance of his earlier remarks, or innuendos, about Sister Ord and the purser vis-à-vis Crump's duties, and went along to his pantry. Just as he reached it the purser's buzzer sounded.

Crump knew Mr Pemmel's habits: he already had the sandwiches and coffee ready, two cups and saucers, two plates. A mixed lot of sandwiches, tastefully decorated with parsley which Crump grew himself in a couple of flower pots that lived in the pantry and were taken on deck to get some sun and air whenever possible. He went along to the purser's cabin and knocked discreetly.

'Come in, Crump.'

Crump went in, stood at attention, one hand holding the tray, the other stiffly in line with the seam of his trousers. When speaking to officers, Crump was still the colour-sergeant and training died hard. 'You rang, sir. The usual I don't doubt, sir. Good evening, miss.'

Jackie Ord smiled at him; Pemmel said, 'Thank you, Crump. A man in a million. You'd be ready with the sandwiches even if the ship was going down.'

'That's right, sir.'

'Care for a drink, Crump?' Pemmel asked suddenly and surprisingly. The purser was not normally a generous man and he'd never offered Crump a drink before, though he tipped reasonably enough at the end of each voyage. 'Whisky, is it?'

'On duty, sir –'

'Never mind that and if there's any trouble from Mr Rockett, refer him to me. Sit down, man!'

'Well, sir, I don't mind if I do. Whisky, please, sir.' Crump sat on the settee, his bottom right on the edge and his long, good-humoured face showing that he was ill at ease because he had sensed that both Mr Pemmel and Sister Ord were also on edge. He didn't know why, unless they were worried about the nests of U-boats said to be ahead, and they were all more or less worried about Hitler's antics. At a time like this Crump himself would have given his Royal Marines pension to be back aboard a battleship, say the *Nelson* or the *Rodney* with their bloody great sixteen-inch gun-turrets.

Pemmel got up and brought out a bottle of John Haig, poured Crump a measure and after some slight hesitation added some to his cup of coffee, glancing at Sister Ord as he did so. 'You?' he asked.

She shook her head; her answer was abrupt. 'No, thanks.'

'Suit yourself,' Pemmel said. He raised his cup towards Crump. 'Bottoms up,' he said.

'Your good health, sir.' Crump drank, feeling more and more uncomfortable. He was sure something was up, felt something in the atmosphere.

'You were in the navy,' Pemmel said.

'Royal Marines, sir.'

'Same thing, more or less – no, don't bother to explain the difference, Crump. Point is . . . you were in the last lot, weren't you?'

75

'I was, sir. Gunner Royal Marine Artillery in them days, sir, the Blue Marines. Royal Marine Light Infantry, they were the Red Marines –'

'Yes, Crump. You were in action, I believe.'

'Yes, sir.' Crump drank some more of his whisky, and wiped the back of a hand across his lips. 'On Y turret I was, sir, aboard the *Good Hope* – armoured cruiser, sir. We got it. I ended up in the drink for a bit, sir. Got picked up, of course.'

'Yes. So you know what it's like.'

'To be in action, sir?'

'To be bloody well sunk, Crump!' Pemmel voice was high, very much on edge.

'Yes, sir. It happens. Nothing you can do about it. Except swim, sir.'

'You were all trained men – seamen. Trained for war, Crump.'

'We were that, sir, yes –'

'Not aboard the *Ardara* we're not.'

'I don't know about that, sir. I don't honest. We've no passengers embarked – *that*'d be scary. But we've faced it ever since the war started, sir. Nothing different now. And you can rely on the deck officers, sir. Specially now Captain Kemp's with us.'

Pemmel gave a nervy laugh. 'Captain Kemp can't stop torpedoes. He may be a bloody marvel but he can't jump overboard and ride 'em away like a horse.'

Crump didn't like that, didn't like any sort of implied disrespect towards Captain Kemp. His normally kindly eyes hardened a little. He didn't know quite how to react; he was about to drink up his whisky when the nursing sister got to her feet and said she was going to turn in. Pemmel nodded, and she left the cabin. There was a funny look in the purser's eyes and after Sister Ord had gone he seemed to lose interest in Crump, who took the hint, drank up, thanked Pemmel again, stood briefly at attention, and went away. Odder and odder, he thought; it was as though he'd been brought in to defuse a delicate situation, be a sort of gooseberry to prevent something developing. When Sister Ord had gone, Pemmel had no further use for him. Crump moved along the alleyway, thinking, his face puckered. What Rockett had said – of course it was basically true. The purser was, or had

76

been, running a hot affair with Sister Ord, Crump couldn't help but be aware of that. Likewise, Mr Pemmel's drinking habits – they were common knowledge, of course. Could be just the whisky, Crump supposed, and the purser was looking for a way out of bedding the girl just because he was incapable.

[ii]

Still some distance to the east of the OB convoy's position and a little south, HMS *Prince of Wales* with her destroyer escort headed at speed for Placentia Bay in Newfoundland. The security was still one hundred per cent and would remain so if the combined efforts of British and American Intelligence could enforce it. Even the American press had been diddled: it was believed that President Roosevelt was aboard the *Potomac*, the presidential yacht, whereas in point of fact he was aboard the USS *Augusta* which would rendezvous with the *Prince of Wales* in Placentia Bay.

With the British Prime Minister aboard the battleship were Harry Hopkins, Roosevelt's confidential aide, together with Field Marshal Sir John Dill: a useful bag for Adolf Hitler. Winston Churchill, revelling in being aboard a warship at sea, seemed to have no worries about his safety. His curiosity was intense: he explored every part of the battleship, asking probing questions, gesticulating with his cigar as he put officers and ratings through analytical interrogation. He worked or played cards in what would normally have been the Admiral's quarters or he watched films in the ship's cinema or he walked the decks as the great screws thundered him westwards for a vital meeting. He was usually awake early, turning out to smoke a cigar on the quarterdeck and chat to the after turrets' crews and breathe the morning freshness; either that, or get down to some early work before breakfast.

During one of these quarterdeck walks, something seemed to be happening. The Prime Minister became aware of signalling between the extended escort and the flag deck of the *Prince of Wales*. He asked what was going on: no one appeared to know. It could be that a U-boat had been reported, an Asdic contact. But there was so sign of the battleship going to action stations.

77

The Prime Minister climbed many ladders, making his way to the compass platform, where he found the Captain, the navigator, the Officer of the Watch and the chief yeoman of signals staring through binoculars towards the destroyer escort.

'Good morning, Captain.'

The Captain swung round. 'Good morning, sir. I –'

'What's going on, pray?' Cigar smoke drifted across the compass platform. 'A submarine?'

'No, Prime Minister. A merchant ship fallen out from the last OB convoy – she's been having engine trouble, but that's been sorted out. Now there's other trouble – her master's in a bad way.'

'Sick, Captain?'

There was a nod. 'Suspected gangrenous leg. High up in the thigh. Probably not much hope, if the diagnosis is correct.'

'But all possible must be done.'

'Yes, sir. It will be. One of the destroyers will embark him, and he'll be attended by a doctor.'

'Ah. What sort of doctor, Captain?'

'A surgeon lieutenant, sir.'

'Yes. And the medical facilities aboard a destroyer?'

The Captain shrugged. 'Bare necessities.'

'And little room or comfort for an injured man. I beg to suggest, Captain, that your sick bay and your surgeon commander might be more welcome . . .'

'With respect, sir, I think not.' It was not reasonable, the Captain said, to hazard either the Prime Minister or the *Prince of Wales*. To embark a sick man would mean reducing the speed of the battleship and if there were undetected U-boats in the vicinity she would be placed at much risk. Then there was the known presence of surface raiders to the south, who might well elude the heavy ships detached from the OB convoy and make a sudden appearance at a moment when the *Prince of Wales* was unready and not immediately manoeuvrable. The Prime Minister, knowing very well that only the Captain commanded the ship, that only the Captain could make the decision, grew visibly angry. The pugnacious jaw came out, the cigar made stabbing motions. Churchill's mind was made up: the merchant Captain must have the best attention, and that attention was aboard the *Prince of Wales*. Surgeon lieutenants were no doubt competent but their experience was not that of surgeon commanders, and there was presumably a chance that the leg might be saved.

The Captain assessed the situation as a destroyer detached from the escort towards the *Stephen Starr*, now visible to the naked eye. Winston Churchill would seethe and fulminate all the way across the North Atlantic and would arrive at his rendezvous in a fractious mood, and he might quarrel with Roosevelt, himself often not an easy man. The ramifications of a quarrel, of ill temper, would be catastrophic, all Britain's hopes shattered. The Captain conceded: signals were made accordingly and the smile came back to the Prime Minister's face.

[iii]

Redgrave was a very sick man; he was delirious almost all the time now, with just brief periods of lucidity, and in those periods the pain was more than agony. Chief Officer Hardy had still not taken the decision to operate, to amputate. He had agonized himself, sweating blood in an attempt to reach the right decision. Then his problem had been resolved when the lookout high in the foremast had reported a strong force coming up astern. They might be Germans in which case the *Stephen Starr* would be sunk. If they were British there would be succour. It was in the lap of the gods. Hardy recognized the British destroyers with relief, and answered the challenge on his Aldis lamp.

EIGHT

'Mouncey!' Kemp's voice was sharp.

'Yessir?'

'Look alive, man! Destroyer signalling.'

'Sorry, sir.'

Kemp glowered: inefficiency depressed him; signalmen were the eyes of the convoy and they couldn't afford to blink. He had a premonition as to what the signal was: already the escort had indicated that the time was not far off when both destroyers would need to refuel from the tanker in company but there had been general agreement that the ocean swell was still too great for the manoeuvre to be successful. It was a tricky business at the best of times, to refuel at sea. The vessels concerned had to approach dangerously close – dangerously, that was, in adverse weather conditions. Now the swell had decreased and the U-boat packs might not be all that far ahead. It was time to take a risk. As always it was a case of weighing one thing against another, the Commodore's responsibility again.

Mouncey reported. 'From leader, sir, to Commodore: Request permission to make alongside oiler.'

Kemp lifted his binoculars towards the fleet oiler, RFA *Wensleydale*. She was a big ship, had been the Mediterranean Fleet oiler just before the war, but well down now to her marks so that her size didn't show other than in her length. Her master and ship's company would be well practised in oiling at sea, and she had something of the manoeuvrability of a cruiser – twin screws, for instance, to assist in turning short round when necessary, and plenty of reserve power to give her some twenty-two knots of speed. But she was dipping a little to the remains of the swell and

80

Kemp knew the job was going to be a matter of crossed fingers throughout.

'All right, Mouncey. Make to the leader: Approved. And make to *Wensleydale*: Stand by to fuel destroyers in succession.'

'Aye, aye, sir.' Mouncey operated his shutters, using the big SP. The signals were quickly passed: the *Wensleydale* carried signal ratings and was not slow to respond as so many of the purely merchant ships could be at times. The Royal Fleet Auxiliary vessels were a mixture of two services, RN and Merchant Service. Owned and managed by the Admiralty, they carried Merchant Service officers and men. When *Wensleydale* had sent the acknowledgement, Kemp signalled the destroyer leader to start the ball rolling, then watched as she turned under full helm to race back through the convoy lines, her bows thrusting the North Atlantic aside and bringing up a big bow wave that washed aft from her fo'c'sle-head.

'They're like racing cars,' Kemp remarked. 'All swagger and a sharp pull-up as if they'd rammed the brakes on hard!'

Williams said, 'Showing off, sir.'

'Well, I don't blame them. They have the power, and usually their judgment can't be faulted.' Surreptitiously Kemp laid a hand on the teak guardrail in front of him, touching wood: this was no time to tempt fate. A scrape of hulls wouldn't be any help. Aboard the RFA, as Kemp saw through his glasses, they were lowering heavy fenders over the starboard side, heavy beams with lines attached at each end, the beams themselves thrust through a continuous line of old motor-car tyres, a type of fender known as the *Brambleleaf* fender, officially noted and recommended as such in Admiralty Fleet Orders and named after the *Wensleydale*'s predecessor in the Mediterranean Fleet, whose master had invented it. Very effective, as Kemp knew from past experience, and very necessary even though the destroyers wouldn't approach the oiler's side so closely. Precautions were never neglected at sea.

By now the leader had come round the oiler's stern and was turning to make her approach along the starboard side. Already a big gantry had been swung out from the *Wensleydale*, carrying the fuel pipeline, and as the destroyer came into position and the speed of the two ships was synchronized the gantry was lowered over the warship's deck, where the engineer officer and an

81

engine-room artificer were standing by with four stokers to take the pipeline and make the connection to the bunkers.

'Expeditiously done,' Kemp said as the pipeline was connected. He spoke to Captain Hampton, who nodded.

Hampton said, 'Not something I'd care to do myself. I don't like other vessels too close . . . being in convoy's bad enough as it is! Just one lift of the sea . . .'

'Quite. That's when the fenders come into play, of course.' Kemp was watching closely. Every now and again the destroyer's stem swung, either to port or starboard, and was quickly righted. Too large a swing to port and she could cut in and smash her bows into the oiler's side. If there was damage, then the Commodore would be faced with problems. Kemp had already considered this and had formulated his orders in his mind, but he knew that nothing ever went quite as visualized and he would have, as it were, to think on his feet if the unexpected happened. For now he thrust it from his mind and said to Hampton, 'It's something we never had to think about in the old days, isn't it? Fueling at sea.'

Hampton laughed. 'You're right, sir. I wonder we didn't really, or the company didn't – something to amuse the passengers!'

'Yes.'

Keeping the passengers amused was always important. They were all very well in small doses but there were a lot of them at the Captain's table, mostly elderly and often full of their own importance. Kemp had frequently envied the junior officers. Their companions tended to be much younger and much less important, and Kemp had grown inattentive at his table, looking across at laughing groups getting along splendidly while his own gaggle of decrepits munched steak with false teeth, thought about their digestions, and explained in detail to Kemp how they had got to the top in their various spheres. Often their wives did that for them and the husbands themselves were embarrassed. Of course there were exceptions. Kemp himself was happiest on the few occasions when he had carried a retired admiral or general out to Egypt or Ceylon or all the way to Australia. They had something in common with him, and his last-war medal ribbons had meant something to them, as had his then rank of Captain RNR.

He reverted to Hampton's last remark. He said, 'I doubt if I'll enjoy retirement when it comes, in spite of all. What about you, Hampton?'

They knew one another very well. Hampton said, 'Same as you, sir. I'll miss the sea. I'll miss the companionship of men who go to sea. I'll miss the Line – as such. They're a good outfit. But I won't miss the passengers. What was it the pursers used to say? One thousand passengers equals one thousand bloody stupid questions a day.'

'Yes, do I not know!' Kemp swept a hand around the convoy, the ships pushing into the North Atlantic, heading towards danger. 'All that . . . it makes the peacetime days fall into some sort of perspective, doesn't it? All frivolity, people with too much damn money wondering how to get rid of it in the most pleasurable way. That was cruising anyway – the long run to Sydney was all right.'

'There was a different element creeping in even to that. We'd started to become gin-palaces and floating brothels! Maybe the war saved us, I don't know.' Hampton paused. 'If I had my time over again, I'd go for the cargo liners, the twelve-passenger jobs. Best of both worlds. More variety and nicer people.'

Hampton turned as the senior second officer came up to him with the result of the noon sight. He excused himself from the Commodore and went into the chartroom, where the position had already been noted on the chart by a neat pencilled cross. The convoy was now well westward of Cape Farewell.

[ii]

Pemmel sat in his private office leading off the main office, with his head in his hands. Another hangover, headache, red-rimmed eyes, parrot's-cage mouth, white-furred tongue, and a general feeling of creeping death and dissolution. By some sort of alchemy or thought-transference his mind had been running along lines similar to Kemp's reflections on the pre-war days and he had thought of the depressing sameness of the stupid questions that Kemp had talked of to Captain Hampton.

Pemmel could hear them now.

'Oh, Purser, do tell me, how much is a penny-ha'penny stamp?' They all thought prices were different at sea, like duty-free.

83

'Oh, Purser, where's the next deck up and how do I get to it?'

On embarkation: 'Oh, Purser, is this the right ship for Fremantle?' Just like a bus stop.

'Oh, Purser, which is the tender between this and the next, and what time does it go?'

That sort of thing; it used to be said that passengers marked their brains 'Not Wanted On Voyage', like their heavier baggage destined for the holds. Nevertheless passengers, at any rate the female ones, had had their compensations and Pemmel was wishing for the days of peace and promiscuity back again. He was having a bad time with Jackie Ord, who was slipping through his fingers. His own fault – he knew that; he had no illusions. He drank too much but he couldn't stop it now, couldn't get by without it, couldn't face the day. The doctor had spoken to him about it again, reprovingly, doing his duty as a medico but not managing to avoid the suggestion of the pot calling the kettle black and thus having no effect. Yet it was a funny thing: the doc had cut it down a lot in the last twenty-four hours. Rumour had said he'd taken it badly when he'd failed to follow his Hippocratic oath in buggering off to the heads when wounded men needed him. Something had penetrated, it seemed; but it was early days yet and he would probably have a relapse before long.

Pemmel gave a low groan as a knock came at his door. It was the second steward. 'Yes, Mr Portway, what is it? Overtime sheets again?'

It wasn't the overtime: behind Mr Portway loomed Master-at-Arms Rockett. It was Rockett who reported: 'Case o' theft, sir. One o' them stewards.' He jerked a hand towards Mr Portway, managing to infer that all stewards were thieves and layabouts. 'Have to be investigated, sir.'

Pemmel groaned again: a purser was ship's dogsbody. Banking, catering, sports and pastimes, money changer, tour organizer at *en route* ports, passenger appeaser, Captain's secretary – CID, too, when something like this happened. He didn't feel up to it. 'Too busy,' he said. 'See the deputy purser.'

Neither Rockett nor Portway argued; but Pemmel saw the look that passed between them as they withdrew to the main office.

The oiling of the leader was successfully completed and she drew away to resume her protective station while the other destroyer prepared to take on bunkers herself. As the leader settled on the convoy's starboard bow, her consort turned and headed for the *Wensleydale* and the performance was repeated, the gantry going out and down and the pipeline connections made. Kemp, watching as before, could see the pulsing of the heavy pipe as the oil-flow was switched on aboard the *Wensleydale*. A breeze was coming up now, nothing much but enough to ruffle the water – nothing much yet, but it could increase. Kemp was only faintly concerned, however. The oiling should be finished long enough before there was any real weight of wind to bring danger and perhaps force the termination of oiling.

Kemp's assistant had something to say; Kemp knew Williams had had something on his mind ever since the leader had asked the Commodore's approval for oiling and now he came out with it.

'Mouncey, sir.'

Kemp turned. 'What about Mouncey?'

'Slackness, sir. Having to be told the senior officer of the escort was calling us.'

'Yes.' Kemp's tone was off-putting.

'I was wondering if he was up to the mark, sir.'

'His first lapse that I'm aware of, Williams.'

'Well, sir, I've noted signs before.' Williams coughed. 'Do you want him charged, sir?'

'What with?'

Williams said carefully, 'I've been preparing a charge as a matter of fact. I suggest simply inattentiveness to his duty whilst signalman of the watch in convoy, sir. Whereby he could have endangered ships and lives.'

'But didn't.'

Williams gaped. 'Sir?'

'I think you heard, Williams. I don't deal in ifs and buts. The matter was not serious – though I agree it could be if it happened again. But, you see, I've already dealt with it and it *won't* happen again.' Kemp was looking his assistant straight in the eye. 'I see you don't consider a rebuke to be an effective way of dealing with it. Let me tell you something. There is a tone of voice that carries in it more than the words of the rebuke. Remember that, Williams. There will be no charges. Mouncey is a good signalman. That's all.'

Williams realized that Kemp's tone of voice was being used once again, with intent. Kemp turned his back and concentrated on the refuelling scene. He had a shrewd suspicion that there was more behind Williams' wish to make a charge than had appeared on the surface. He was aware of a touch of surliness in Leading Signalman Mouncey when addressed by Williams: Mouncey was a shade bolshie when it came to Williams, a different Mouncey from the one who jumped to it when spoken to by the Commodore or the ship's master. Although that was to be deplored it wasn't up to Kemp to interfere: Williams alone had to earn Mouncey's respect, all by himself.

[iv]

Captain Redgrave was aware of very little now and was barely conscious of the great camouflaged side of the *Prince of Wales* as a motor-boat from the destroyer escort brought him alongside in a Neil Robertson stretcher and he was hauled to the battleship's quarterdeck. He was unaware of the identity of the stocky man in civilian clothes and a yachting cap who was watching the embarkation and smoking a cigar. When Redgrave had been taken below to the sick bay and the attentions of the surgeon commander and his staff, Churchill said that he was to be kept informed of Captain Redgrave's progress.

'Such brave men,' he said to the battleship's Executive Officer. 'Armed with popguns . . . and always at sea. Without them, Britain would starve.'

Already the *Prince of Wales* was moving at speed again, heading west with her escort, zig-zagging continually through the seas. The Prime Minister remained on the quarterdeck, his mind projecting ahead. A message came for him, brought by a surgeon lieutenant from the surgeon commander: there was no gangrene – it would have been unlikely at sea in any case – but there was septicaemia and it was now too late to operate. Recovery was not expected.

Late that afternoon Redgrave died. No time was lost in disposing of the body. The battleship's captain came down from the compass platform to stand with the padre, and watched by the Prime Minister, Redgrave's body slid from under the folds of a Red Ensign provided by the chief yeoman of signals. When the *Prince of Wales* reached safe harbour in Placentia Bay the news would be sent home to Redgrave's owners who would inform the family, what was left of it – the father and sister, that lonely pair in York.

[v]

Jackie Ord had worked tirelessly in the *Ardara's* sick bay, fighting off weariness as she looked after the injured men. The burns cases were horrifying, pulpy flesh all red and blue, burned through to the bone in some instances. Pain-killing drugs were having their effect but there would come a limit to their use: the build-up could be dangerous. The ship's surgeon had come back after a while to do his duty and no one mentioned his lapse, but he was useless: very likely he hadn't seen a serious burns case in his life, or anyway not since his student days many years in the past, added to which he was running again on alcohol power and the fumes were wicked, enough to set light to. Dr Barnes was the saviour – him and Jackie.

When he saw she was almost out on her feet he told her to go off and have a zizz.

'But I can't –'

'We'll manage. We've already done all we can – you know that.'

She nodded; from now on it was a case of watching and keeping them under and re-bandaging when necessary. So Jackie went along to her cabin and dropped on to the bunk fully dressed. But she couldn't get to sleep; she was over-tired and her mind was too restless. After a while she gave it up, sat up in the bunk and lit a cigarette. She picked up a book: *Gone with the Wind*, which she'd started back in the Clyde anchorage whilst awaiting the forming-up of the convoy. But she found she couldn't

87

concentrate. She was thinking of the injuries, the burns, the terrible screaming when the merchant seamen had been brought aboard and transferred below. It had been harrowing. Jackie was young still, her experiences had not been those of war. Trained at Addenbrooke's Hospital in Cambridge, she had done time as a staff nurse in casualty after qualifying, and there had been traumas – road accidents, would-be suicides, burns too – but nothing to compare with this. She forced her thoughts to happier, easier days, which meant Cambridge: she was a local girl from Cherry Hinton, so she'd not been far from home, and she loved Cambridge and its particular atmosphere – the Backs in summer and winter, King's College Chapel and the Christmas carols, tea at The Whim in Trinity Street with a gaggle of probationers – or with Tom. Tom Bulstrode had been an undergraduate at Clare, doing medicine the long way round – BA first, three years at Cambridge then on to St Thomas's in London for his medical degrees. They were probably going to be married, though they'd both agreed not to rush it. Soon after qualifying Tom had joined the RAMC and had been killed at Dunkirk. So had ended – so young – a chapter of her life. She had been devastated.

She was thinking of Tom now. Had he been like her current patients, before he died, screaming in agony, perhaps calling for her? Of course she would never know: the official bulletins, the notifications of death in action, didn't go into that sort of thing. Even his parents wouldn't know. She'd been back to see them – they, too, lived locally, in a small house in Fenstanton on the old Roman road that ran from Cambridge to Huntingdon. It had been a sad and harrowing visit. There were so many memories, days off, when they coincided, often spent bicycling around the villages, Hilton, Elsworth, Conington or through St Ives to Needingworth and other places, sometimes as far as Ely and back along the A10 to Cambridge. It was good flat country for bicycling and always the sun had seemed to be shining on the dyke-crossed fens. In his last term Tom had bought a small car, an MG, and they had extended their range to King's Lynn and Hunstanton and Cromer. Tom had once deviated off the A10 to show her the flood-control system near Littleport, the Old Bedford and the New Bedford, and had bored her with a long explanation of how it all worked and what would happen if it didn't.

Tears came to her eyes: she would have given anything to be

bored again.

She lit another cigarette: chain-smoking, which was bad. She thought of Andy Pemmel, so different from Tom, so dissolute – though he could be nice. She had drifted into that, seduced by sheer loneliness and unhappiness and Andy's attentiveness, though she knew very well that the attentiveness was directional, one end only in view. Dr Barnes had tried to warn her off – purely disinterestedly she knew, since he was engaged to a girl, not a nurse, whom he'd met when at Bart's, and he was so obviously the patient, faithful sort, a plodder in love and medicine – conscientious but unimaginative . . .

In the end she found sleep, deep and dreamless, really flat out to the point of unconsciousness, as though drugged. She was aware of nothing, didn't stir when there was a knock on the cabin door and Pemmel entered, more or less on spec. But she did wake when she heard him shout at her.

'Jesus, what the *hell!*'

On the heels of his words she found herself being drenched with a fine spray of water, she saw the flame and smoke and she felt burning, a sharp pain in the flesh of her shoulder. The cabin seemd to be full of smoke and Pemmel was dragging her from the bunk. There was a fine mist of water: the sprinkler system had gone into automatic action. At first, coming so quickly from deep sleep, she thought there had been an enemy attack. Then she heard Pemmel shouting at her again, something about how bloody daft it was to smoke in bed.

[vi]

The alarm had gone automatically through the ship as the sprinkler operated: Mr Portway, who had turned in for a late-afternoon nap, woke instantly and ran out of his cabin pulling on his uniform jacket. The working alleyways were crammed with stewards and galley hands, bar staff, laundry staff, all the denizens of the bowels of the ship surfacing at the threat of fire. Mr Portway pushed through, shouting at the top of his voice and causing worse confusion until the junior third officer appeared at the head of a ladder and took charge, after which Portway gathered his hose party and once again ran out the flat reels of canvas from the fire hydrants. No one seemed to know quite what was happening, not until the senior nursing sister's cabin sprinkler was isolated as having gone off.

For a while the Commodore was equally in the dark. The fuelling operation was finished by this time and both destroyers were back in their proper positions ahead of the convoy and out to either bow and aboard the *Wensleydale* the gear had been stowed away and the tanks trimmed by use of the pumping system that allowed transfers between one tank and another. The report of fire below on C deck had come as a shock: fire at sea was one of the worst hazards, for fire, once it had taken a grip, was devilish hard to get under control and if the flames should reach the upper decks then they would be fanned by the wind beyond any ship's resources. When fire came as a result of enemy attack, that was one thing and had to be accepted. But when it came internally as it were, then nine times out of ten it was due to one thing only: sheer damn carelessness, unforgivable aboard a ship at sea.

Kemp was livid when the report reached him: fire in a nurse's cabin, due to smoking and falling asleep.

'Is the girl hurt?' was the first thing he asked.

It was Pemmel, making the report in person since he had been first on the scene. 'No, sir. Shaken but not hurt, apart from a little burning.'

'Doctor's report?'

'Nothing serious, sir. He's dusted her with boracic powder, I believe.'

Kemp said, 'Well, well! I shall dust her with something else, Purser. Send her up to the bridge.' He remembered his own position aboard and turned to the master. 'Have I your permission, Captain, or will you see her?'

Hampton made a gesture of negation. He preferred to leave this to the Commodore. He was as furious as Kemp; the girl deserved the weightiest of brass-bound wrath, and the Commodore was the Commodore, an extra sort of God. Kemp turned back to Pemmel. 'Thank you for what you did, Purser.'

'It was nothing, sir. I just –'

'You smelled smoke, did you?'

Pemmel hesitated: he'd gone to Jackie's cabin for quite different reasons. He said, 'Yes, sir.'

90

'And you took immediate action. I dare say that girl owes you her life, or anyway her lack of burns.' Kemp paused. 'I don't believe we ever met before the war.'

'No, sir.' Pemmel seemed suddenly embarrassed. 'Different ships . . . we didn't cross.'

'And your last ship?'

More embarrassment: Pemmel began to stammer. He had been, he said, deputy purser in the *Aramac* just before the war had broken out. Kemp remembered then, but said nothing. The DP of the *Aramac* – there had been a scandal, a minor one, involving a female passenger. Minor it might have been but Kemp was surprised that Pemmel had made full purser after it; the exigencies of war, perhaps. Other pursers – he knew a couple – who were paymaster lieutenant-commanders RNR had been called up to the fleet. The scandal wouldn't have been a scandal if Pemmel hadn't been caught in the act, of course – the one unforgivable crime was being found out. So to some extent it had been bad luck. But Kemp was old-fashioned and didn't approve of cabin-crawling, certainly not on the part of senior officers who had a responsibility to the Line. Now, as he gave Pemmel a dismissive nod, he came close to the truth: it hadn't, in all probability, been smoke that had attracted the purser to Sister Ord's cabin. He smiled, grimly. No smoke without a fire!

His remembrance of Pemmel's past did nothing to soften his attitude when Sister Ord reported to the bridge. He took her into the starboard wing; everyone else moved away discreetly.

'Now, Miss Ord.' She was pretty – damn pretty! Lovely figure – but that couldn't weigh. 'First of all . . . have you anything you wish to say?'

'No, Commodore Kemp.'

'No excuses?'

'No . . .'

He liked that, not that there could have been any possible excuse. But she'd probably been dead tired and could have said so. He went on, 'I see. No doubt you realize just what might have happened.'

She nodded but didn't say anything. Her eyes were very bright. Kemp began his rebuke. He told her what fire at sea could be like, the many deaths that inevitably resulted when a fire got a hold. The damage to the ship, a valuable ship in time of war, much needed for trooping. The fact that they were part of a vital convoy and that a fire aboard the Commodore's ship would have played havoc. The fact that the ship's company had already been warned that the enemy lay ahead across the convoy's track, that attack could for all anyone knew come at any moment.

She nodded, didn't meet his eye, held her hands clasped in front of her body, a schoolgirl getting a blasting from the headmistress. *Was* he becoming headmistressy, or was it just because he had a girl to deal with this time?

Anyway, he laid it on thick. It was heinous. So many lives at risk from thoughtlessness.

She began to cry and Kemp broke off in mid sentence. Now he was out of his depth. Did he bring out his handkerchief, say 'There, there,' and wipe away the tears? He coughed, cleared his throat, and lifted his voice.

'Williams!'

Lieutenant Williams approached at speed. Kemp inclined his head towards the girl and Williams took over, very efficiently. Kemp glowered as they went down the ladder, Williams' hand on the girl's undamaged shoulder. Williams was proving his use: crying women looked as if they were right up his street. Kemp gave an impatient grunt. All *he* did was scare the pants off them . . .

[vii]

Dusk began to descend, the approach of any convoy's worst hours, the night hours when the zig-zag became a nightmare for the officers on watch as they altered course according to the laid-down pattern and kept their eyes on a number of things at once, the shaded blue stern lights, the great black bulk of ships moving across their bows as the convoy altered its formation. The escorting warships were now at dusk action stations, as were the naval gunners aboard the merchantmen. The convoy had been steaming slap into the sunset, a brilliant one, all colours of the rainbow and great streaks to either side, almost like those you saw, Petty Officer Frapp thought, east of Suez, the sort that struck you with awe if you had any imagination at all. Frapp had not, in fact, a great deal of imagination but he'd always been very impressed with spectacular sunsets because in his view they said something about God. Their beauty was way beyond anything that man could produce. There had to be some power beyond this life and this world to produce anything like that.

And perhaps, coming tonight, it was an omen, or rather a promise that all would be well. Frapp removed his cap and stared into the last flickers of the dying sun, into a sort of purple look that lay over the water; to the leading hand of the gun's crew behind him it looked like an act of obeisance . . . perhaps old Frappy was a sun worshipper. In fact the cap's removal was simply to facilitate the scratching of an itch on Frapp's bald skull, as the leading hand realized a moment later. Frapp, forgetting sunsets, got to work on his guns, keeping the crews busy, exercising action, laying and training on different ships of the convoy, depressing the angle of sight to bring the gun to bear upon an imaginary conning tower which would in fact be the actual point of aim if they should go into action against U-boats during the night.

When the stand-down came half an hour after full dark Frapp relaxed, pushed his cap back from his forehead and felt for a fag which he didn't light, not on the upper deck: the strike of a match, even just the red glow from the fag itself, could be seen through a periscope. But it was nice just to feel the cigarette between his lips.

'All right, you lot, fall out. Stand fast the duty watch.' Frapp smacked a hand against the breech of the six-inch as though saying goodnight, sleep tight, hope the bed-bugs don't bite . . . Frapp didn't want to have to turn out during the night and he didn't want to have to fire his guns in anger. For why? Because he fancied they might simply blow up and fragment the gunners. They were poor old has-beens, stored in the arsenals for years and years, dragged out of ancient cruisers long gone to the breaker's yard. Not long after leaving the Clyde PO Frapp had been visited whilst exercising action by an old bloke from the liner's crew, a night steward who'd been a Royal Marine in the last lot – Crump by name. Ex-Colour-Sergeant Crump had almost talked to the after six-inch and said he believed it had come from the old cruiser *Glasgow*, built back in 1909 and present at the battles of Coronel and the Falklands and partly responsible for sinking the German cruiser *Dresden*. Well, if that was true, it was something, though Frapp didn't know quite what beyond senility. It certainly wasn't going to sink another *Dresden* . . .

A shaded signal lamp began flashing from the escort on the port bow and on the heels of the message the alarm rattlers sounded throughout the *Ardara*. Alongside Frapp the telephone from the bridge whined and Frapp answered. 'Six-inch aft –'

It was Lieutenant Williams' voice. 'Alarm port, Frapp – contact! All guns' crews stand by. I'll be down as soon as possible.'

'Aye, aye, sir,' Frapp said into a line that had already gone dead. He sounded sour and was; the Commodore's assistant, at exercise action, had fancied himself as a gunnery officer and gone into several flat spins yelling out such orders as 'Still, misfire, carry on,' and 'Shoot, shoot, shoot,' and 'Check gun-ready lamps,' just as though the *Ardara* was fitted with a director. It sounded efficient, or Frapp supposed it did to Williams, but he thought the two-striper was a right tit. Meanwhile the six-inch crew was coming back to the gun, fast.

Frapp said, 'All right, lads, this is it or looks like it.' They took up their stations and Frapp saw the gun trained round to port. He waited for the next order from the bridge.

NINE

The minutes passed. Nothing happened. The ships moved on.

Kemp asked suddenly, 'What d'you make of it, Hampton?'

Hampton shrugged. 'Getting into position?'

'The bugger's already in position. Just ahead of the convoy and ready for the flank. Perfect!' All eyes watched from the bridge but there was nothing to be seen. The night was dark; as yet there were neither moon nor stars to give some light; just the faint glow that was always present over the sea. Yet it would, Kemp believed, be possible to spot a torpedo trail unless the setting was exceptionally deep. So far there were no trails. They went on watching and waiting. The port escort had gone in to investigate but nothing seemed to be developing.

'It's a bloody mystery,' Kemp said.

'False alarm?' Hampton suggested.

Kemp laughed. 'Could be. Echo off a whale – it's been known before now!' With a massive attack foreshadowed in the Admiralty cypher, there would be jittery men aboard the escort, Asdic ratings who might jump a mile if they got an echo from a sardine. And there had been, so far as Kemp was aware, just the one contact. It didn't quite represent a whole U-boat pack. The starboard escort was still standing guard and hadn't reported anything, so it could be assumed the right flank was clear and nothing ahead either. The destroyer would be sweeping all round, through three hundred and sixty degrees.

Then the shaded signal lamp came up again and Mouncey reported to the Commodore. 'From the leader, sir: "Lost contact. This I do not like."'

Kemp said, 'No more do I! But it's somewhat cryptic I fancy. I

95

wonder what's in Phillips' mind, precisely?' The question was rhetorical. Kemp moved over to the telephone to the after six-inch and got Frapp on the other end. 'Frapp, is Mr Williams there?'

'No, sir. 'E went for'ard, sir, to take charge there.'

Kemp rang off, went to the fore screen and called down in a carrying voice. 'Lieutenant Williams?'

'Sir?'

'On the bridge, please. Pronto.'

Williams came up. Kemp said, 'You've served in destroyers. So have I, but in the last lot. We didn't have Asdics then – lots of things we didn't have. I'm out of touch, you're not.'

'No, sir . . .'

'Get inside Commander Phillips' mind.' Kemp repeated the leader's last signal. 'What do you think he doesn't like about the situation? I don't propose asking him – the fewer signals the better, in regard to certain matters. But I want to make an assessment.'

'Yes, sir. You say he's lost contact . . . and there haven't been any more contacts.'

'Not yet, no.'

'Well, sir, of course it's easy enough to lose contact –'

'I know that, Williams. That wasn't what I meant. If you've no ideas, let's try this for size, shall we? I'd like your reaction. The packs have drawn off, they're not interested in an empty convoy – I don't know what that one contact was, maybe it *was* a false echo. But the Nazis could be waiting for something else.'

'The HX homeward, sir?'

'No. I answered that question earlier. They won't hang about. They could have had a report about other matters. The *Prince of Wales*, Williams.'

Williams' lips framed a whistle that didn't emerge: it was a tradition that you didn't whistle at sea and Kemp was the sort of man who would jump on a whistler, hard and fast. He said, 'Yes, that could be right, sir. That's what Commander Phillips doesn't like.'

Kemp grinned. 'Great minds! I think it's a fair bet. The U-boats just aren't around any more. *We* don't know the actual course or position of the *Prince of Wales*, but Berlin could have had their ears to the ground. We all know about their bloody spy networks,

Williams. And there's something else we don't exactly know but can have a damn good guess at: the Admiralty won't know the U-boat packs have drawn off and are heading for bigger game.'

Williams said, 'We don't know for sure either, sir. We can't be sure we were spotted by a periscope. That's really only guess-work too.'

'Wars are often won on guesses, Williams, they're the very stuff of decision! However, we'll know before long. If no attack develops, they've gone.' Kemp blew out a long breath. 'That's when I'll have to decide whether or not to warn the Prince of Wales.'

'She'll have been alerted same as us, sir. By the Admiralty.'

'Yes. But she won't know the U-boats' whereabouts or that an attack may be developing, Williams.'

'But wireless silence –'

'Yes, I know. It's not a decision anyone can make yet. I shall make another assessment at first light. If there's to be an attack, then it'll come during the night, I fancy. And if that happens, there'll be no need to worry about wireless silence. That's all for now, Williams, thank you.'

'Yes, sir.' Williams paused. 'Will you be remaining on the bridge, sir?'

'Yes, Williams.'

Williams turned away and went down the starboard ladder to the Captain's deck and on down to the boat deck, making aft for the 6-inch. From behind the gun-shield, PO Frapp saw him coming. Frapp sucked at a hollow tooth and spat disdainfully and skilfully over the side to leeward. 'Here comes Johnny-come-lately,' he said to the gun's crew. 'Watch out.'

Williams halted by the gun. 'We remain closed up, Frapp.'

'Yes, sir. All-night job, d'you reckon?'

Williams nodded. 'The Commodore expects an attack to develop during the night.' He didn't add that the chances were no attack would come: no point in encouraging the guns' crews to slack off, he considered them a sloppy lot at the best of times. What they needed wasn't Frapp but a rasp-voiced gunner's mate from the Whale Island gunnery school in Portsmouth. Frapp was something of an old woman and a bit past seagoing. Williams looked him over, superciliously. 'Keep them up to the mark, Frapp.' He peered closer. 'That man. He's not in the rig of the day.'

Frapp said, 'No, sir. It's night.' Then he, too, looked: Williams was right, one hand wasn't in night clothing – still had his blue collar on. It should have come off after 1630 hours, as though it mattered when the gun's crew were wearing their anti-flash gear. Frapp made a pretence at bawling the man out, more than ever convinced that Williams was a prat.

'See it doesn't happen again, Frapp. We can't have slackness in wartime, you know.'

He turned away to go for'ard again. Frapp said nothing; if he had done so, it might have been a mouthful that would have put him slap in the rattle and endangered his rate. He wouldn't chance his arm to that extent. Officers could be rude to ratings but not the other way round.

The *Ardara* moved on, the dark shapes followed in their columns, the destroyers' wakes streamed back on either bow. Stars began to show, and a moon. The convoy became silvered with light, standing out sharply to any watching periscope. Throughout the convoy the guns remained manned on the orders of the Commodore, their crews weary but watchful, walking up and down where there was space, keeping themselves awake throughout a long night, most of them thinking thoughts far removed from their present environment. Home, women and beer . . . the pubs of Queen Street and Commercial Road in Pompey, the dockside pubs in Liverpool and Birkenhead, Sauchiehall Street in Glasgow, pubs in other parts where at the start of the war the canny Scots had produced whisky made from wood alcohol that had sent seamen blind – literally. Ladies of easy virtue loomed as large in their thoughts as the pubs, since the one led frequently to the other, a natural progression for a seaman ashore. Throughout the convoy the collected experiences of the land would have been a guarantee of hell's everlasting fires, far too powerful to be redeemed by all the prayers of all the nuns and monks throughout the world since time began. But they were men and they were fighting a long, hard war against tyranny and dictatorship, and they had men's desires. Perhaps God would not use too heavy a hand when they mustered at the last Defaulters.

po Frapp was one of those who might not make it: he hadn't always been what Lieutenant Williams thought of as an old

98

woman. He'd been quite a lad with the girls, once, before the fires had died down. A sweetheart in every port, had Frapp: Pompey, Guz, Chatham, Gibraltar, Malta, Singapore, Hong Kong . . . currently he was thinking of Hong Kong, where there had been more than the one – Frapp had done two commissions China-side and the second time the first girl hadn't wanted to know, having got married to a cook aboard an RFA, and he'd had to find another. He couldn't even remember their names now, one had sounded like Hoo Flung Dung . . . but the Chink women were wonderful in bed, nothing like them anywhere else. When he was a young AB he'd been told the Chink women were built different, that it went athwartships rather than fore and aft, but he'd soon found out that was just bull.

Below in the bowels of the ship Mr Portway, whose experiences and far-flung womanizing were not dissimilar from Frapp's, was thinking, or rather dreaming since he'd sat himself down in an alleyway near his fire hydrant and had fallen asleep, of Thurrock and Grays, of his wife and Mabel. It was Mabel's fault that he awoke suddenly: he had an erection. Embarrassed, he shifted to conceal it, but went on thinking about Mabel and what they would do next time he was in Tilbury, and God knew when *that* was likely to be, what with the war having shattered all the schedules. Next time in, it would in all probability be the Clyde again, not that anyone ever knew until they got there since no one was told anything of that nature, you just arrived somewhere and that was that, and then you sailed again and you didn't know where for until you'd left port. The uncertainty made things very difficult for a man with two women to consider, both of them near each other and far south. Mrs Portway, once she had realized that Thurrock wasn't going to see much of her husband while the war lasted, had made noises suggestive of wanting to shift up to Greenock or somewhere else handy. Mr Portway had dealt with that easily enough by hinting darkly at official secrets and the death penalty for careless talk that cost lives, and Be Like Dad Keep Mum as all the posters advised. If she went north, Mr Portway said, they'd be sure to pin it on him: she wasn't supposed to know where the *Ardara* was.

He wouldn't in fact have said the same to Mabel, but Mabel had her job and he couldn't afford to keep two women. Mabel had to pay her way. Currently Mr Portway was racking his brains as to

how he might get her a job somewhere on the Clyde; he'd made a
few contacts up there, useful contacts in hotels and so on, and
something might be brought about. Mr Portway, as it happened,
had no regular woman in or around Greenock, though there had
been a few odd nights in Helensburgh . . . Scots girls didn't
really appeal to Mr Portway. They were too direct, too outspoken
and often abrasive, and for some reason or other he'd found the
ones he had pursued had been Scottish Nationalists with a dislike
of the English and the way their country had been taken over for
war purposes by the navy. One of them, the last of his forays, had
poked fun at his stomach, and that had hurt him. She'd
wondered when he'd last seen his little willy other than in a
mirror . . .

The junior third officer came along the alleyway and Portway
scrambled to his feet.

'All right, Mr Portway?'

'Yessir. All's well, sir.'

'Good. It's all quiet up topsides. With any luck . . .'

'Funny, no attack, sir.'

'It wouldn't be if there was.' The officer passed on, stepping
clear of the run-out fires hoses. Mr Portway remained on his feet
and decided it was time he made his rounds again. He did so; in
the course of his tour of inspection he came upon Master-at-Arms
Rockett with his long torch, seeking sin. Mr Portway reckoned
that Rockett, too desiccated for the real thing, did it by proxy.

[ii]

The next day's dawn was as splendid as the last evening's sunset,
a splendour of many colours. On the *Ardara*'s bridge the
Commodore rubbed at tired eyes and stretched his arms, longing
for his bunk. No attack: now the time for decision had come and
couldn't be delayed. The fact that there had been no attack must
mean there were no U-boat packs, at least not where the
Admiralty had expected them to be.

'Williams?'

'Here, sir.' Kemp's assistant emerged from the wheelhouse,
where he had just got up from a catnap on the deck.

'I shall have to warn the *Prince of Wales* – break wireless silence.'

100

'It's risky, sir. For the convoy, I mean.'

'Yes. But there's a greater prize for Hitler, Williams, as I've said before. Make a signal to the destroyer leader, by lamp: Propose warning . . . propose warning prisoners-of-war of likelihood of their getting what we did not. How's that?' He saw the look of incomprehension and added testily, '*POW*, Williams. Phillips'll get the drift. There's still a need for secrecy within the convoy. God knows why, but I have to assume there is.'

'Yes, of course, sir. I think that's fine, sir, if you really do –'

'Really do what?'

'Really do think it's wise to break wireless silence, sir. As I said before, the Admiralty's signal –'

'Yes. And as I said before, neither the Admiralty nor the *Prince of Wales* is aware of the current situation.' Anger grew in Kemp: he was desperately tired. 'I've already made my decision, Williams.'

'Yes, sir, but –'

'But what?' Kemp's voice cut hard.

Williams said stubbornly, 'It's my job to make representations, sir. Point things out.'

The tone irritated. 'You're an assistant, Williams, not a consultant.'

Williams flushed. 'I'm sorry, sir. I just –'

'That'll be all, thank you.' Williams went off to pass the signal order. Kemp knew he had been unfair and was already regretting it, but Williams was the sort who grated on a man when he was dead tired . . . so damn tired, Kemp thought, that there was a possibility he wasn't thinking straight. That was no use to anybody. In a gentler tone when Williams came back he said, 'Let's just hope it's going to be in time.'

'Yes, sir. Depends on how far off . . . U-boats haven't all that much speed submerged.'

'No. And they won't know the precise position.' Kemp waited for the response from the escort commander. If Phillips came up with some cogent reason for not breaking wireless silence even for the Prime Minister, then maybe he would accept it, though since Phillips was RN he was probably to some extent hidebound about the use of w/t at sea in wartime. Kemp paced the bridge, so weary now that he cannoned off the screen at the extremity of the bridge and saw the look Williams gave him, the look that said the old buffer was past it.

The leader was flashing now. Signalman MacCord reported the reply. '"Your 0433. Concur, sir."'

'That's all?'

'Aye, sir.'

Kemp gave something like a sigh. He said, 'All right, Williams. Make: To *Prince of Wales* from Commodore OB 418, U-boat packs believed to be closing your position from west. All right?'

'Yes, sir. Prefix?'

'Most Urgent and Most Secret. Get it encyphered as fast as you can and transmit immediately.'

'Yes, sir.' There was something smug about Kemp's assistant and a moment later Kemp knew why. 'I've already encyphered it, sir, during the night, word for word as it happens . . . I anticipated –'

'You anticipated well, Williams. Well done!' Kemp was astounded and in a way humiliated: Williams had hidden depths of efficiency tucked away and Kemp thanked God for it. This was something Kemp should have thought of for himself; perhaps he really was getting past it. Every second was vital – yes, he should have been more on the ball. It wouldn't happen again. Williams, who had lost no time in taking the encyphered signal to the radio room, was quickly back to say the message had been transmitted. Naturally, there would be no acknowledgement: the *Prince of Wales* would not risk giving away her own position. The message had been transmitted three times to make as sure as possible that the telegraphists aboard the battleship picked it up.

'That's all, then,' Kemp said. 'Nothing more we can do now. I doubt if we'll know the result until we reach Halifax.'

But in that he was wrong. That same day, as the sun went down the sky to bring another brilliant painting to hang above the waters, the lookout at the foremasthead, sweeping round a full 360 degrees through his binoculars, reported a light signal from the rearmost ship of the convoy. Leading Signalman Mouncey read it off: ships, as yet unidentified, were closing from astern.

Kemp said, 'Sound the alarm, Williams.' Once again the *Ardara* went to action stations, the ship becoming a busy beehive of running men above and below. As the overtaking ships, moving at high speed, came within visual distance, the challenge was made and answered, and soon after this Kemp recognized the

102

silhouette of HMS *Prince of Wales* behind her escort, bringing her massive gun-power to head straight through the lines of the convoy. On she came, her escort parting to steam up the flanks of the outer columns, the great battleship herself passing between the two port columns to come close by the *Ardara* and the Commodore's broad pennant that flew from the mainmasthead. There was enough light for those aboard many of the merchant ships to see the officers clustered on the compass platform, and to see someone else: a stocky figure wearing an overcoat and an odd-shaped black hat that was half-way between a bowler and a topper, standing for everyone to see, right for'ard in the eyes of the battleship, ahead of the centre-line capstan and the fourteen-inch turrets.

As a gale of cheering swept across the darkening sea, Winston Churchill lifted his right hand high above his head, two fingers standing out in the familiar gesture.

'And up Hitler and all,' Petty Officer Frapp said at the after six-inch. 'Good old Winnie!' He roared the last three words out with all his voice, and the shout was taken up all along the decks. On the bridge Captain Hampton was standing with the Commodore as the *Ardara*'s ensign was dipped in salute.

He said, 'He's blown it, sir. All by himself. Indiscreet?'

Kemp laughed. 'Not a bit of it! It's a grand gesture – and it doesn't matter now. He'll be in Newfoundland waters long before we make Halifax.' As he spoke the battleship's flag deck came alive with a flashing lamp. Mouncey read, and reported.

'From *Prince of Wales* to Commodore, sir. "Your 0445 appreciated. U-boat attack repulsed with bad news for the Führer. Surface raiders as reported earlier failed to show. Your escort will rejoin soonest possible."' Mouncey wiped a hand across his lips and added, 'Message ends, sir.'

Kemp nodded. 'Thank you, Mouncey. Make back: Good luck to all aboard you and a safe passage.' He turned to his assistant. 'Read *Prince of Wales*' signal over the Tannoy, Williams.'

As Williams went into the wheelhouse another signal came from the battleship: the *Stephen Starr* had been encountered, the master had been transferred but had died. Kemp felt a curious emptiness inside. Poor Redgrave, so much endured for so little purpose in the end, another of the war's heroes to be quickly forgotten, probably by the time the convoy reached Halifax.

103

TEN

Various domestic matters were to engage the attentions of a number of the men in the convoy once they had entered the blessings, the mixed blessings for some, of the land. One of the less fortunate was to be Mr Portway, for events had stirred up trouble back across the sea in Essex, trouble that arose for no other reason than the fact that there was a war on and Mrs Portway's laundry had been put out of action by a bomb. Mrs Portway had never done her own washing: it was infra dig for the wife of the second steward of the *Ardara*. The trouble was that hers had been the only laundry left in business in Thurrock and she had quarrelled with the only one she knew in Grays. But she knew there was one in Tilbury, for that was where the second steward of the *Ardara* had on occasions negotiated for the laundering of his underlings' white jackets, so Mrs Portway went personally to Tilbury: she had tried telephoning but the instrument was out of order; Hitler again, no doubt. But it wasn't far by train.

The moment she set eyes on the fat girl with the poor skin she had the feeling she'd seen her somewhere before but at first she couldn't think where. Then she had been asked her name.

'Portway,' she said. 'Mrs Portway. Thurrock.'

The girl's face had been a picture – a picture of guilt Mrs Portway knew, for suddenly it had come back. The girl outside the Co-op, and the funny look that had passed between the girl and Herbert. A pity she hadn't tackled him about it there and then. Her face suffused and her jaw came out and she grasped her umbrella like a lance.

'You seem to know the name,' she said.

104

'Oh no – no I never –'

'Never what?'

'Never heard the name,' Mabel said, almost in tears already.

'I don't believe you, girl. What's your name?'

'Miss Tucker.'

'Tucker. I'll remember that. Now let me tell you something: I saw you once, not long ago, in Grays. You all but bumped into my husband. I sensed something then, I did.' It was odd, the way things went, the way the human mind and memory, or awareness, worked: all of a sudden other things had all come back to Mrs Portway – the times Herbert, when in Tilbury between voyages in peacetime and when somewhere up north after the war had started, hadn't been home when he should have been. Always some excuse, harder to find once the *Ardara* had quit her Tilbury base, but he always found something and here before her, in the laundry, was the cause. It stood to reason and Mrs Portway was convinced she wasn't imagining anything.

'You little bitch,' she said. 'You dirty little whore!'

Mabel found strength, hidden reserves of pride coming to the surface. 'Old cow,' she said as the tears ran. 'Give it him yourself and he wouldn't have wanted me. I'm not all that attractive, I know that.'

'No, you're certainly not,' Mrs Portway said. 'In any case, you've seen the last of him now.' With that she marched out of the laundry, head high and followed by astonished and intrigued stares. Going home to Thurrock as fast as she could she wrote a letter to Mr Portway, addressing it HT *Ardara*, c/o GPO London. This was two days before the Prime Minister in the *Prince of Wales* left Scapa Flow; and the GPO, efficient as always, delivered the letter via the RN postal service to Rosyth in time for it to join the mail being placed aboard one of the cruisers of the Prime Minister's escort, joining from the Firth of Forth.

[ii]

Four days after the *Prince of Wales* had passed through the lines of the OB convoy, the telephone rang in Mason Kemp's home in Meopham and Mary answered with her heart in her mouth: in wartime the telephone could be an instrument of torture. You never knew what the news might be.

'Mrs Kemp?'

She recognized the voice of the chairman of the Mediter-ranean-Australia Steam Navigation Company and she braced herself. She said, 'Oh – yes, Sir Edward.'

There was a chuckle: that was one hundred per cent reassur-ing. 'Home to roost, Mrs Kemp – not home exactly, but I'm sure you understand. All's well, anyway.'

'Thank you so much –'

'Rubbish, least I can do. Is everything all right your end – boys well?'

'Oh yes, Sir Edward, thank you. I –'

'Anything you want, any time. Just let us know.' Sir Edward said a brief goodbye and rang off. There were tears in Mary's eyes, tears of relief and gratitude. The Line was always caring, never more so since war had broken out – even though her husband was at least temporarily away from the Line, they still regarded him as one of their own, and herself as well.

She went upstairs to tell Granny Marsden the good news. The old girl was looking rather peaky she thought, but she was, as ever, as bright as a button mentally. She said, 'Well, I never doubted Johnny would get wherever he was going. *Where* is he, do you know?'

'Of course I don't, and you should know better than to ask.'

'I'm not likely to tell Hitler,' Granny Marsden said tartly.

'That's not the point and you know it. Careless talk –'

'All that rubbish! In the Great War –'

'That was a different war.'

'Yes, it was.' The old lady gave a heavy sigh. 'And even then I was an old woman. I doubt if I'll be here much longer, Mary.'

Mary laughed. 'You'll be here for ever. You know that too.'

'I don't,' Granny Marsden said, and all at once Mary Kemp realized she meant it. Something was up, but no use asking questions. Granny Marsden kept her own counsel. But she would ask Dr Ford to look in. Mary went downstairs, thinking that the old girl's age made the end inevitable soon and it was silly to pretend they couldn't do with the room and an end to constant attention that kept Mary largely tied to the house – help was getting harder and harder to find, with all the women doing war work of one sort or another, munitions, conducting buses and so

106

on, or in the women's services. But Mary would miss her, she was often good company, and John would be really sad if anything should happen. She wrote to him that night, care of the GPO like Mrs Portway, but she didn't worry him about his grandmother. The letter was largely news of the boys.

[iii]

After arrival in Placentia Bay and the rendezvous with the USS *Augusta* carrying President Roosevelt, HMS *Prince of Wales* passed the news to the shore authorities that Captain Peter Redgrave, master of the SS *Stephen Starr*, had died aboard and had been committed to the sea. This was passed by the Admiralty to York in the form of a telegram addressed to Redgrave's father, but it was the sister who opened it and sat staring at it for a long time, in silence. Then she took it to her father's bedside and read it out.

He seemed uninterested, far away. He said, 'Now they're all gone. Just you and me left.'

'Just you and me,' she said, her voice without expression. There would be no help with her father now, no one to share the mental strain, not that Peter had come home much. But he'd always been available, could be contacted somewhere, and that had been something to hang on to. No more now. She wanted to cry but couldn't: she felt dried up inside. Damn this war! Where was it getting anybody? Past scenes moved across her mental vision, long-gone childhood days, excursions out in the moors and dales to the north of York, the whole family going out by train and bus until her father had bought an old car which made things easier. She remembered driving through Wensleydale from Bedale and Leyburn to the little market town of Hawes, where once they'd spent the night and next day gone on to Clapham and Ingleborough, by way of a wild, mountainous road, and had then climbed up through woodland and past a lake, all the way up to the huge pothole of Gaping Ghyll, deep enough, it was said, to take St Paul's Cathedral into its great stomach. Peter, adventurous even then, had gone close to the brink and they'd all held their breath . . . she and Peter had been great companions in those days. Wonderful days that would never come again. She had been about to write to her brother when the telegram had

107

come and now the sudden realization that there was no longer any need came like an awakening blow and she began to cry. She envied her father, with his mind so far gone that the news would never really penetrate.

[iv]

Without the *Stephen Starr* which had not so far rejoined, the OB convoy slid to its anchorage off the port of Halifax, Nova Scotia, under a grey, windswept sky with low cloud and an unpleasant, damp atmosphere though it was not currently raining. The Commodore remained on the bridge, watching as the ships' cables rattled out and the many anchors took the sea bed, watching a pinnace of the Royal Canadian Navy cutting across towards the *Ardara* from the port.

'Here comes the brass,' he said to Williams.

'Yes, sir.' Williams sounded eager and was wearing his best uniform: the starched white collar was elegance itself and he was showing a lot of cuff. Best cap too, but with the gold badge nicely tarnished to prove his sea-time: the young officers, Kemp was aware, frequently left a new cap-badge in a cup of salt water until it looked as though it had been round Cape Horn half a dozen times.

Kemp grinned. 'I said, brass. There won't be any Wrens aboard the pinnace.'

'No, sir. But later on –'

'If you're asking permission to go ashore, Williams, you'll have it the moment all the bumph and bull has been sorted out. Satisfied?'

'Yes, thank you, sir.' Williams, anxious for the shore's as yet unknown offerings, also wanted the mail to come aboard. You never knew: there might be something from a girl and hope sprang eternal in his breast. He stood there with Mason Kemp as the chief officer reported that the ship had got her cable. The Captain passed down the orders to secure the slips and stoppers; Kemp rubbed at his eyes and left the bridge after a word with Hampton, making for the latter's day-cabin put at his disposal for the reception of the naval brass, which consisted of a commander RCN and two lieutenants of the Royal Canadian Naval Volunteer

108

Reserve. Not, in fact, as brassy as all that; and, as it turned out, there was a Wren as well. She was an attractive girl and Kemp was aware of his assistant making what he believed were called sheep's eyes at her but without much success. Kemp was glad he was no longer young himself: it was an awful strain on young officers trying to fit the war around their love lives. Kemp knew: he'd been young in the last one.

[v]

The mail, sent across the water from Newfoundland by the Prime Minister's escort on its arrival in Placentia Bay, reached Halifax and was distributed by boat around the ships in the anchorage. Kemp read his letters after the navy had gone back inshore with his convoy report for forwarding to the Admiralty. A bill from Gieves, the inevitable accompaniment of life in the navy: uniform was not cheap but Gieves never minded waiting so long as you paid a little on account now and again. In fact they hated it if you paid it all off: that could mean you'd shifted your custom to Miller, Rayner and Haysom. A letter from his brother, who was a solicitor in Worthing, doing good business on wills in an area where the average age was sixty-five plus. Some bumph from the Officers' Federation and the Master Mariners' Association and a reminder about increased subscriptions to a golf club.

Nothing from Mary, which was the one letter he wanted.

Well, that was the war. She would have written, of course, but the letter could have missed the mail, just missed a sailing. It was largely a matter of putting home out of your mind, but you couldn't do that entirely and now there was a nagging worry that something could have happened. Bombs could come down even on such unlikely places as Meopham when the Luftwaffe bomb aimers jettisoned their remaining loads on the way home to report the flaring bonfires to Hermann Goering. But if that had happened he believed Sir Edward would find a way of letting him know speedily, faster than anything from the Admiralty.

In his cabin in the bowels of the *Ardara* Mr Portway, together with a bottle of beer, read his fate. He read it from two sources, his wife and Mabel Tucker, and he didn't care for what he read. Mrs Portway appeared to be in a state of shock at the time of

109

writing her letter: she never wanted to see him again and she was going to find out about a divorce. The loss of Mrs Portway would in fact be less disastrous but she wasn't the only consideration: Mr Portway owned his house, or rather he and his wife owned it jointly; and that fact came in for heavily underscored threat in the letter. So did alimony. Mr Portway felt already bankrupt and turned for comfort to Mabel's letter. This he found to be a sort of Dear John: Mabel had had to go off work as a result of the attack in the laundry, she was ever so upset about what had been said in public, she was already finding the deception something of a strain, what with the war and all, and now she felt that it had better end.

Mr Portway, pale-faced, said, 'Bugger,' and screwed up both letters and flung them viciously into his waste-paper basket. Then, since his wife's had uttered those threats of divorce and sequestration, he retrieved that one and smoothed it out. It might be needed.

That evening Mr Portway went ashore on the binge.

[vi]

Lieutenant Williams also went ashore, his objective a little different. For him there had been none of the hoped-for letters from such girlfriends as his imagination could drum up as likely correspondents: just the usual long letter from his mother, full of nothing in basis. The war was dragging on and on, wasn't it, and the queues were awful and people were so rude in shops and on the buses. She had bumped into Mrs This and Mrs That and they'd asked so nicely after him and she told them he was assistant commodore of a convoy and that so much depended on him, she was really ever so proud, but it just went to show. Williams didn't know what it went to show but evidently it showed something to his mother. There was mention of his father: Dad was working ever so hard, what with the City and the ARP, he was dead on his feet most of the time and had become bad-tempered and, it was funny, but he seemed to get worse every time she talked about Paul being an assistant commodore. His mother thought he might be jealous – jealous of his own son, did you ever!

110

Shoving the letter into his pocket, Lieutenant Williams reflected that old man Kemp might get equally bad-tempered at mention of the title.

The mail for Petty Officer Frapp brought mundane tidings of home. Portsmouth hadn't suffered much just lately from the bombings but things were getting hard and the prices in the shops were enough to give the cat kittens and Mrs Frapp didn't know how she was going to manage, she didn't really. Frapp's allotment note went nowhere, neither did her wages – she'd just changed her job to get a bit extra and had got taken on at the Landport Drapery Bazaar as a cleaner, and *that* wasn't doing her arthritis any good at all.

'Moan, moan, bloody moan,' Frapp said angrily to himself. What a welcome to a sodding place like Halifax after sweating his guts out across the bloody North Atlantic . . .

[vii]

The mail brought real anxiety to Leading Signalman Mouncey and with a shake in his hands he sought out Lieutenant Williams, who aboard the *Ardara* could be considered his Divisional Officer and as such someone to turn to, though in all truth that wet weekend wouldn't be able to help a snail off a dandelion. But Williams, he found, had already pissed off ashore; and after that it became a case of an ill wind blowing a bit of good his way.

Leaving Williams' cabin door, he all but bumped into Mason Kemp.

'Sorry, sir,' he said, backing off.

'All right, Mouncey.' Kemp looked at him hard. 'Is something the matter?'

'Yes, sir,' Mouncey said. His voice, like his hands, shook. 'The mail, sir. I was looking for Mr Williams, sir.'

'News from home, is it, Mouncey?'

'The missus, sir. A neighbour wrote, like. She's poorly . . . in hospital, she is, in Devonport, sir.'

'I'm sorry to hear that, Mouncey. Come along to my cabin.' Kemp turned and strode along the alleyway. Mouncey followed, suddenly feeling a great weight easing off a trifle: the Commodore might do something.

111

In his cabin Kemp said, 'Sit down, Mouncey. Let's have it all.'
He paused. 'Like a drink?'

'Thank you, sir. Thank you very much, sir.' Mouncey sat on
the edge of a chair, his cap on his knees, his weather-beaten face
screwed up like a monkey's, his eyes showing the gnawing
anxiety. He took the glass of whisky, imbibed a large gulp, and
coughed and spluttered. 'Beg pardon, sir –'

'That's all right, Mouncey. Now – tell me the facts and we'll see
what we can do.'

'Yessir.' It all came out, the words tumbling over each other in a
torrent, so fast that Kemp could make neither head nor tail of
them. But he didn't interrupt, didn't hurry the man; when
Mouncey paused for breath he asked if he could read the letter for
himself.

'Course you can, sir.' Mouncey passed it over, a crumpled
sheet of Woolworth's lined paper from a pad. Kemp read that
Mrs Mouncey had been knocked down by a double-decker bus in
Fore Street, Devonport, while it was turning short of the bomb
damage. The neighbour didn't know the full extent of the injuries
but she said Mrs Mouncey was still unconscious at the time of
writing. An ambulance had come along fast; the neighbour had
happened to see Mrs Mouncey being lifted aboard and fancied
there were head injuries, a fact that had been confirmed to her by
Freedom Fields hospital.

That was all; Kemp had a feeling the neighbour was softening
the blow. So had Mouncey. Mouncey said, 'I reckon she's bad,
sir.'

'She may not be, Mouncey. Don't jump to conclusions.' Kemp
tapped the letter. 'This was written some while ago. If there had
been . . . well, worse news, then you'd have been informed. A
telegram from the Commodore at the Devonport depot.'

'Yes, sir.' That hadn't occurred to Mouncey; now he looked a
shade happier, but he said, 'She'll be wanting me, sir.'

'Of course she will. I understand that, Mouncey. But the
exigencies of war – you must understand that too. What I'm
saying is, it's impossible to get you home faster than by
remaining just where you are.'

Mouncey nodded. 'Yes, sir. But we're going to be in Halifax a
fair time –'

'I've no comment on that, Mouncey.'

'No, sir.' Mouncey sat there, looking expectant since Kemp wasn't throwing him out yet and looked as if he might have some more to say. Mouncey looked at the broad gold band on the Commodore's cuff: if that meant anything at all, Kemp might be able to pull something out of a hat.

But all Kemp said was, in a kindly voice, 'Leave it with me, Mouncey. I'll see what can be done, though I don't hold out a lot of hope. I'll send for you later. I take it you won't be going ashore today?'

'No, sir. I'll wait for news, sir. Me and the missus . . .' He couldn't go on, there was something in his throat. He saw Kemp's sympathetic look and he left the cabin with a mist before his eyes. Commodore Kemp, he was all right; Mouncey knew he would be doing his best. Half an hour later he saw the Commodore leave the ship in a tender that had come out with some dockyard mateys or whatever they called them in Nova Scotia to attend to some job or other in the engine-room.

[viii]

There were no letters for ex-Colour Sergeant Crump: he had no relatives left. He'd been a widower for some years and had no children. The ship was his life and he didn't go ashore except when he had to. The shore didn't appeal; Crump didn't go much for the drink and he was well past women, and what else was there ashore? So he retired to his cubby-hole and looked after his parsley for the purser's sandwiches. That early evening, taking the air on deck, he watched the libertyboat leave from the starboard accommodation ladder, taking among others Master-at-Arms Rockett, who if past form could be relied upon, and it usually could, would return aboard late and blotto. With him was Mr Portway, looking distrait.

Purser Pemmel didn't go ashore: there was too much to do, things he should have seen to at sea. Pemmel wasn't much of a shore-goer any more than Crump, since drink was so much cheaper and more plentiful aboard. Most of the assistant pursers went, all except one who was required by Pemmel for duty aboard. Jackie Ord went ashore, not because she was on pleasure bound but because she felt she would go mad if she didn't get a

113

change of scene. Once the wounded men from the ships sunk in the convoy had been discharged ashore in a hospital tender she had nothing to do. The ship's surgeon went with her, leaving her at the jetty and mumbling something about paying a call on the hospital and his former patients, but she knew he would in fact make for the nearest hotel and sit boozing in the bar and trying to forget his session on the bog seat.

That was where Lieutenant Williams, who had gone ashore earlier, met him. Williams had looked in at the naval offices in the port, seeking Wrens and looking what he was, just in from sea, though he looked it differently from a man like Mason Kemp. He put on a sort of world-weary look as though he'd borne the whole weight of the convoy and wanted the Wrens to know it. It didn't work; he was being a nuisance and they all but said so, being busy.

Williams drifted away and tried some shopgirls with equal lack of success. They seemed to sum up his wants with an extraordinary accuracy. In the end, down by the sleazier areas around the docks, he found a prostitute. She was a gold-digger and he couldn't afford the all-night tariff: the British Navy wasn't paid on the same scale as the RCN. He settled for a short time, maximum half an hour and away whatever stage you'd got to, unless you brought out more cash. Romance over for the night, Williams made his way towards drink and found the doctor. The doctor seized upon him as a long-lost friend, though they'd met but briefly aboard, recognizing, perhaps, someone equally lonely and willing to get drunk.

'Delighted to see you, young feller. Delighted!'

'Nice of you to say so, sir.'

The doctor looked surprised but pleased. No one with a gold stripe had called him 'sir' for years. He offered Williams a gin.

'Thank you, sir.' They drank large gins, then more large gins, no suggestion that they might eat, eating being a waste of time when you were enjoying yourself. The gin began to cost Williams a great deal of money at shoreside prices, for after a while the doctor stopped paying. But Williams grew reckless and paid up, drowning his sorrows and looking more and more war-weary as the time passed. Eventually, bleary-eyed and smelling like a couple of distilleries, they staggered back to the docks and the last boat back to the *Ardara*. They arrived clutching at each other for

114

support and singing loudly. Something about the nocturnal proclivities of Old King Cole, who sent for his wife and his retinue in the middle of the night.

'Whop it up and down, up and down said the painters,
Move it in and out, in and out said the barmaids,
Screw away, screw away, screw away said the carpenters,
Throw your balls in the air said the jugglers,
Very merry men are we,
For there's none so fair as can compare
With the boys of the King's Navee . . .'

They were still singing as the boat came alongside the *Ardara* and the racket disturbed Commodore Kemp and Captain Hampton. It continued as the two officers staggered along the alleyways to their cabins. Master-at-Arms Rockett was unavailable: he, too, was drunk.

[ix]

Kemp himself was having a couple of large whiskies with Captain Hampton and feeling more relaxed than he had felt since leaving Meopham. He looked forward to all night in his bunk and waking refreshed but he had a good deal on his mind. Not just the dangers of the homeward run for the Clyde and the responsibilities of his appointment; there was the nagging anxiety about Mary and the boys – no letter. He could think up all the reasons in the world, and had; they were all logical but the nag remained and wouldn't go away. And he felt very much for Mouncey; his understanding was complete. Going ashore that day as seen by Mouncey, he had made for Naval HQ and had talked first to a Captain RCN and then to a Rear-Admiral. He had put Mouncey's case and had strengthened it by some observations of his own.

'He'll worry himself sick,' he said.

'So would we all, Commodore.'

'I know. But I'd rather not have to rely on a signalman with only half his mind on the job, sir. I don't need to stress how vital the Commodore's signalmen are.'

'No, I take your point.' The Rear-Admiral drummed his fingers

115

on the desk in front of him. 'The same could apply to you, you know – God forbid, but if you had similar news . . . you'd have to carry on.'

'True enough. But I've been trained to it for so many years, and I think there's a difference between a commodore and a leading signalman. Hard to put it properly, but –'

'Yes, all right, I think I follow. The bigger responsibilities concentrating the mind more – something like that. Again I take your point. But what do you suggest, Kemp?'

Kemp looked down for a moment, studying his fingers, noting the heavy nicotine stains: he was smoking too much. Then he looked up directly and said, 'The Prime Minister's escort, sir. I don't know when they're sailing, of course, but Mr Churchill won't hang around for long, and they'll get home a damn sight faster than the HX will.'

'H'm. A transfer?'

Kemp nodded. 'So long as your drafting commander can let me have a replacement.'

'Well, we'll see. No promises at all. But if I can bring it off there's to be full secrecy – even your man himself is not to know where he's going till he gets there.'

Kemp had returned aboard feeling he'd done all that could be done. The war wasn't going to wait for a leading signalman and his wife but something might happen now, like a miracle. He wasn't going to say anything definite to Mouncey yet but since he knew Mouncey would be waiting to hear something he sent for him and told him to keep his fingers crossed. Just that. Kemp said nothing to Hampton either when they had their whiskies together: it wasn't his concern, the signal ratings were firmly on the Commodore's staff. From the master's accommodation they heard the racket as the boat from the shore came alongside. Kemp recognized the song and also believed he recognized his assistant's voice. He would be having a word with Williams in the morning.

Hampton said with a grin, 'Not all that different from passengers really!'

'Only when cruising – be fair! My God, they were a mob, some of them! Cruising was my idea of hell.'

They yarned as they had yarned before about old times and different days, reliving their early years at sea. Both Kemp and

Hampton had done their time in sail and both held square-rig masters' certificates. Master in sail – that had been something. Neither of them had held actual command in sail, even then sail had been on its last legs and in any case they hadn't stayed in the old windjammers for long enough before following the trend and going into steam for the sake of their careers. But both of them remembered the crash and thunder of the seas off Cape Horn, the days, sometimes weeks, spent beating into the westerlies off the pitch of the Horn, seeking a shift of wind to carry them on and past and eventually into the calmer waters of the South Pacific *en route* for Chilean ports and the long haul to Sydney. Those had been vastly uncomfortable days of wet and cold, with no hot food, days of laying aloft with the fo'c'sle hands, out along the yards with the windjammer rolling so far that the yardarms seemed about to touch the water, desperately keeping a hold on the foot-ropes with seaboots that slipped continually, one hand for the ship and one for themselves as they fought the gale-blown canvas, often enough stiff with ice.

Really, Kemp thought, they all had it soft now. Apart from the war, that was, and even that was worse for some than others: the men aboard the *Stephen Starr*, for instance, of which there was still no news.

[x]

Like Lieutenant Williams, Mr Portway, that first night ashore, had found women hard to come by. In fact he was more bereft than Williams, for there was a fastidiousness about Herbert Portway that wouldn't let him go to a prostitute. It wasn't just the dangers of disease: he saw no reason why he should pay for it when it was all there for free. Or mostly it was; not in Halifax, not yet anyway, but there was time yet, and he could bide it. Anyway, he had plenty of women in other parts of the world, currently minus two if you counted Mrs Portway, and he could practise abstinence as he was forced to at sea. That evening he moved around Halifax like a zombie, worrying about the Tilbury-Grays-Thurrock situation. Trust his wife to shove her proboscis in and stir up trouble, bloody bitch . . . and Mabel, caving in at the first obstacle! It made you sick. You just couldn't trust women. They were all the same, married or single, you were just a meal ticket to them and when things got rough they upped sticks and away.

Just as he was coming out of a bar, rather the worse for wear by this time, shifting berth to another bar where there just might be a decent woman, he bumped into the senior nursing sister.

'Evening, Sister,' he said.

'Good evening, Mr Portway.' Jackie Ord looked him up and down, a smile on her lips. 'Been enjoying yourself, I see.'

'Not really I haven't. Not really like.'

'Oh. I'm sorry to hear that, Mr Portway.' Then she saw his worried look, the look of acute anxiety. 'Is there anything wrong?' She knew what the arrival of the mail could do to seamen in from deep water, sometimes good, sometimes bad.

Tears came to Mr Portway's eyes, maudlin, drunken tears with a basis of good, solid trouble behind them. He said, 'Oh, my, Sister, yes there is. It's the wife.'

'Oh dear, I'm –'

'Bitch. That's what she is! Bitch.'

'Really?' Jackie was shaken: she'd expected a tale of illness or worse. Perhaps Mrs Portway had been unfaithful and it had all come out. Often enough, nosey neighbours caused trouble with the best of intentions. She went directly to the point: nurses so often did, it was part of the training. 'Is it another man, Mr Portway?'

'Like fuck it is,' Mr Portway said, then realized who he was talking to and apologized profusely. She cut him short; the wind was cold and filled with creeping wetness and it was blowing round her legs and up her skirt.

'If you want to talk, we'll talk. But no more drink, thank you very much.' She looked around: she remembered she had passed a Salvation Army citadel some way back along the street. That would offer comfort and sobriety and perhaps a hot drink. She took Mr Portway's arm and propelled him up the road, more or less quiescent but having difficulty with his legs. Mr Portway was trying to visualize his wife with another man – trying without success. The two just didn't go together. He entered the doorway of the Salvation Army without protest. Jackie Ord sniffed: certainly the place was teetotal but only by the skin of its teeth. Drunk seamen were everywhere, sobering up. There was a strong smell of beer recently taken. There were a Major and Mrs Moline in charge and they seemed delighted to see Jackie, who had obviously not been drinking herself, and they produced steaming hot cups of tea.

'The cup that cheers,' Major Moline said, beaming through gold-rimmed spectacles. 'That's what I always say.'

Mr Portway gave him a glare, wishing he'd bugger off so he could open his heart. As soon as the Major had withdrawn, he did. And began to get ideas: after all, the nursing sister was a woman – a woman without a man. All women except his wife wanted it and you could often play on their sympathy. There was just one snag: their relative positions aboard the *Ardara*. He was of the lower deck, the rank and file, she was an officer. It was all right for male officers to hump female ratings, but not the other way round. The world was a funny and difficult place.

[xi]

Halifax absorbed them all: not the town but the fact of being there and having to make preparations for the homeward run, the forming up of the HX convoy and the embarkation of the troops, the loading throughout the ships of the stores, ammunition and general supplies for home. RFA *Wensleydale*, which had not after all detached – the returning naval escort ex-*Prince of Wales* had brought changed orders – filled her cargo tanks so that she could fuel the destroyers on the homeward run. Aboard the *Ardara* life became hectic as the days passed. Purser Pemmel was glued to the office, scanning regimental lists of officers and men, organizing the cabins and the troop-deck accommodation, his staff of assistant pursers making out the meal sittings and allocating tables to the military officers who would embark for the war in Europe. The chief steward's department worked around the clock, ordering and loading foodstuffs for the galleys, getting the ship cleaned through all ready to be made dirty again. The surgeon checked his medical supplies of drugs, bandages, splints, aperients – there was always much constipation at sea owing to lack of exercise – and ointments. After the first two or three days there was little shoregoing except as a duty for the Commodore and Williams, who seemed to be needed constantly

119

at conferences and discussions of the convoy's tactics under the attack that they all knew was bound to come as they neared home waters and came within the range of the U-boats and the air armadas that Goering would send out to try to halt the army reinforcements in their tracks.

On the second day Leading Signalman Mouncey left the *Ardara*, bound he knew not where and by this time not caring all that much: the dreaded telegram had come, telling him the worst. Notwithstanding this, Kemp had held to what had been arranged: Mouncey should get home as soon as possible and he wouldn't have been much use to the convoy had he remained. A replacement joined, a leading signalman who had been landed sick into hospital from an earlier convoy.

Six days later the troops embarked: thousand upon thousand of them pouring up the accommodation ladders of the *Ardara* and the other hired transports, milling men in an unaccustomed world afloat, getting lost along the alleyways and up and down the ladders and main staircases, chivvied by raucous-voiced sergeants and sergeant-majors as lost as their charges, and by an OC Troops, a brigadier named O'Halloran, MC and Bar from the last war, a loud officer who announced to Commodore Kemp that, by hokey, he was no hanger back and intended to keep him company on the bridge all the way through. Knowing this would prove unlikely, Kemp responded in a friendly fashion, but took an instant dislike to a bellicose, blustering man who showed all the signs of believing that the OC Troops commanded the ship.

As soon as the troops were aboard the big ships of the convoy, the Rear-Admiral commanding the rejoined cruiser squadron asked permission to proceed. One by one the ships, their cables already shortened-in, weighed their anchors and secured them for sea; and one by one they moved out from the port, out into the North Atlantic behind the old battle-wagon and the leading cruisers of the escort. It was a grey day and there was some wind and rain. Kemp's prayer was that the weather would worsen by the time they came into the main danger zone past the longitude of Cape Farewell. But that was too much to hope for.

120

ELEVEN

More mail from UK had come aboard before the convoy's sailing and Kemp had heard from his wife, to his immense relief: one worry the less as he set out across the seas for home. It was a homely sort of letter, the sort he liked to get. The daily round, so far removed from his life at sea if not from the war: there had been some raids but not close enough to Meopham to worry about. The boys were well and sent their love; he wished they would write more often, but there it was, they were young and had their own concerns. Rufus, just finished with Pangbourne, was enjoying his last summer holiday before being appointed to the fleet as a midshipman RNR. His first appointment was likely to be for further training and courses, probably at one of the naval barracks. Harry, the elder, had been some while in the navy now, an ordinary seaman with a recommend for a commission as sub-lieutenant RNVR. He was finishing his qualifying sea-time in the flagship of the 15th Cruiser Squadron in the Mediterranean, no quiet place to be and another anxiety to nag away at a father. And the war looked like going on interminably, a long haul ahead yet. Kemp thought back to the outward voyage. Those losses – each ship that went down was a sad blow to Britain's heart, another nail in the coffin that Hitler saw for the British Empire. Starving out was no empty threat. The country was so vulnerable, so dependent upon its seamen and upon keeping the trade lanes open.

There was brief news of Kemp's grandmother: she'd worried about him but was happier now. From that Kemp understood that Sir Edward had been in touch and Mary knew he'd made it one way in safety.

And now they were back in it again. The *Ardara* was a different ship now, she had come alive again as compared with the emptiness of the outward voyage, alive with a huge complement of passengers as compared with pre-war days, far too many for comfort. The smell of sweaty serge had pervaded the accommodation from the moment the Canadians had embarked with their rifles and heavy packs, so had the language as the close confines of an overcrowded ship brought friction and temper – and seasickness. The *Ardara* had only just put her nose out into deep water when the seasickness had hit, and hit hard. Bodies were everywhere, so was vomit.

Four hours out and Kemp was still on the bridge. So was Brigadier O'Halloran, keeping his promise so far. He walked up and down the bridge with the Commodore, talking about his lads and what they were going to achieve, which was total victory. Fair enough; Kemp wouldn't dream of denigrating anyone's enthusiasm. But the Canadians aboard were fresh, no experience yet of war. Few even of the officers, O'Halloran said, had seen action in the last lot, certainly no one below the rank of lieutenant-colonel.

'A lot to learn,' he said, 'but they'll be okay. I guess Hitler's not going to like it.'

Kemp asked, 'Where d'you think your troops'll be used?'

'Wherever they're needed.'

'Yes. But have you any views? A new attack, a second front?'

O'Halloran shrugged. 'Can't say. Wouldn't say if I did, you know that. But I can make guesses, Commodore, and my guess would be raids, forays along the occupied French coast, keep the bastards busy and not knowing where they're going to be hit next.'

Kemp nodded. He had heard rumours that the Canadians were to be based in Brighton, or many of them were, and Brighton on the south coast was a good place from which to carry out raids across the Channel. The brigadier talked on and on and Kemp lifted his binoculars to scan the convoy, which by now had sorted itself out into its proper formation, with the cruisers disposed ahead and to either beam, and the destroyers acting as the extended screen, the old battleship ploughing along behind, a massive seagoing fortress to provide the heavy gun-power if any surface raiders should turn up.

122

Kemp caught Hampton's eye. 'I'm going below, Captain. Usual orders.'

'Aye, aye, sir.'

'If you'll excuse me, Brigadier.'

O'Halloran looked surprised: Kemp grinned inwardly, thinking that perhaps brigadiers were superhuman. He went below; paper-work awaited him. He left Williams on the bridge: Williams was officiously instructing the new leading signalman, by name Mathias, in the duties of a convoy signalman. Mathias was being polite but clearly knew it all better than Williams did. After a while O'Halloran called out to Williams.

'Hey there, sonny.'

It was Williams' turn to look surprised and a shade offended when he realized it was he who was being addressed. He went across and saluted smartly. 'Yes, sir?'

'At ease,' the brigadier said automatically. 'What's your job aboard here?'

'Assistant Commodore, sir.'

O'Halloran gave a whistle and said, 'Jesus Christ.'

[ii]

Jackie Ord had started something: Mr Portway was almost, she believed, paying court. The excuse was his marital problems but he was growing matey little by little, having started the morning after their chance meeting ashore and the cup of tea with the Salvation Army. Mr Portway, whenever the senior nursing sister was off duty, seemed to appear at her cabin door. If Purser Pemmel was there, which he was on two occasions, Portway made an excuse and vanished.

The second time, Pemmel asked irritably what Portway wanted and Jackie told him about the wife and Mabel.

Pemmel grunted. 'Nothing unusual,' he said.

'Perhaps not, as an abstract thing. When it happens to yourself, it looms large.'

'How do *you* know?'

She disregarded that. 'I'm sorry for him. It's all got too big for him.'

'Let him stew, Jackie. No one's fault but his own.'

123

'And Hitler's, for bombing the laundry in Thurrock. Or was it Grays?' She giggled.

'Well, never mind Portway. What about us?'

'*What* about us?'

'Oh, come off it. You know what I mean. Look, I'm sober –'

'Yes. You're busy again now. How long will it last?'

Pemmel shrugged: he was a man of few self-illusions. 'As long as I'm kept busy, I suppose. I don't get all that pissed anyway.'

'No?' Jackie lit a cigarette and drew a deep lungful.

'No.'

'We'll agree to disagree on that, Andy.'

'How about the doc? If I'm –'

'I'm not going to talk about my boss.'

'Loyal girl,' he said with a grin. He put a hand around her shoulder and was about to pull her towards him on the settee when there was tap at the door and an assistant purser came in. Pemmel said, 'Well, young Bates? Looking for a cough cure – or something more personal?'

'No, sir. It's you that's wanted. The troops – the orderly officer with a complaint about the troop decks. If you'd come to the office, sir –'

'God! Can't anyone else cope?'

'The orderly officer's creating hell, sir.'

'Damn.' Pemmel got to his feet; Bates held the door open for him and he flicked a hand at Jackie and left the cabin, with the AP following. Jackie gave a sigh, stubbed out the less than half smoked cigarette. Time to turn in; she was thinking she would do just that when another tap came at the door. It was Mr Portway, back again and smelling a little of whisky.

Jackie frowned. 'Yes, Mr Portway?'

Portway came in and shut the door behind him. He said, 'It's my problems, Sister.'

'Yes, and I'm sorry. But I don't see –'

'I just don't know what to do, I don't really. Soon we'll be home and I don't know what to do.'

'You'll have to face up to it then, won't you?'

'Yes, I know. That's what worries me.' Suddenly Mr Portway was slumped on the settee; he seemed almost to have collapsed on to it, a sack of potatoes that was coming apart at the seams. Jackie moved away a little. 'I'm all twisted up inside,' Mr Portway said piteously. 'People don't seem to understand. My wife, she never did.'

'Never did what, Mr Portway?'

'Understand me. And then there was the – other. What she never did either.'

He seemed, she thought, to be approaching some point and she didn't find it hard to guess what. Portway had not previously revealed what he was now evidently revealing – a lack of zeal for sex on the part of his wife. Before Jackie could utter the second steward spoke again. 'Frigid, she is. Frigid. Like a blooming codfish. Stood to reason I 'ad to find someone else.'

'Did you not tell her?'

Portway blinked. '*Tell* her? Tell her what? About Mabel?'

'No. That you found her frigid. It's better to come out with these things . . . and avoid the other complications, surely?'

Portway said, 'Try telling the wife she's frigid. Just try! She wouldn't know what it meant.' He paused and there was some heavy breathing. 'Not like you, Sister. Not at all like you.' He shifted closer, hefting a lard-like bottom along the settee. 'You and I –'

'I can be far more frigid than your wife, Mr Portway,' she said calmly though her heart was going like a steam-hammer. 'When I try. And right now I don't even need to try.'

'That's a change of tune.'

'It isn't! I've never . . . all I've done is listen and try to help. I think it's time you left, Mr Portway.'

'Come off it, Sister.' He moved closer, a lecherous whale with whisky breath and a pawing fin.

[iii]

Ex-Colour-Sergeant Crump was in his pantry and had the purser's sandwiches nearly ready, just in case. Now the ship was full the purser could be busy even at this hour and the sandwiches might have to go to the office and not to Mr Pemmel's cabin and if he was too busy to bother with them at all, then Crump would finally eat them if none of the office staff wanted them.

There was quite a roll on the *Ardara* by this time; she was well

125

out into the North Atlantic and the weather was restless. Things shifted about in Crump's pantry and from beyond its confines there came sounds of distress as troops made for the lavatories or the upper decks. Crump grinned to himself. Pongoes at sea were a bit of a joke; they didn't appreciate a moving, rolling barrack-room at all. Not like the Royal Marines – His Majesty's Jollies as they used to be known – who, though it was true they were half soldiers, looked upon themselves as sailors first and reacted as such. Crump looked out from his pantry and saw an infantry sergeant staggering along the alleyway, bouncing off the sides, a handkerchief crammed into his mouth. The sergeant just made it into one of the wash-rooms, going in with a rush as the *Ardara* rolled heavily to starboard and the door clanged shut behind him. As Crump withdrew back into the pantry a bell rang: not the purser, but the senior nursing sister. No ordinary ring, not the sort that meant sandwiches. A long, long ring as though Miss Ord had collapsed against it.

'Oh, dearie me,' Crump said aloud, and moved fast for Sister Ord's cabin, his face crumpled in concern. Reaching the cabin he knocked hard and went in, to be confronted, if such was the word, with the second steward's bottom. Mr Portway was on the bunk, so was Sister Ord. The bottom was clad certainly, but the attitude was eloquent. Sister Ord was weeping, as Crump saw when Mr Portway did a fast shift and thumped off the bunk on to the deck, his eyes wild and hair all over the place.

'Now what's all this, Mr Portway?' Crump asked, using his colour-sergeant's voice. 'Are you all right, miss?'

Jackie Ord had sat up. 'Just about, Crump. You were just in time. And thank God for it.'

'Yes, miss. That's all right, miss. Now, Mr Portway, sir, if you'll kindly leave the cabin I'd be obliged. We don't want trouble. But it's my duty to enter this in my night report and inform the purser.'

'You bloody do,' Mr Portway said threateningly. 'Bloody do, that's all!'

'Leave it, Crump, *please*,' Jackie said in distress. 'I can cope. It won't happen again.'

'No, miss.' Crump's heart went out to her. Nursing sisters . . . angels of mercy they called them. She wouldn't want the talk, all the nastiness. Maybe he could forget about his report – maybe.

126

But it wasn't to be that way. There was a step in the alleyway and the purser came in. He took in the scene at a glance: the bunk was ruffled, so was Jackie Ord, and Mr Portway's flies were still undone.

[iv]

It was all left until the morning. Jackie was in a state of distress still. Mr Portway spent the rest of the night shaking like a jelly. He knew he was done for; Pemmel had called it rape, or anyway attempted rape. When the *Ardara* reached UK Mr Portway would be given a bad discharge, such as would preclude any future employment at sea, and projected like a spent cartridge towards Thurrock and his ruined love life. Very likely he would find himself subject to the call-up and forced to become a pongo. Pemmel had been adamant: the affair could not be glossed over, for the sake of discipline it had to be reported and dealt with. Jackie had pleaded as much as Portway, but to no avail. Purser Pemmel knew his duty.

On the other hand, Mr Portway knew his onions.

'Led me on, sir.'

'I don't believe that for one moment, Portway.'

'She did, sir. Honest to God she did! Took off her –'

'All right, Portway. You know that's a lie.'

'No one else does.' Portway's eyes, red-rimmed, gleamed with spite and fear. 'I can always say she did. If there's to be charges. No proof either way, and *you* know *that*. There's something else too.'

'Such as?'

'I reckon you know, sir.' Pemmel's eyes flickered at that; he knew he had his Achilles heel. Portway confirmed it. 'Always half pissed, you are. All the stewards know it. Maybe the Captain knows it too. If he doesn't, I can tell him. I can quote times and places. You'll only have yourself to blame. Sir.'

That was when Pemmel peremptorily ordered the second steward to his cabin and told him the matter was far from ended. Pemmel thereafter spent a night as sleepless as Portway himself, wondering whether or not the thing should go any further. He wasn't too worried about the threat re drink, that was just stupid,

127

just fear talking, and Portway could never make it stick – Captain Hampton wouldn't take any action because he couldn't. It was in basis just hearsay. At the same time it was nasty and wouldn't do Pemmel any good in the long run. Hampton would remember. Pemmel would need to be superhumanly careful ever after, for he would be watched closely. No good saying captains didn't pass things on to their fellow captains – they did. And any scandal was a scandal, unwelcome to the Line: which brought him back to the main point of Portway's crime. Report it or not? Rake up dirt, or deal with the matter himself? So far as he knew, it was currently between himself and Portway, Jackie Ord and nightwatchman Crump, the latter being the soul of discretion. It would not necessarily have come to the ears of Master-at-Arms Rockett: in fact it couldn't have, since Rockett would have exploded into action by this time with the charge already framed.

It was a dilemma.

Pemmel had his duty and if he didn't do it Portway would think his threat had paid off and from then on Portway would have the whip hand. But do his duty and the chief sufferer would be Jackie Ord, and Pemmel didn't like that. He was fond of Jackie, could even be in love, he believed. Just the proximity, the being thrown together in war? She had never given him any real encouragement. Perhaps he was being selfish in even thinking he might one day offer himself in marriage to a girl like Jackie – he didn't see himself through rose-tinted spectacles these days – but he wasn't in the first flush of youth and the sea life would come to an end one day; a bachelor in retirement was always a pathetic sight. Selfish was probably the word. Anyway, he didn't want her to suffer on account of Portway.

In the end he dropped the matter quite unconstitutionally and unfairly on the shoulders of Commodore Kemp.

TWELVE

It had been Pemmel's own personal idea. He went to Kemp's quarters after 0800 hours, at which time he knew the Commodore usually left the bridge to wash and shave and have his breakfast, brought from the Captain's pantry by his steward. Pemmel knocked and was admitted.

'I hope you'll excuse me, sir?'

'Pemmel, isn't it?'

'Yes, sir.'

'Well, Mr Pemmel, what can I do for you?'

Pemmel began to explain, intending to leave out only Portway's threat about his drinking habits; but, not unexpectedly, Kemp cut him short. And Kemp was angry.

'What the devil d'you mean by coming to me, Pemmel? This is nothing whatever to do with me – I don't command the ship! This is Captain Hampton's business and in no way can I become concerned. You should know that. Why go behind your Captain's back?'

Pemmel said, 'For the sake of the Line, sir. I'm still a company's man. So were you, sir – and basically still are. I'm certainly not asking you to take any action. I only want advice, that's all. Without involving Captain Hampton, who might be forced to act.'

'From what you've said, he would indeed – I should say.'

'And there's the girl to be considered, sir.'

'H'm.' Kemp got to his feet, leaving the set table to move across to a large square port that looked out beyond the Captain's deck to the fo'c'sle and the heaving greyness of the North Atlantic: the bad weather was holding but Kemp had an idea that wasn't going

129

to last. After all, it was high summer. In his mind he cursed Pemmel and the antics of an over-sexed second steward. In the middle of a troop convoy in wartime!

Just then Pemmel struck the right note. He said, 'An enquiry of that sort, sir, aboard a troopship bound for the war zone. It wouldn't be a good thing.'

'But that's Captain Hampton's business to decide!'

'When it would become official –'

'Yes, yes, I know you made that point. Sit down, Pemmel. Fill me in properly.'

Pemmel did so, appealing to a former senior master of the Line, a kind of father figure and a much-respected one, who by good fortune was aboard a ship where so many had served under him. Kemp ate while he listened: a good breakfast, grapefruit, kedgeree, fried bacon and eggs, toast and lashings of coffee: he ate fast and then lit a cigarette with the coffee. Pemmel was long-winded and was still talking. Kemp thought about Sister Ord, the one he'd bollocked for setting fire to her cabin. Women aboard ship were a blasted nuisance but he'd been quite struck by this one. And Portway was going to say she'd asked for it – that was far from nice.

He cut in on the purser. 'You said only the four of you know.'

'Yes, sir.'

'You're sure of that, absolutely sure?'

'Positive, sir.'

'Right. Now, anything I say, any advice I give, is just that – off-the-record advice, which is what you came for. Understood, Pemmel?'

Pemmel nodded. As yet he had no idea as to which way Kemp was leaning but whichever it was he would act accordingly. Kemp was a wise man and very experienced, and Pemmel knew that he himself needed bolstering. Kemp was about to speak again when the voice-pipe from the wheelhouse whined and Kemp moved for it, fast. Pemmel heard the chief officer's voice.

'Commodore on the bridge, sir, please.'

'Coming up,' Kemp said, and went out of the cabin at the rush. Pemmel was left in the air. A moment later the alarm went.

Kemp lifted his binoculars: a bearing had been pointed out to him but so far nothing was visible. A signal had been made by lamp from a destroyer on the starboard beam of the convoy: the radar had picked up an echo, a surface echo so far unidentified. As a precaution all the ships of the escort and the convoy had gone to action stations. Lieutenant Williams went down to the guns to chivvy Petty Officer Frapp.

Frapp asked, 'What is it, sir?'

'Suspected commerce raider, Frapp.'

'One of them pocket-battleships, sir?'

'Don't know. Just keep on top line, that's all. It could be anything.' The term commerce raider covered a lot of ship types. Williams stared around, the eagle-eyed look of a genuine gunnery officer. 'Frapp . . .'

'Yessir?'

Williams pointed. 'The gun barrel, Frapp. Seagull droppings. Have it cleaned up.'

Frapp bared his teeth and muttered *sotto voce*, 'Need bloody stuffing you do.'

'What was that?'

'Nothing, sir.'

'I heard –'

'I said, needs some buffing up, sir. See to it right away, sir.'

'You do that, Frapp.' Williams moved away for'ard.

When Williams was out of earshot Frapp said to one of the guns' crew, 'You there. Officer has birdshit on his mind. Get rid of it, son.' He looked out to starboard. He couldn't see anything, except that the escort was redeploying. Three of the heavy cruisers were heading out for the bearing, moving fast, with great swathes of sea sweeping back from their knifing bows, and the old R-Class battleship was moving ponderously astern of them. Frapp said, 'If it's a bloody Hun out there it won't bloody linger. The raiders don't attack escorts the size of ours. Not unless they've gone clean round the bend like Harpic.'

On the bridge Kemp had come to the same conclusion. 'Just shadowing, I fancy.'

131

Hampton nodded. Brigadier O'Halloran, whose promise about bridge-keeping hadn't lasted all that long, had come up when the alarm rattlers had sounded; now he asked questions in a somewhat hectoring voice. He knew little of sea warfare, in fact he knew nothing, but was keen to learn.

'Mean they'll report back to Berlin, Commodore?'

'Most likely to the U-boat packs direct. Submarines can receive whilst surfaced for battery charging and so on.'

'Uh-huh. How come they shadow inside our radar range?'

'Because they have to, it's inevitable. They shadow by means of their own radar and the range is the same as ours. Or they catapult off their spotter aircraft and the effect's the same. They'll just have picked us up and now they'll be getting out at maximum speed.'

'Just buggering off, eh?'

'Yes.' The radar reports had confirmed this already: the range was widening fast, very fast. It was possible the raider was one of the German battle-cruisers, the *Scharnhorst* or the *Gneisenau*. If so she was going to get away; the escort wouldn't leave the convoy too far to the north, in case the German ship proved to be a decoy. The convoy was the main concern. But Kemp knew that from now on the unknown ship would remain in spasmodic contact, approaching to get its radar echoes and then making off again at speed, breaking wireless silence with impunity to report to the U-boat packs. With her presence already known to the convoy, there was no point in attempting anonymity . . .

There was a low rumble from across the sea, like thunder.

O'Halloran said, 'For Christ's sake. That's gunfire.'

Kemp nodded. 'Very distant. This begins to look like an attack on someone else, not us.'

'A westbound convoy?'

'I don't know. So far as I'm aware there shouldn't be an OB at sea just now. And the escort's radar would have –' Kemp broke off as an urgent report came from the radio room abaft the wheelhouse and chartroom.

'Mayday, sir. Reads: "Am under attack by heavy German ships."'

'Call sign?'

'Ss *Stephen Starr*, sir.'

'Oh, my God.' Kemp blew out his breath. Arse-end Charlie

from the OB – up to the time they'd left Halifax there had still been no news and the assumption had been, as day after day had gone by and the freighter had failed to show, that she'd fallen to a U-boat. Not so, evidently: she'd struggled on, plagued with her doddery engines, doing her best to reach Halifax and load for home, without her master who had died aboard the *Prince of Wales*. Now she was being blown out of the water . . . Kemp's grip tightened on the bridge rail and he cursed aloud into the teeth of the wind blowing across the North Atlantic.

O'Halloran asked, 'What's the *Stephen Starr*, Commodore?'

'A small ship. Just a small ship with not much speed and engines that should have been taken out and scrapped years ago.'

'Uh-huh. Not much loss, then. That's fortunate.'

Fury swelled in Kemp's head. The veins stood out, but he contained the explosion. It would be bad for the convoy Commodore to fall out with the OC Troops, very bad. There was plenty Kemp wanted to shout at the soldier, to talk of courage and guts and determination and a sense of duty to an island nation facing the threat of starvation if ships, small ships such as the *Stephen Starr* as well as the bigger ones, didn't get through Hitler's U-boat blockade. But he had the feeling O'Halloran wouldn't understand how seamen felt about these things. The brigadier had the look of a dug-out, a real relic of the last war, almost a blimp. Possibly he had served under Douglas Haig or the other top generals, men who accepted enormous casualties with a shrug of the shoulders, regarding the men as no more than cannon-fodder to form a vast platform of corpses over which one day the Allied armies would march in victory upon Berlin.

No more gunfire was heard after that single salvo, and within the next half-hour the cruisers of the escort were to be seen returning once more, appearing over the southern horizon. As they came closer the signal lamps began flashing from the flagship and Leading Signalman Mathias reported.

'To Commodore, sir. "Enemy out of range. No survivors ex *Stephen Starr*."'

She must, Kemp thought, have gone in one God-Almighty burst of flame and torn metal. He felt deathly cold inside, imagining the horror of the holocaust. There was nothing unusual about it, in terms of the war at sea, but he felt a special

133

responsibility for the game old ship that had been a lame duck almost from the start. As more signalling came from the flagship, Kemp passed another order.

'Secure action stations.'

The convoy moved on, once again under full close escort.

'Beg pardon, sir.'

Pemmel, in his cabin, looked up from his desk. His visitor was Mr Portway. 'Well, Mr Portway?'

Portway shuffled and coughed into his hand. 'I was just wondering, like. What decision you've reached.'

'I haven't.'

'Still considering, like.'

'Yes.' Pemmel hadn't been sent for by Kemp as he had half expected to be, to receive the advice cut off by the action alarm earlier. No doubt the Commodore was busy: by all accounts Kemp wasn't the sort of man to forget conveniently. Pemmel said sourly, 'You'll be told in due course, Mr Portway.'

'Yes, sir.' Another cough. 'That young woman, she flaunts herself. It's not right. A man's a man all said and done.'

'That'll be all, Mr Portway.'

'Now look, don't you forget –'

'Out!' Sheer anger brought authority to Pemmel's voice, and a sudden red blaze to his eyes. Portway looked startled, opened his mouth, shut it again and backed away to the door. He went out. Pemmel sat on, chest heaving, face flushed, fists clenched on the desk top, hammering. Damn it, he was the purser, he wore three gold bands on his cuff with white cloth between, he was in charge of the whole catering department from the chief steward down. And now he believed he might have the measure of Portway. Fat and flabby and full of spurious bravery when he thought he had his superior in his grip – but a basic coward who could be put in his place by a show of authority? Or by a counter threat: Pemmel had had those earlier words with Jackie Ord and knew a thing or two. His hand shaking with the anger that was still in him he took up his telephone and called Kemp's cabin. He was in luck: Kemp answered.

134

'Commodore here.'

'Purser, sir –'

'Yes, Pemmel.'

'Thank you for seeing me, sir, and listening. I've found an answer, so –'

'I'm glad to hear it. The best way is for you to make your own decisions, you know. From now on, I don't want to know any more about it.'

Kemp rang off. When he had done so he wondered if he had sounded too peremptory, too much as though he was washing his hands. But it had never been his concern and Pemmel had vastly overstepped the mark by talking to him about it in the first place. On the other hand a fellow officer of the Line had been in difficulties . . . but what he had just said was true: a man in the position of a purser should make his own decisions without wanting his hand held.

Below in his cabin, Pemmel used his telephone again, this time to the main office. 'Purser here.' An AP had answered. 'I want a word with Crump, the night steward – when he wakes. No special hurry. See to it, please.'

[iv]

The rumours ran round the ship: word about the sinking of the *Stephen Starr* had spread and most of the ship's company felt as Kemp had done. Arse-end Charlie was a special mate, a flaming nuisance to the escort and the convoy's safety but a plodder who'd done his honest best to catch up. So there was a good deal of talk about the *Stephen Starr*'s fate and much speculation as to who had sunk the ship. There was no hard information about that, but it was obvious that something heavy was at large, and according to the navy as represented by Petty Officer Frapp the chances were that it was a pocket-battleship such as the *Deutschland* or the *Admiral Scheer*, carrying six 11-inch guns in her main armament, plus smaller guns and torpedo-tubes.

But according to Frapp, who was talking to Bosun Bush at the after end of C deck, even a pocket-battleship was unlikely to attack. 'Escort's too strong,' he said. 'The buggers don't like being out-gunned, Bose. I'm not worried.'

135

'Pongoes are,' Bush said, grinning.

'Sod them,' Frapp said disinterestedly. 'Brown jobs get on my wick, all that stamping and saluting!'

'And puking. My lads spend all day with the deck hoses, sluicing down. Still, you get used to it. Fare-paying passengers, they puke too.'

'Been long in the liners, have you?'

'Forty years, about,' Bush said briefly. He wiped the sleeve of his tunic across his nose. 'I was an AB in the *Titanic*.'

'*Was* you?' Frapp looked at Bush with a new interest. The *Titanic* was history and high drama, an unsinkable ship, a bloody great iceberg, the band playing and all those deaths – and succour in fact not all that far off if there hadn't been some sort of communications balls-up. 'What was it like that night, eh?'

'Bloody,' Bush said. 'You've no idea . . . and I don't ever want it to happen to me again.'

'Don't blame you, mate!' Frapp said with feeling. 'But at least there won't be any women and kids. That's apart from the nursing sisters, of course. But it's not going to happen anyway. Like I said – we've got a nice strong escort.'

Bush gave a sardonic laugh. He'd been in a sight more convoys than Frapp had, in the merchant ships at any rate, the sitting ducks, the main target for attack.

The day wore on, taking the HX nearer home, beginning once again to close the sea area to the south of Cape Farewell, moving homeward slowly through waters that would become more and more dangerous as the sea miles fell away behind, the wakes streaming back towards the New World. That New World was in evidence on the bridge throughout the afternoon watch; and with apparent peace around the convoy for a while Kemp took the opportunity to get a couple or so hours' sleep. He would be on the bridge throughout the night. For now he left the brigadier to Lieutenant Williams, who strode from one side to another briskly, at O'Halloran's military pace, like a dog trotting by his master's side. Williams tended to be rank conscious and although he regarded the brigadier as a has-been like Kemp the air was thick with sirs.

'Young, to be Assistant Commodore, son.'

'Yes, sir.'

'Responsible job . . .'

136

'Yes, sir.'

'A lot of sea experience?'

Modesty would be in order. 'A fair amount, sir.'

'RNVR. They call you the Saturday-afternoon sailors, don't they, son?'

'Er . . . yes, sir. But there've been a lot of Saturdays since the war started, sir.'

'Oh, sure there have. Still.' O'Halloran chuckled. 'Like God, maybe.'

'Sir?'

'Your navy. Moves in a mysterious way – get it?'

This was O'Halloran's idea of a joke; he chuckled again. Politely, Williams laughed. But he didn't like being patronized; and the brisk walk was wearing him out. It was, however, interrupted half an hour later when another message reached the bridge from the radio room, this time a cypher from the Admiralty. When broken down this proved to be another warning: as on the outward voyage, a strong presence of U-boats was believed to lie across the track of the HX convoy to the south-east of Cape Farewell, and this time no one at the Admiralty had any doubts that they would attack. Later an air strike might come. The fleet aircraft-carrier that had been standing by with fighter squadrons embarked had been ordered to sea from the Clyde to rendezvous with the HX convoy. In the meantime Kemp was to alter course to the south in an attempt to outflank the U-boat packs.

THIRTEEN

Kemp broadcast the word throughout the ship; after that O'Halloran addressed his troops. Everything was okay for the moment, but before the next dawn they might be in the thick of it, he said, repeating what the Commodore had already told them. They had to be ready for anything and before dusk action stations that evening there would be an extra boat drill to ensure that every man knew exactly where to go in an emergency. The ship's Captain, he said, would say a few words about that.

Hampton went to the microphone. 'Captain speaking to you all, but with special reference to the troops.' He paused: there was a silence around the ship, above and below. 'If we're hit, we may have trouble with the generators – that has to be considered. The alleyways could be in darkness. My ship's company will of course assist with torches if that happens, but some of you may have to feel your way to your boat stations. You should make very sure you're familiar with the ship's layout. Above all, act calmly. We don't want panic – I'm sure there won't be, but for the great majority of you this is your first experience of the sea, and I understand the difficulties of an unfamiliar background. There is a first time for every one of us. One more thing: if it should happen that I have to give the order to abandon, then there will be strict and absolute discipline along the embarkation deck – the deck from which you embark into the lifeboats. For the purpose of abandoning ship, or any other emergency in a sea sense, the orders of my officers, petty officers and leading hands will take precedence over those of your own officers and NCOs. There will be total obedience to those orders for the sake of every soul aboard. That is all.'

138

The broadcaster clicked off and throughout the ship the men took stock. To the troops, an unfamiliar world it certainly was, and one that wouldn't keep still. Some had got their sea legs, many hadn't. Almost to a man they were from the rolling Canadian prairies, a few from towns such as Edmonton or Calgary, none at all from the coastal areas. They had never before been confined in a steel can that rose and fell and lurched from side to side, criss-crossed with alleyways and filled with ladders and stairways, the air itself noisy with the continuous hum of dynamos and forced-draught blowers and vague engine sounds from deep below, and with the peculiar smell that always filled a ship at sea, compounded of wax polish, a vague oiliness, tinned air and, in a troopship, human sweat and its effect on serge uniforms.

There was a decided nervousness along the troop decks. Aboard a ship you couldn't get away. Not that many of the men would think of running from action; but if you did want to when aboard ship, there was nowhere to run to other than a leap overboard. That was something they might have to do anyway if the worst happened. One of the sergeants had had a word with a bloke who looked important and knowledgeable: Master-at-Arms Rockett, ex-Regulating Petty Officer RN. The pongo had asked a question: what would happen if any of the lifeboats got damaged by a torpedo explosion?

That got a sour answer: 'Use one o' the others, that's what. You'll be told . . . and no torpedo hitting below the waterline's all that likely to damage the boats. Though it could 'appen. What's more likely is that we'd get a list one side or the other and if the list's big enough, well, then likely we couldn't get the boats away on the *other* side, not unless we slid the buggers down the plates like a load o' kids on a playground slide. All right?'

'Then what?'

MAA Rockett moved up and down on the balls of his feet, like a bobby. ''Ave to jump, wouldn't you? But no panic, now. This is all 'ypothetical. We'll cope, you'll see. We're used to it, mate.'

Nevertheless the word spread. Not via the sergeant; but the conversation had been overheard and the galley wireless went into instant operation and there was just the tinge of a fear-smell as the *Ardara* moved on towards boat drill, dusk action stations, and nightfall.

139

A knock at the purser's cabin door and Crump appeared. 'You wanted to see me, sir.'

'Yes, Crump. Come in. Sit down.'

For the second time since leaving the Clyde Crump sat in the purser's cabin. This time, no drink: Mr Pemmel was being formal – formal yet friendly and a shade oily with it. Crump knew what it was all about. But he wasn't going to speak till he was spoken to.

'Crump . . .'

'Yessir.'

'You were a primary witness. You know what I'm talking about.'

'Yessir.' Crump sat with his hands on his knees, staring over the purser's head at the white-painted bulkhead behind.

Pemmel said, 'You saw it all.'

'From a certain point, sir, yes. My statement –'

'Yes, I know. You got there – at that certain point. You couldn't really say what had gone on up to then – that's to say, how it came about.'

'That's right, sir.'

'You know what Mr Portway's saying?'

'No, sir. I'm not party, sir, to Mr Portway's statement.'

'No, quite.' Pemmel fiddled with a pencil on his desk. 'Then you don't know – and this is strictly between you and me, Crump – you don't know that he's trying to make out Miss Ord led him on?'

'No, sir, I do not.' Crump stared back at the purser, shaken. 'That's a lie, sir. A dirty lie, and –'

'Of course it is. But can you shoot it down, Crump? In your fuller evidence, shall we say, if it came to an enquiry by the Captain?'

Crump seemed to consider; then he said reluctantly, 'No, sir, I can't. I only came upon the scene . . . later as you might say. Result of Miss Ord's bell, sir.' He paused. 'That bell, sir. Wouldn't that be enough? If the young lady had been a willing party, she wouldn't have pressed the bell, sir.'

'Not good enough if Mr Portway takes his line further, Crump.

She could have changed her mind . . . and that doesn't shoot down the lie that she led him on in the first place. We need something more substantial than that. I want the nearest thing possible to proof positive – something to stop Mr Portway.' Pemmel looked down at his desk, avoiding Crump's eye. 'A statement from you, Crump. It could save all the unpleasantness. Do you see what I'm getting at?'

'I think I do, sir, yes.'

'Well?'

Crump made a business of clearing his throat. He said, 'A statement, sir, that I saw Mr Portway . . . make a grab, sir, if I may put it that way.'

'Something like that.'

'A false statement, sir.'

'Not all that false, Crump. That's what happened in actual fact. That is, if we believe Miss Ord. Which we do – don't we?'

'Yes, sir, of course we do.' Crump was looking really distressed. 'I'd like to help all I can, sir –'

Pemmel pointed out, 'I'm giving you the way to do just that.'

'I know, sir. But it'd be a *lie*, sir! Bad as Mr Portway, sir. That's not right.'

Pemmel sighed: he knew he'd lost. He said, 'Only a *technical* lie, Crump.'

'Same thing, sir. And even if I did, Mr Portway might bowl it out. It's hard to tell a lie, sir, and not show it.'

Yes, Pemmel thought, it is, for a patently honest man, very hard indeed. Crump's face was too open. But that wasn't the point: as he'd already hinted, all Pemmel wanted was a lever to threaten Portway with. Maybe he was being too devious: and there was nothing devious about Crump. A little thick, perhaps: Pemmel couldn't get him to take the point. Perhaps he didn't want to, Jackie Ord notwithstanding. Lies were not in his character: obstinate old fool! Pemmel realized now that he should have known. And he had a feeling he'd fallen several notches in Crump's estimation. He dismissed the nightwatchman; there was another way and he would use it. Portway, it appeared from what Jackie had said, was a womanizer who'd just been caught out by his wife. It might be hard for a known womanizer to make anything stick about being led on in innocence . . . after Crump had left his cabin Pemmel suddenly wondered why he was

141

bothering. All everyone wanted was to have the whole thing hushed up. Portway certainly wasn't going to press for anything like an official enquiry. Pemmel knew that he was being propelled by his own obstinacy: he wasn't going to have the second steward believing he'd got the purser to back down, caught in the cleft stick of threat, of statements being made about his drinking habits. Portway was the one who had to be forced to back down.

[iii]

After the decyphering of the Admiralty's signal, the orders had been passed by lamp from the Rear-Admiral commanding the cruiser squadron and from the Commodore. The new course was indicated; and a new zig-zag pattern was put into effect once the vast body of ships had steadied on its southerly course and, after much backing and filling and some anxious moments as one ship cut across another, was back in its steaming formation under cover of the warships. The orders were that the convoy should head due south for four hours and then alter to the eastward. Kemp was doubtful about the effectiveness of the manoeuvre. As he said to O'Halloran, who was back on the bridge with him, the packs would be well extended to north and south of the track.

'You mean they'll be expecting an alteration, Commodore?'

'Very likely, yes. And it only needs a couple of U-boats to play merry hell.'

'How many have they out there?'

Kemp shrugged. 'Your guess is as good as mine. All I know is, Hitler has plenty and to spare.'

'So what do we do?'

'Follow orders, Brigadier. Nothing else we can do.'

O'Halloran said, 'Well, I guess that's right. But once again, talking about orders . . .'

Kemp said, 'Yes.' He knew what was coming because they'd had it out already, before the *Ardara*'s captain had made his broadcast, but O'Halloran was a sticker and as obstinate as a mule, a mule that wouldn't let things rest or take no for an answer. 'We've been into all that, Brigadier –'

'I know we have. Now we're going into it again, all right?'

'Not all right,' Kemp said, bristling beneath his bridge coat. 'Orders at sea must be given by seamen.'

'My officers –'

'I've nothing against them. But they're not seamen, Brigadier.'

'You've denigrated them by telling their own troops not to take their orders.'

'Not exactly what Captain Hampton said. And remember I don't come into that. Hampton commands the ship, not I.'

'You told Hampton –'

'I *advised* Captain Hampton – or would have done had I needed to. As it happened I didn't even need to do that. Hampton has sailed in plenty of convoys.'

O'Halloran persisted, as dogged as ever. 'I still say it's my officers and NCOs who know how to control troops. I'm not having you or –'

Kemp's interruption was crisp and authoritative. 'I repeat, Captain Hampton commands the ship. He also commands you while you're aboard. Your time will come after you're disembarked. Currently you're a passenger. I suggest you remember that, Brigadier. And I'll tell you something else: if you complain when you're safe in Britain, you'll get no support from any quarter at all. The conduct of convoys and of the individual ships in the convoys is very clearly laid down as a wholly naval responsibility under the orders of the Trade Division of the Admiralty.'

He almost felt like adding, so there. But he grinned to himself when O'Halloran, as if in anticipation of some such suffix, said angrily, 'God, how childish can you get!' and stumped away to the bridge wing on the other side.

Kemp thought good riddance and wondered which of them was being childish, though it didn't take very much wonderment in fact. And he thanked God he'd gone to sea himself. He was sorry for the troops, destined for bloody battle against Hitler's Third Reich under O'Halloran's command. He'd watched them embark in Halifax: they were young and eager, a fine-looking lot, leaving for the unknown but not letting the fear of it dampen their spirits. Kemp hoped they would manage to survive such as O'Halloran . . .

'Kye, sir?' The voice came from behind him: Williams. Kemp swung round. Kye, the navy's term for a steaming hot cup of

143

cocoa, was always welcome.

The mug in his hand, Kemp said, 'Thank you, Williams. You can turn in for a spell so long as you keep an ear and a half listening out.'

'That's all right, sir. I'll stay.'

'Just as you like.' Kemp's tone was noncommittal but he was pleased by his assistant's sense of duty, even though it was unnecessary – in Kemp's view no attack was likely while the convoy was on its southerly course. The U-boat packs would wait on their possibly extended station for the ships to steam into the net. That was how it usually went, when you didn't know where the net was. They were a shower of bastards, loosing off their tin fish from the depths against helpless merchantmen, but a shower of bastards who were only doing their duty. Kemp wouldn't want their job. To be beneath the surface in a steel canister under depth-charge attack, lying deep in the hope of avoiding the shattering explosions that would spring plates and open seams, damage the batteries to bring poisonous fumes to claw at throats – such a life was not, in Kemp's view, one for any man of the sea. Too claustrophobic, too confined. One of Kemp's own reasons for having gone to sea was his love of open spaces and the feel of wind and weather on his face. To watch the sunrise and sunset in all their differing moods, to see the scud of cloud before the wind, racing across a blue sky. Much as he loved his home he sometimes found even Meopham claustrophobic. Thoughts of home and family obtruded . . . day-dreaming as the night came down into full dark.

Williams stood silent by the Commodore's side. He had earned a rebuke from Kemp the morning after he'd staggered up the accommodation ladder with the ship's doctor, bawling out 'Old King Cole' at the top of his voice. Bad for discipline, Kemp had said. Officers didn't get so disgustingly drunk in the full view and hearing of ratings. Kemp was no killjoy and he'd said so. But some steam was best let off in private, and noise was an abomination wherever it took place. Always aboard a ship, there was a watchkeeper, many watchkeepers, trying to sleep during their watch below, and such excruciating dins carried. Williams hadn't tried to excuse himself and had apologized and Kemp had found a new liking for his assistant, who had obviously been suffering from a filthy hangover, looking like death warmed up.

Now, up there on the *Ardara*'s bridge, Kemp said suddenly, 'A penny for 'em, Williams.'

'Sir?'

'You're unusually silent.'

'Am I, sir? I didn't . . . I thought perhaps you didn't want to be bothered.'

Kemp laughed. 'A kindly thought, but misplaced as it happens. I wasn't thinking about the convoy, though no doubt I should have been. Thoughts of home, nothing more . . . I'm perfectly human beneath my brass hat, Williams. Just like any OD.'

'Yes, sir.'

'No doubt you think of home. I don't know much about you – another example of my remissness. Where's home to you?'

'London, sir. Hounslow.'

'H'm. Family?'

'Parents, sir, that's all.'

'Your father in the service – or retired?'

'Neither, sir. ARP warden.'

'I take my hat off to him,' Kemp said, and meant it. 'Those chaps have had a bellyful, all slog and plenty of danger. No doubt you worry.'

'Yes, sir,' Williams said, and sounded what he was: surprised. In point of fact he hadn't worried at all. Kemp's words made him realize something – that his father could be killed in an air raid over London. Strange he hadn't thought of that before, but he hadn't, his thoughts being all of women and his urgent desire to have someone he could regard as a girlfriend, worrying about him every time he went to sea. Silence fell again between the Commodore and his assistant; Kemp once again went through the actions of lifting his binoculars and scanning the darkened ships of the convoy and the water to port and starboard. Speed of spotting the tell-tale feather of water from a periscope scraping the surface was vital, though of course the Asdics would, or should, spot the presence of a U-boat long before the human eye. Tonight the sea was moonlit, very unkindly, and the weather was just right for attack, an almost flat sea with the wind having dropped away, but something of a swell that wouldn't bother the enemy much though it kept the *Ardara* rolling fairly heavily. Williams said, 'I'll make rounds of the guns, sir. Just to keep them on the hop.'

'Right. But not so much of the hop, Williams. Alert's a word I like better. Don't make good men hopping mad!'

'No, sir.'

'I trust you understand what I mean?'

'Yes, sir.'

'Off you go, then.'

Williams left the bridge, a little puzzled and ruffled. Old Kemp . . . one moment he yacked about discipline, the next he didn't want the hands chivvied. To Williams, discipline meant chivvying and being the efficient, soft-soled officer who caught ratings out. He had the idea Kemp would clump round in clogs, just so that the lower deck would know he was coming and crush out their fag-ends and get their arses off the deck. Williams saw no point in that. There was a lot of satisfaction in a sudden pounce and it was always effective. The men had a respect for you when you appeared suddenly and bowled them out, the officer with the eagle eye over whom nothing could be put . . .

'Watch it,' Petty Officer Frapp said to his gun's crew. 'Johnny-come-lately's on the loose again.' He had caught a glimpse of an RN cap badge as a moonbeam slanted across the deck, a cap badge emerging from behind a big bell-mouthed ventilator. 'Daft bugger – looking for birdshit again, I s'pose.'

That episode still rankled with Frapp: young Williams, he'd be better off and less of a liability if he spent the whole war on the parade ground at Pompey barracks, done up in sword and gaiters and marching matloes around and back again, practising ceremonial drill. Plenty of the RNVR officers, the Wavy Navy as they were known on account of their wavy gold stripes, were very good indeed and had done wonders in adapting quickly from civvy life to the war at sea, and all honour to them in Frapp's view. But Williams struck him as just a mobile uniform, a tailor's dummy with gold lace. Or maybe he was simply prejudiced – that birdshit again.

Williams halted, 'Well, Frapp.'

'All's well, sir. Any news, sir?'

'News, Frapp?'

Frapp was patient. 'Of the Jerries, sir. The packs.'

'No.'

146

'Ah. Just thought something more might 'ave come through, sir.'

'Well, it hasn't. Keep on top line, Frapp.' Williams moved away again. Low sounds came from Frapp and his lips mouthed the silent words: *Fuck off for God's sake and drop dead.* Suddenly and involuntarily Frapp emitted a very loud belch across the open deck and saw Williams halt, stiffen and look round. Frapp had difficulty in not splitting his sides. The officer had thought for a moment a gun had gone off somewhere and had almost shit himself.

[iv]

'I think,' Jackie Ord said carefully, 'the bridge believes there may be an attack tonight, Doctor.'

'Oh . . .'

'If there is, we're going to be needed.'

'Yes, yes.' The doctor's hand shook and whisky slopped over from the glass. The doctor looked at it without interest; at three and sixpence net to the ship's officers per bottle, the expense was no consideration at all. 'We shall be ready, Sister.'

You won't, she thought. She did her best without being too insubordinate. He wasn't a bad old stick and she was sorry for him, for the way he was sliding down the drain: no doubt he'd been a good doctor once, young and keen and efficient, and it was always sad to see this sort of thing. She said, 'If I were you, I wouldn't have another, Doctor.'

'A small one, Sister.'

'Think of your liver, Doctor.'

'I do. Though I try not to.'

Cirrhosis of the liver, she thought, it gets them all in the end, though gin would be worse. There was something therapeutic about whisky: perhaps the silly old bloke was practising self-therapy or something. And God knew, he *did* need his stiffener. Jackie sighed as the doctor reached unsteadily for the bottle and poured a shot that was scarcely small. She'd said her piece and that was that, she couldn't be his keeper. But she had a terrible vision of a torpedo taking the *Ardara* and causing an explosion inboard, deep in the ship, and all the burns cases, all the shattered bodies and broken limbs, and a drunken doctor

147

staggering about with a hypodermic and adding to the confusion and agony – but there were army doctors aboard, of course, and army nursing sisters too. Perhaps one piss-artist wouldn't be missed after all and he might as well make a job of it and pass out, out of the way. Jackie left him to it, tippling away in his cabin, and went back to the sick bay.

The doctor finished the whisky and poured another. He lit a cigarette, taking a long time over it, for the end of the cigarette appeared shy of the lighter's flame, veering away from it again and again. At last he managed it, dropped the result on his carpet, fished about for it, picked it up and put it between his lips, where it trembled up and down. Why had that woman mentioned his liver? It was a sore point; he knew he wasn't doing himself any good and despite what he had said to the girl he did in fact spend a good deal of time thinking of his liver. He read books about it, diagnosing himself after every likely, or possible, symptom – he was years out of date in his medical knowledge and he knew that too. Too many years at sea, vegetating. And drinking, of course . . . frontal lobes of the brain and all that, they wore out, eroded by the constant drip of alcohol or its effect. Very nasty: he could even be in for early senile dementia for all he knew. It could have started already. He never felt too good, at any rate until he'd taken a fair amount of whisky into his system. Fortunately the diminishing of his medical expertise didn't matter all that much: it was seldom anything difficult cropped up at sea. No childbirths, not even in peacetime since the Line always demanded to know about pregnancies before female passengers were booked. Few diseases – the days of shipboard epidemics were largely past. Gippo tummy, mal-de-mer, VD among the crew, these were the mainstays of the surgery. These and boils and so on, simple ailments that could be left to the assistant surgeon and the nursing sisters.

Of course it was different now that they were at war.

A little more whisky to drown the thought of what might happen at any moment. A stiffener was in a sense a duty . . . for a moment the doctor put his head in his hands, a prey to sudden and terrible depression. He felt very much alone, alone in a ship filled with seamen and troops, a ship whose alleyways were never entirely silent. He'd enjoyed that night ashore in Halifax, when he'd encountered that friendly young fellow – what was his name? No idea. But he was aboard. Assistant Commodore – that was the young man's job. The doctor slithered along his settee and took up his telephone.

[v]

On the bridge Kemp saw the blue-shaded lamp from cs29, an urgent look about it. Leading Signalman Mathias was on the ball, acknowledging. 'Number of contacts on the port bow, sir,' he reported.

'Thank you, Mathias.' Kemp went at the double into the wheelhouse where the senior second officer was on watch. 'Captain on the bridge,' he said crisply. The lid of the voice-pipe to Hampton's day-cabin was wrenched up: the Captain wouldn't be sleeping, he'd gone down for a call of nature only. Unusually, as Kemp started to pass the order for the alarm to be sounded every one of the telephones and voice-pipes demanded attention at once: radio room, gun positions, engine-room . . . and something else. Kemp himself happened to take up the phone on that one.

'Bridge, Commodore here.'

'I want the . . . the Ashishtant Commodore.'

Kemp's face was grim. 'Who the devil's that?'

'Ship . . . ship's shurgeon. I want –'

The telephone slammed in the doctor's ear. He had a hurt look, a surprised look. Some people . . . so damn rude! A fraction of a second later he became aware that the alarm rattlers were sounding, an appalling din, and then the ship seemed to come alive with pounding feet.

FOURTEEN

Hampton reached the bridge as the alarm rattlers started. Kemp was in the port wing, with Williams. He put Hampton in the picture. 'This is it, Captain. Sounds like a whole hunting pack. I'd like your engines to stand by for maximum power – it'll be needed within the next minute.'

'Aye, aye, sir.' Hampton nodded at his messenger, who went at once to the wheelhouse. The word went down to the engine-room, to Chief Engineer Burrows already on the starting-platform. On the bridge Kemp gripped the rail ahead of him: so many U-boats, so many torpedoes to be loosed among the ships, too big a target – they couldn't possibly miss if they simply fired blind into the mass. In Kemp's view the time had come for the extreme order: with misgivings he gave it in a firm voice.

'Scatter the convoy, Williams. Inform cs29 and Captain(D).'

Williams passed the order to Mathias, who got busy with his shaded masthead lamp, remote controlled from the bridge. Now the ships would begin to move into independent sailing, diffusing the target while the warships went into the attack. In a few minutes would come the testing time, the time when collisions might well be almost inevitable as the ships altered course and speed, some this way, some that, a great disintegrated monster flailing about the North Atlantic.

'Rendezvous, Williams. Work out a position on the chart, south-east from Cape Farewell. Thirty-six hours' steaming.' Kemp searched the surface through his binoculars, eyes straining through the moonlit night. Nothing to be seen, but signals were coming again from the flagship. There were some twenty contacts, all of them on the port bow but some of them now

150

moving across. The convoy, course having been altered east-wards after the four hours stipulated by the Rear-Admiral, was steaming virtually slap into the packs. As Kemp watched out, a message from the radio room was reported to him: the Rear-Admiral had broken wireless silence to the Admiralty, reporting the HX about to come under potentially heavy attack. Still nothing showed, no feather on the surface, not in the *Ardara's* vicinity.

'Buggers are taking their time,' Kemp said.

Hampton asked, 'What about that battleship?'

'Sitting duck. Useless! But I'd hate to see her go. Part of Britain's history.'

'Psychological effect?'

'Precisely. At home as well as here. Household names, all those battlewagons. Remember the sense of doom when the *Hood* went?'

Hampton said, 'Yes, very well indeed. My wife . . . she had a nephew aboard, an RNR snotty. Went down with the ship.'

'I'm sorry,' Kemp said.

'Not to worry, sir. It's in the past now.'

They were talking for the sake of talking, a human reaction as they waited, since all they could do was wait now. The relevant orders had been passed, the formation of the convoy was breaking up, the cruisers of the escort were moving across with the destroyers, the protective greyhounds of the seas, steaming fast into the attack, following their Asdics, the depth-charges ready in the racks and throwers aft, their main armament manned to finish off anything that was forced to the surface, to shatter the U-boats with gunfire. No survivors on either side would be picked up: the remnant of the convoy, if it came to that, would steam at its best speed, independently, for the rendez-vous. Then would come the count.

'Hey there, Commodore.'

Kemp turned: Brigadier O'Halloran, conspicuous by his ab-sence after the contretemps about orders, had come back to the bridge. Kemp said, 'This is it.'

'Sure, I know that. I'm reporting all my soldiers ready, Commodore.'

'Thank you.' Ready? Kemp wondered: what for? Ready to slide over the lifted side of a stricken transport, ready to gasp their lungs out in spilled oil fuel, to try to swim for the lifeboats, to

151

die horribly in a series of explosions and escaping steam if they failed to make the boats before she went, or die more slowly, trapped, carried down into the depths until the water pressure crumpled all that was left? He gave himself a shake: those were defeatist thoughts. But it was the waiting that gave rise to them, the sense of helplessness, of being a sitting duck like that pathetic old battleship with her maximum speed of around twenty-one knots.

And the *Ardara* had little more. Perhaps, with luck, twenty-three with the holding-down bolts in danger of shearing under the stretched thunder of the shafts. Below in the engine-room, the chief engineer was bringing her up to that maximum, standing on the starting-platform, watching his dials and gauges, a mess of cotton-waste in his hands, his white overalls spotless in a hell of heat and din and spider's-web ladders criss-crossing the space above his head, right up to the airlock into the engineers' alleyway.

Burrows thought about what was going on up top, in the fresh air. He was thinking about some of the things that could happen – they didn't often, but there had been a time in his experience when they did, and aboard a certain merchant ship, not the one he was in himself but he had imagination enough to see it all, the engineers and greasers and firemen had suddenly found steel bows knifing in, with ton after ton of seawater pouring in around them as the plates buckled. The engine spaces would have filled, lifting the engine-room complement to the deckhead far above, lifting them to impact and drown. The normal procedure when one ship hit another was for the hitting ship to remain in the hole to act as a kind of collision mat, something to plug the damage until, say, a cement box could be prepared as a running repair; but that hadn't happened in the case Burrows had in mind. The hitting ship had been a neutral that had attached herself to the convoy without invitation – that had often happened in the earlier days of the war – and she'd hauled off to the accompaniment of panic-stricken shouts and wails, a load of native crewmen dancing about on her bridge and rushing up and down the deck getting in each other's way and the Captain literally tearing at his hair.

Nasty!

There had been just a couple of survivors from that engine-room, two greasers who'd managed to find the air-lock and get through with seawater acting as a thrust . . . and soon after that the ship had been torpedoed anyway, and had gone down.

Burrows turned over the starting-platform for a while to his senior second engineer and moved around, having a word here and there, eyes darting, looking at bearings and such, ears attuned to every sound, any small interruption to the sweetness of the running that might be a forewarning of trouble. A chief engineer needed all his senses alert, sight, sound, smell, touch. Machinery was Burrows' life but he knew it had a life of its own and was very temperamental. To be a good chief engineer you had also to be a machine doctor, a diagnostician first class.

[ii]

Hampton was conning the ship: that wasn't the Commodore's job. Hampton was having his work cut out: in the circumstances of convoy scatter, the precise letters of the regulations for preventing collision at sea didn't always apply, simply because they couldn't. No ship could alter three or four ways at once and still obey the regulations, and often three or four ships could come close and need to be stood clear of.

If possible.

It was when it became impossible that collisions happened; avoiding one ship, you stood foul of another.

Fortunately Captain Hampton had a cool mind and a clear brain with a capacity for instant decision. Just once during the early stages of that scattering operation did Commodore Kemp feel his blood run cold. A big freighter loaded to her marks with high explosive came suddenly across the *Ardara*'s bow, surging from port to starboard as she attempted to give clear passage to another ship that in its turn had come across her own bow.

Kemp had to bite back the order, but Hampton gave it in good time: 'Engines emergency full astern, wheel hard-a-port!'

The telegraphs were hauled over on the bridge, from full ahead to full astern twice, two pulls being the emergency signal. Bells rang and were repeated from deep down in the ship as Burrows, back on the starting-platform, reacted. There was a momentary lull in the spinning of the huge steel shafts that ran through their

153

tunnels to the screws, and then they went into reverse and a shudder ran through the ship, a shudder that became a violent vibration, and water boiled beneath the *Ardara*'s counter. Churned sea, milky white, rushed for'ard as the way began to come off. On the bridge the Captain ordered the wheel amidships. Below, Burrows wiped his cotton-waste across his sweaty forehead and waited for the crump. Throughout the ship the tension had mounted. The *Ardara*'s crew guessed the score: the soldiers didn't. To them the sudden vibration that had taken their steel box in its grip brought another dimension of the unknown. Anything could be about to happen – like an explosion. They stood fast because they were soldiers and not boys or women, but a good many prayers were said and a good many stomachs got the runs until, as suddenly as it had started, the vibration ceased and a member of the transport's crew came shouting along the alleyways and troop decks: Master-at-Arms Rockett.

'It's all right, no panic.' The loud voice carried and brought comfort. 'The ship's all right, just a near miss, almost hit a silly bastard but didn't.'

Rockett was brought to a halt by a sergeant-major, an infantry RSM resplendent with the Royal Arms on his right sleeve. 'You, there!'

Rockett stopped. 'Yes?'

'Who are you?'

'Ship's master-at-arms, Sar-Major.'

'What actually caused the vibration?'

'Engines going astern.'

'You'd think,' the RSM said, 'the Captain'd have given some bleeding warning,' He looked shaken, grey in the face.

Rockett stared at him, face blank. 'Waste time doing that and he'd have hit. Result – you might be bloody swimming now.' It was an exaggeration but it seemed to put the RSM out of his misery. He wiped his face and marched off, left-right-left, and began shouting at his troops. Rockett moved on, no longer on the snoop for sin but helping to spread confidence. Moving through the troop decks and then down to the working alleyways he found Mr Portway and his fire parties, standing by the fire hydrants and their hose connections.

'All well, Mr Portway?'

Portway nodded, seeming oddly startled to be confronted by

154

the master-at-arms. Maybe not so odd; Rockett had heard funny rumours . . . things always circulated aboard a ship, nothing could ever be kept entirely secret, and Rockett was aware that there *was* a secret though he couldn't get at the truth. Nothing had been said officially so there had to be a cover-up in progress. God alone – or God and a handful of others perhaps – knew what the facts were re Portway. But the buzzes! Portway had got rotten drunk and attacked the purser, Portway had attempted rape, Portway had attempted buggery against a young private of the army draft, Portway had seven wives like the man who'd been going to St Ives and he'd gone round the bend with the strain, gone berserk and tried to jump overboard . . .

Never mind, Rockett thought. One day it would come out and since whatever it was had never been reported to him it would be no skin off his nose. What intrigued him was where the sod the buzzes had started. In his view it all added up to Crump's section, and he'd interrogated Crump and Crump wouldn't say a thing, not even when Rockett approached him on a man-to-man basis, an ex-RPO to ex-colour-sergeant basis. Crump was always like a clam. Obstinate old twit.

Rockett went back up the ladders, feeling the tension again as he moved for'ard along the troop deck. The soldiers were all ready, all fallen in with their kitbags and rifles as if about to go on parade – and they might just as well ditch their ruddy kitbags here and now, Rockett thought, because no deck officer was ever going to allow the lifeboats to be cluttered up with personal possessions if they had to abandon.

Through the troop deck, up three decks to the purser's office in the for'ard square, along the port alleyway past the surgery and the purser's accommodation and then, away ahead and dimly seen in the blue police lights, the unsteady lurch of a figure out of a cross-alleyway followed by its total collapse to the deck.

Bloody Norah, Rockett thought, it's the quack! He put on speed and shone his torch down on the heap. It was the doctor, all right, out cold but breathing, breathing noisily. Poor old bugger, Rockett thought, all grey and rumpled, always with soup-stains down the front of his uniform . . . but he should have known better considering he was a qualified quack. Rockett clicked his tongue, bent and grabbed the doctor's shoulder.

'Come along now, sir. Come along, get up. I'll take you to your

155

cabin, sir.'

There was an indistinct utterance that sounded like 'splurge' but couldn't have been, but no other response. The doctor was physically inert.

Pemmel came along from aft. 'What's that?' he asked.

'The doctor, sir.'

'Oh, my God,' Pemmel bent. 'Out for the count.'

'Yessir. Wonder what did it.'

'Don't try to be funny, Rockett.'

'Sorry, sir. Just thought it might be tactful like.'

'Oh – yes! I see what you mean. The sudden vibration, a fall and a bump on the head. Give me a hand, will you?' They lifted and dragged, the heels slid along the polished corticene, and the doctor was sick. They got him into his cabin, lifted him to his bunk, removed his tie, loosened his collar and took off his shoes. He appeared lifeless though he still breathed.

'Nasty colour, sir. His face.'

'Yes. Get Sister Ord here, Rockett. Fast.'

Rockett lifted the telephone. 'She'll be in the surgery, sir.' He called the surgery, passed his message and rang off. 'On her way, sir.'

'Right, thank you, Rockett.'

'Want me any more sir?'

'No. I'll cope. Er . . .'

Rockett understood. 'Soul of discretion, sir.'

Pemmel thought: I wonder! That remained to be seen. Rockett was inclined to be bolshie at times but he was basically an arse-crawler whose future lay in the hands of the ship's officers. Soon after Rockett had left the cabin, Jackie Ord came in.

She looked at the bunk and said, 'Lovely sight. I did warn him.'

'He's past heeding.'

'He is at this moment.'

'I mean all the time.'

'Yes, I'm afraid that's right.' Jackie examined the motionless body, pulling back the eyelids, feeling heart and pulse. Pemmel asked if they shouldn't get Dr Barnes along, but she said that wasn't necessary. 'Just drunk, nothing else. He'll live.'

'And the less that know . . .'

'We all know already,' she said crisply. 'It's not that. It's just . . . well, I've got a lot of time for the old soak, Andy. I just

156

don't want to expose him to a junior who's not long out of medical school, that's all.'

Pemmel nodded. 'Yes, I get you, Jackie.' He paused. 'Look, isn't it about time you got out of all this? I mean . . . pissy-arsed doctors in charge, all the social boozing . . .' His voice tailed off. 'I know I'm not the one to throw stones.'

She looked at him, a quizzical expression showing. 'Are you suggesting I ought to retire?'

'In a way, yes, I am.'

'Bit young, aren't I?'

He said, 'If you got married, Jackie . . .'

'Is this a proposal?'

Pemmel sounded defensive. 'Yes.'

'Weird setting – quite original!' Mid-Atlantic, convoy scattering, attack likely at any moment . . . one drunk doctor and a lot of work potentially looming. But she laid a hand on his arm and her answer was gentle. 'I'm a qualified woman, Andy, an SRN, and I'm needed. Even if I did get married, I'd want to carry on.'

'But surely –'

'Andy, there's a war on. Remember?'

There was a smell of vomit again. Already Jackie had turned the doctor's face to one side so that the vomit wouldn't remain in his throat and suffocate him. Pemmel left her to clean up.

[iii]

Before the convoy had moved very far apart the officers on the *Ardara*'s bridge had heard the series of explosions from the port bow of the original line of advance, the explosions as the depth-charge patterns blasted the ocean aside in their search for the submerged attackers. They seemed to go on without cease and Kemp wondered how any U-boat could survive. Wondered, but knew they would. Submarines were not easy targets to find and not all that easy to sink when found. They could go deep, and silence could be ordered throughout the boat, not even a rattle against the hull that might be picked up. Always the settings on the depth-charges were a matter of guesswork: they could go off too near the surface or too deep, and submarines were capable of surviving quite a number of close explosions. Also they could fool

157

their attackers into thinking they had been hit, fool them by disgorging quantities of oil and bits of wood and clothing to rise to the surface so that the attack would be broken off.

But tonight could be different: Kemp knew this was the massive attack, the one scheduled to halt the convoy in its tracks and destroy the troop lift before it could be deployed against the armies of the Third Reich. There would be many targets and the attack would be kept up indefinitely, or at any rate until the dispersal of the convoy was complete and the ships away on their separate courses. Even so, many of them were going to be sunk. That was inevitable. Certain of the ships were going to be marked by the U-boat captains, the bigger units, the troopships especially.

The *Ardara* was one of those most at risk.

Kemp watched for torpedo trails. All the lookouts were glued to their binoculars. The moon was bright now, an unkind quirk of fate that illuminated the targets for the Nazis. Each ship stood out sharply, silhouettes inviting attack. The destroyers were concentrating around the area of the most echoes, but Kemp knew that not all the U-boats would be in that area – some would have sneaked away to carry out isolated attacks. The cruisers were moving around, apparently aimlessly but doing their best to stand between the heavy ships and the likely direction of the enemy, a constant movement in and out, a tricky and dangerous movement calling for a consummate ship-handling skill. Away now on the port quarter as the *Ardara* steamed on her new course away from the attack concentration, the old R-Class battleship could be seen pushing her great bulk through the water, slow and solemn and stately with her battle ensigns hoisted – before the *Ardara* had moved farther off Kemp had seen the huge, over-size White Ensigns creeping to the mastheads in glorious defiance of Adolf Hitler's killers. The old battlewagon could possibly succumb to just one torpedo if the Nazis aimed a lucky shot clear of the anti-torpedo bulges that ran along both her sides in protection of her magazines and engine spaces. But not all the way along: if she was hit in the bow or stern she could flood and never mind the watertight doors and bulkheads, never mind the efforts of the damage control parties. Certain things had been rumoured about Britain's ageing battle fleet, the old-timers from the last war. Their so-called watertight divisions were said to leak like sieves . . .

Kemp wasn't looking towards the battleship when the first torpedo hit was scored for Germany: he was looking right ahead and had in fact spotted the torpedo trail seconds before it hit. He had called an automatic and totally useless warning, and then hell appeared to lift from beneath the living world and shatter it into an inferno. Immediately ahead of the *Ardara*, an ammunition ship went sky high as something approaching twenty thousand tons of high explosive blew up.

FIFTEEN

Heat blasted back; Kemp's eyebrows singed and his exposed skin felt red-hot. All the windows of the wheelhouse shattered. Debris, flung into the air from the ammunition ship, began falling from a great height. Slivers of steel had sliced across the *Ardara's* fo'c'sle and bridge, some of them at white heat. Hampton was lying on the deck, quite still and bleeding. Two other of the ship's officers were reeling about. Kemp ran for the wheelhouse. The quartermaster was all right, a lucky man.

Kemp shouted the order: 'Wheel hard-a-starboard!'

'Wheel hard-a-starboard, sir.'

Kemp ran for the engine-room telegraphs and once again the bells rang and the indicators, the tell-tales, ordered full astern. The heat was increasing, could be felt all along the open decks. Petty Officer Frapp felt it, though he was to some extent protected as were the guns' crews by their anti-flash gear. Frapp looked for'ard, saw Lieutenant Williams on the bridge with the Commodore. It didn't look as though Williams was coming down to start fussing and that was something to be thankful for. Frapp looked with horror at the shattered, blazing freighter so close ahead, beginning now to draw away as the *Ardara's* helm took effect and the engines thundered her astern and clear. He saw men, ablaze themselves, jump from what was left of the decks. He fancied he could hear screams even over the roar of the flames, coming back to him through rolling clouds of red-licked smoke. It was total devastation, total obliteration of a big ship that had been steaming intact only seconds before, carrying some fifty men each with his own hopes and thoughts of homecoming. Many of those men would have been fried by now, reduced to

160

running fat or blackened crisps. And many were in the sea, the red-lit sea, some swimming, some lying motionless with their heads down in the water.

As Frapp looked in horror and anger, he saw the next torpedo trail. On the port beam and headed straight for the *Ardara*. He cupped his hands, yelled a warning to the bridge, then followed it up by use of the telephone, the communication between gun and bridge.

Kemp, too, had seen it. As Frapp put down the telephone the *Ardara*, with sternway on her and with her bows swinging, presented her counter to the approaching torpedo. Kemp, watching closely from the port wing of the bridge, checked the swing so as to maintain a position stern-on to the torpedo trail.

'Wheel amidships . . . hard-a-port. Stop engines . . . engines to full ahead. Midships . . . *steady!*'

Sweat streamed down his cheeks, not from the heat of the burning ship alone. For a moment he lost the torpedo and stood with fists clenched, waiting for the stern to blow out of the ship. Then he heard Williams' voice.

'It's all right, sir! You've done it!'

Kemp felt far away. 'Done what, Williams?'

'Torpedo passing down our port side, sir.' Williams pointed; Kemp looked. Down the port side was right – the tin fish could be seen, or its trail could, a matter of half a dozen feet from the *Ardara*'s plating.

Kemp said, 'Thank God.'

'Yes, sir. But that'll be the first, only the first.'

'I know.' Kemp stared down into the water, at the men struggling for their lives, men now drawing astern fast but still visible in the bright glare from the ammunition ship. Not for long: the light went quite suddenly as the rising water doused the fires, and left a hiss of steam behind as the freighter sank, steam and a great bubble of air. No one spoke of picking up survivors: no one would expect to hazard a troopship for the sake of a handful of men who might well have little longer to live in any case. The *Ardara*'s task now was to keep floating and clear the danger area – but that danger area extended across many square miles of the ocean depths. Kemp said, 'We're not the only target, Williams.'

'No, sir.'

'And I don't mean that as a kind of hope for ourselves.'

161

'I realize that, sir.' Williams spoke with sincerity; he knew the strains on the convoy Commodore, knew that Kemp was thinking of all the others, of his responsibility that continued overall even though each shipmaster was now under individual orders. The Commodore couldn't be everywhere at once. But that wouldn't lift the weight from a man like Mason Kemp. Williams had learned quite a lot about Kemp since the convoy had left the Clyde; Kemp had proved he was no has-been, no dug-out like Brigadier O'Halloran. O'Halloran, to give him his due, had remained quiescent in a corner of the bridge wing throughout, but now, as the *Ardara* drew away on a zig-zag course to the south, he thrust himself back into the picture.

'Somebody's balls are going to be had for garters,' he said.

Kemp turned and stared briefly. 'Whose, may I ask?'

'Oh, not yours. The skipper of that freighter.' O'Halloran seemed to realize he'd said something out of place. He coughed. 'Poor bloke . . . he'll be dead most likely.'

'Yes. And not to blame in any way, Brigadier.'

'That torpedo should have been spotted.'

'Try it some time. It's all luck. We could get one at any moment.'

O'Halloran said, 'All that wasted ammunition!' He sounded disgusted.

Kemp turned his back: inside, he was boiling. What did a man like O'Halloran know of the war at sea? Then Kemp took a grip and simmered down. The answer to his unspoken question was: about the same as he, Kemp, knew of the war on land. The difference was that Kemp, if caught up in a land battle, wouldn't shoot his mouth off.

Kemp looked at his watch: the whole thing had taken no more than two minutes. Now there were things to attend to: the transport's Captain and the two watchkeeping officers. Kemp said, 'Williams, get the doctor up at once.'

'Message already sent, sir.'

'Good. Have you had a look at them?'

'Yes, sir. Captain Hampton . . . he's dead, sir. Caught in the neck . . . a steel splinter by the look of it.'

Kemp reeled a little: an old friend and shipmate. He asked, 'The others?'

'Just knocked out I believe.' A minute later Dr Barnes, the

162

assistant surgeon, reported to the bridge. Kemp, with sharp memories of the slurred telephone call, refrained from asking why his senior wasn't attending. Barnes made his examination and confirmed what Williams had said. Barnes had Sister Ord with him. Kemp recalled the last time they'd met on the bridge, the time he'd had to deliver a broadside at her. She had been ill at ease then. Now she was the spirit of confidence, the ship's nursing sister doing her professional job.

Barnes said, 'The chief officer, sir. He'll need rest in his bunk.'

'See to it, then, Doctor. What about the senior third?'

'Fit enough, sir, just knocked about a bit by the blast.'

'Fit to take over the watch?'

'I think so, sir.'

Kemp nodded. 'Right. I'll be here myself, of course.'

Barnes looked at him critically. 'You need rest yourself, sir. I –'

'I'm all right, Doctor.'

'But you –'

'I said, I'm all right. Doctor's orders don't always apply at sea.'

Barnes was stubborn. He tried again. 'Benzedrine, sir. A tablet would keep you going.'

'*Drugs?*'

'You could call it that, yes. But with a difference.'

'You can put them where the monkey put the nuts,' Kemp said tersely.

'Waste of much-needed medical stores,' Barnes said with a grin. 'The point is, benzedrine helps concentration when you're tired. As Commodore, you need –'

'Don't you tell me my duty, young man!'

'It's *my* duty to do so, sir.'

'God . . .' Kemp came near to an explosion but held on to his temper. Barnes was persistent, and certainly he had a duty as much in his own sphere as the Commodore in his. One should not be too old-fashioned in this war; keep-awake drugs could help. And Kemp respected anyone who did his duty and stuck to his opinions in the face of seniority and rank. He came to a decision, for the good of the convoy. He said, 'Very well, Doctor. Produce your confounded bloody tablet!'

Barnes fished in a pocket and brought out a phial. He also produced a flask. Kemp asked, 'What's in that? Whisky?'

'Water, sir. For sending down the Benzedrine.'

163

Kemp laughed. 'You come prepared!' He put a tablet on his tongue and took a swig at the flask. A pity it wasn't whisky . . .

[ii]

Hampton's body was taken down from the bridge by two seamen with a Neil Robertson stretcher and laid upon his bunk in his sleeping-cabin. Kemp wondered about committal: it would have to be done, of course, but not before they were clear of the danger zone. He could not risk stopping engines while the body went overboard. So that was something for the future, a grim and unwelcome business that he didn't want to think about too much. He put it from his mind. There were other considerations: Staff Captain Greene would now take over command as master of the *Ardara*. Greene was in general charge below during action stations and had better remain there until he was relieved by another officer. Kemp sent Williams down to report the facts and ask Greene to make his arrangements. Kemp himself would do no more, could not interfere with the master's conduct of his ship. Poor Hampton . . . Kemp took a grip on his mind, forced down thoughts of pre-war days, of a lasting friendship, of a first-class shipmaster who very likely, if he'd been given the chance, would have preferred death at sea while still in command to the slow disintegration of old age and the gabbling of senility, the repetition of stories of old times that no one wanted to hear any more. Kemp thought suddenly of his grandmother: if she survived much longer she too would probably outlive her wish to go on. He knew all her yarns by heart, had often prompted her in the telling, bored stiff but not wanting to hurt. It was hard to grow old. Well, Arthur Hampton wouldn't be doing that. Kemp would find time to write a letter to Hampton's wife, for posting in the Clyde if ever they got there. Hampton had lived not far from Meopham; Mary would go and see her, do what she could – they'd liked each other and there was the sea's and the Line's bond between them . . .

The *Ardara* moved on, zig-zagging at full speed, coming clear of the convoy as the ships scattered in all directions. The senior second officer had come to the bridge to take over the watch; the senior third remained to act as second watchkeeper. Distantly

164

there had been more attacks, more torpedo hits: Kemp had counted no less than thirteen and currently had no information as to whether the ships concerned were afloat or sunk. There had been only three mayday calls and it could be assumed that those three ships had gone down: the calls had not been repeated.

Greene came to the bridge and saluted the Commodore. He reported, 'Taken over command, sir.'

'Thank you, Captain. I'm sorry it had to be this way.'

'Yes indeed.'

'What's it like below?'

'Everything under control. No panic. All troops at their boat stations, sir.'

Kemp nodded, lifted his binoculars and once again studied the sea's surface, sweeping all around. So far as could be seen, there were no torpedoes running. He could have chosen a lucky course, but that couldn't be banked upon. He looked away towards the destroyer escorts: he couldn't pick them out now, but he saw the evidence of attack, the results of the exploding depth-charges. Some of them must surely reach their targets, the U-boats wouldn't get away without losses. Kemp thought ahead: such ships as remained to re-form the convoy at the rendezvous later would still not be in the clear. Soon after they had re-formed, they would come within the range of Goering's *Luftwaffe*, the reconnaissance Focke-Wulfs and the bombers and the torpedo-bombers that in many ways were worse than the U-boats. Kemp sent up a prayer that the aircraft-carrier from the Home Fleet would reach them in time. Her fighters would be more than welcome as a better bet than the anti-aircraft fire from the escort.

[iii]

'All right, Crump?'

'Yes, Mr Portway, thank you.' At emergency stations, Crump became one of the below-decks fire parties working in the second steward's section. Currently he was standing by a fire hydrant, ready to spin the handwheel and bring the water to swell out the hoses.

'Nasty, that ammo ship,' Portway remarked. The word had spread to the troglodytes below decks as to what the vast

165

explosion had been due and all hands were expectant of something similar happening at any moment to themselves; but Portway's thoughts were still centred mainly around his personal problems and he was being nice to Crump, just in case. He said, 'I could do with a drink.'

Crump made no comment.

'Care for one yourself, would you? In my cabin.' Portway, in charge of his section, had a fairly roving commission and wouldn't be missed if he made it a quickie. He said as much.

'No, thank you, Mr Portway. Not in action.' Crump's whole bearing was a rebuke. Portway flushed and turned his back, stifling a temptation to tell Crump to fuck off.

[iv]

The purser's staff had all the cash checked and balanced, a nightly routine at sea in wartime, and ready in bags to be sent aboard the lifeboats if they had to abandon. There was plenty of it, in Canadian dollars and sterling, notes and coins, the notes largely fivers all ready for paying off the crew when they reached their home port, preparatory to re-signing the same hands, in the main. Pemmel took personal charge of the Articles of Agreement and the as yet uncompleted Portage Bill, the basis of the crew accounts. These were in his briefcase, and the briefcase was close by his side as he sat in his private office taking sips from his whisky flask.

His telephone went: it was the surgery calling. 'Purser speaking . . . yes, Jackie?'

'It's the doctor, Andy.'

Pemmel sat straighter in his chair. 'What about him?' If the doctor had been taken bad . . . Jackie could be for it, not having called Barnes in. 'Bad, is he?'

There was a brittle laugh. 'Not that! Better if anything – mobile, anyway. He's not in his cabin.'

'Where is he, then?'

'That's just it. I don't know. He's certainly not in the surgery or the sick bay. No one seems to have seen him.'

'Heads?'

'Not there either. Not his own, anyway – bathroom's empty.'

166

Jackie's voice gave away her anxiety. 'I was wondering if I should let the bridge know?'

'Why, Jackie? They'll have enough on their plate – Captain dead, ship in the middle of a bloody great mass of U-boats –'

'Yes, I know all that. Can't you guess what I've got in mind, Andy?'

Pemmel's lips framed a whistle. 'You mean he could be suicidal?'

'Yes! The state he was in, the state he's been in so long, come to that. I'm terribly worried . . .'

'All right, Jackie. I'm all ready here and the DP can cope if the bridge wants anything, which I doubt if they will. I'll have a look around myself, do some questioning. I'll ring you later.'

Pemmel put down the receiver, picked up his cap and briefcase and left the office. He'd talked of questioning but that would take too long and might lead nowhere. He went straight up on deck, to the open section of C deck alongside the square ports of the peacetime staterooms to port and starboard. No sign of the doctor; and the same on B deck, where he looked into the big main lounge, empty but for duty hands. In the lounge he did ask questions: no one had seen the doctor.

He climbed to the boat deck, one deck up from the embarkation deck that was crammed with troops. The boats had been swung out earlier on, their gripes cast off and the lowerers standing by the falls ready for such orders as might come from the bridge. Again, no one had seen the doctor. Pemmel shrugged: the old soak could be anywhere and Jackie was panicking. In Pemmel's view one of the heads was the obvious answer; Doc had done that before, he could do it again. Lavatories meant privacy and a cloak against having to perform duties, a cloak against decision and a drunken state. But this wasn't a time to mount a search of all the heads in the ship – there were so many of them. Another point: suicidal doctors had better means of self-disposal than jumping overboard.

Or had they?

To get at drugs or whatnot would mean a visit to the surgery. The doctor might keep a stock in his cabin but that was unlikely to be the case without his staff knowing of it. There were such things as drug checks, and keys to drug lockers.

Pemmel blew out his cheeks in uncertainty. He looked out

167

from the boat deck, past the naval gunnery rates at the close-range weapons mounted before and abaft the funnel casing and at the after end, looked out at the moonlit sea that covered the menace below, the submarines that even now might be coming to periscope depth to line up their torpedo-tubes on the *Ardara*. Along the deck came Petty Officer Frapp, making contact with his close-range gunners.

Pemmel stopped him. 'Have you seen the ship's doctor, by any chance?'

'No, sir, not that I know of. Wouldn't know him by sight, not unless I saw his uniform like.'

'Oh, well . . .' Pemmel shrugged.

'What would he be doing up here, sir?'

You didn't say the doctor was being half regarded as a potential suicide. Pemmel said, 'I wouldn't know. Taking the air, perhaps.'

Frapp nodded and turned away. Then, suddenly, he turned aside and went at the rush to the port guardrail. Pemmel followed, his heart beating rapidly. 'Christ Almighty,' Frapp said.

'What is it?'

'Man overboard, port side aft.' For the second time that night Frapp raised his voice in a bellow to the bridge, repeating what he had just said.

'Lifebuoy,' Pemmel said, looking about him.

'No, sir.'

'No? Why? What the devil d'you –'

'Prolong the agony, sir, that's all it'd do. Skipper won't stop engines, nor will any other ship, stands to reason. Anyway, likely he'll have been drawn into the propellers by now.'

Feeling sick, Pemmel looked out astern. He couldn't see anything. Frapp said, 'You was asking about the quack, sir.'

'Yes . . .'

Frapp jerked a hand aft. 'I reckon that was him. I just see the gold stripes. Don't know about the red cloth. Not enough light.'

Pemmel turned away and climbed to the bridge. The *Ardara* was still moving ahead – as Frapp had forecast, no checking of her way to look for a man gone overboard. War was war. Pemmel made his report to the acting master. Kemp was listening when Pemmel told the story, and he said, 'Frapp was right. And if what *you* feared was right, then he wanted to go. If it was the doctor.

168

How sure can we be?'

They couldn't; but Pemmel was certain in his own mind. Staff Captain Greene said that a full search of the ship would be made as soon as conditions permitted and if the doctor was found aboard then there would be a roll-call against the crew list. The army units embarked would be told to carry out their own muster.

But that was not to happen.

SIXTEEN

The King was in his counting-house, counting out his money . . .
the line from the nursery rhyme was going through Pemmel's
mind as he returned to his office and walked past the bagged cash
in the main office. Why had he bothered, why did anyone ever
bother? It was only money and if it was lost recompense would
presumably be made by the Admiralty. But you still didn't lose
the Line's money if you could avoid it. Pemmel had looked in at
the surgery and told Jackie what had happened and he'd left her
very upset and blaming herself. If only she'd reported to Barnes,
or done something to ensure that the doctor hadn't been left
alone. Pemmel said if he wanted to go, why not let him? He was
better off now than if he'd lived to get the push, the push into a
living death with no money to keep himself boozed up. Jackie
hadn't liked that; she was dedicated to saving life. So often,
Pemmel thought, the medical profession simply didn't use their
imaginations.

He had left the surgery and gone back to his office just four
minutes before the two torpedoes hit the *Ardara*, one for'ard, the
other aft.

[ii]

The concussion, the flame and smoke, were tremendous. The
two torpedoes had hit almost simultaneously. The hit for'ard was
immediately below the bridge on the starboard side and a lot of
the blast swept upwards. Kemp was sent flying: he had been in
the starboard wing, braced against the guardrail and using his

170

binoculars. For a moment he lay stunned, then felt Williams sitting him upright.

'Are you all right, sir?'

'Yes.' Painfully, his head muzzy, Kemp got to his feet with the assistance of Williams' steadying arm. 'Reports, Williams. State of damage. God! All those troops. Where's the brigadier?'

'Here,' a voice said. The bridge was becoming enveloped in smoke and there were screams coming up from below. 'Guess you'd better get the boats away, Commodore. Or the Captain had.'

'We'll assess the damage first,' Kemp said. He gave his head a shake. 'Signalman?'

Leading Signalman Mathias was already in attendance, waiting for orders. 'Yes, sir?'

'Make to cs29 from Commodore . . . am hit fore and aft. Will report damage soonest possible.'

'Aye, aye, sir.' Mathias ran for his SP and began clacking out the Rear-Admiral's call-sign, raising him at the extremity of vs range. cs29 would get the unspoken part of the message: U-boats in the *Ardara*'s vicinity. It wouldn't be long before the destroyers altered course and began an attack. By now the reports were coming in from the various sections of the ship and to Kemp's ears they sounded bad. There were big holes in the plating and plenty of water had come inboard; but the watertight bulkheads and doors were holding, leaks apart. There was fire fore and aft but the fire parties were in action and coping – that was something. The engine-room was itself more or less intact; the hit aft had not penetrated but it had been close and there was a heavy weight of water piled up against the fore bulkhead. Chief Engineer Burrows couldn't guess how long it might hold. If he was forced to give an answer, it would be that it wouldn't last all that long. The chief steward was one of those who reported by telephone to the bridge: most of the watertight doors had been shut earlier but a few had been allowed open until the torpedoes had hit, for the handling of the hoses and so on. These had now been closed by automatic control from the bridge: and a number of the chief steward's department were shut in behind them. Was there a chance they might be opened to let through those that hadn't drowned already?

Greene looked at Kemp. Kemp, his face a grim mask, said,

171

'Very briefly, by sections. They'll have to be fast . . . we could be hit again. And if water comes through, they're to be shut again immediately.'

[iii]

They said that when you drowned all your past life flashed before your eyes, a sort of fast-run film show just for your personal benefit. Mr Portway just didn't want to know if and when the time came, although it would be a way out. Thurrock, Grays and Tilbury just wouldn't matter any more. Mabel and Mrs Portway would be left to get on with it and Mrs Portway would inherit the house. She'd be glad about that. Mr Portway, fat and flabby and very far now from being any sort of Romeo, pushed ahead of the rising water, or rather through it as it started to reach his armpits, making for the nearest watertight door, all ready to bang and bang and shout himself hoarse. Luck was with him: just as he reached the sealing door, it opened and he flung himself into the gap before it could shut again. Hands dragged him through and a gush of seawater flooded along the alleyway before the door was once again shut. No one else made it. In the section behind the watertight door many men were trapped: soon their bodies would be forced upwards by the rising water to impact against the deckhead and all air would be displaced by the sea's encroachment. One of them was ex-Colour-Sergeant Crump, thinking, as his last moments came, of that other war when he had manned a heavy gun-battery aboard a cruiser. He had little to remember other than his service at sea.

[iv]

In his office Pemmel supervised the transfer of the cash and his briefcase to the embarkation deck, ready to be put into the boats. He and his staff mustered at their various boat stations, where they would be in charge of embarking the troops in their sections under the overall command of the deck officers. That was, if the order came to abandon.

Pemmel was shaking like a leaf. He wished to God Jackie was

with him. He'd looked out for her in the awful confusion, the milling of too many bodies, but hadn't found her. She had her own station, her own part to play. Again – if they abandoned.

Pemmel said in desperation, 'Why the sod don't they give the order?' They would be better off in the boats; you didn't stop the ship in the middle of a U-boat pack to pick up one man gone overboard – true; but the naval escort, and the other ships in the convoy if they were close enough, would certainly mount a rescue operation for the *Ardara*'s vital passengers.

[v]

Kemp didn't believe the time had yet come to abandon. The ship still had power and although she was going lower in the water they might get away with it so long as there was no further attack – the pumps might overcome the apparent leak of the water through sprung plates and watertight sections damaged by the explosions. Kemp knew the *Ardara* and her capacities well enough; but for form's sake he asked Greene's opinion.

'What d'you think, Captain?'

'The same as I believe you do, sir. She's not a goner yet.'

'Right! We'll hang on.' Kemp lifted his binoculars to the *Ardara*'s starboard quarter. 'They're coming. The destroyers. Now we'll see some action.' He picked up the microphone of the Tannoy and switched on. 'This is the Commodore speaking to you all. The destroyers are moving in. If you hear explosions, they'll be the depth-charges. In the meantime the ship is still seaworthy and we're going to try to bring her through.'

He switched off. His face was sombre, the lines more deeply etched than before. It was going to be a long haul to the safety of the Clyde anchorage.

Below in the sick bay Jackie Ord, hearing Kemp's voice, taking in his words of encouragement, was thinking similarly: for many of the men who had been brought to her care the haul was going to be far too long. They wouldn't see the welcoming arms of the land, far from it. Mangled bodies . . . as on the outward voyage there had been screams as the quivering, burned flesh had been brought in. The horrible sounds had died by now; the pain-killing drugs had had their effect. There were too many injured

173

for the sick bay to accommodate; Dr Barnes and the second nursing sister, helped by the army medics, were treating people where they lay throughout the ship and the enclosed decks had taken on the air of a casualty clearing station. Soon after the Commodore had been on the Tannoy the crump of explosions was heard, close explosions that seemed to ring throughout the ship as the depth-charges reached their settings and went up. They clanged through the engine-room where Burrows and his staff were watching the bulkhead and noting the seepage, the water running down the strained seams, a few places where there was a stream of water zipping through holes left by sheared rivets. These were being plugged but Burrows feared there would be more, feared that he detected an ominous bulge that could mean the entire bulkhead might give under the weight and pressure of the water. The section immediately before the engine-room had had the pumps working but the sea was winning.

He got on the telephone to the bridge. Greene answered.

Burrows reported. 'I'm worried about the fore bulkhead. Too much strain. If that goes . . . we all go.'

Greene said, 'I'll send assistance. Shoring-up beams might do the trick.' Orders were passed to the bosun: as many seamen as could be spared, to reach the engine-room at the double, taking timber for the ship's carpenter to rig shoring-up beams, well chocked down to take the strain. Just as Greene had passed the order, there was a shout from Mathias.

'Starboard beam, sir – U-boat coming to the surface!'

They all looked. A cigar shape was breaking surface, bows angled upwards. A gun was seen on the casing, then the conning-tower with water streaming white from the washports. Kemp called for the searchlight to be switched on. When the beam steadied blindingly, men were seen emerging from below, through the hatch into the conning-tower. Some climbed down to the casing and ran for the gun. The U-boat's stern remained beneath the water: she had damage aft. Kemp called for Williams.

'Sir?'

'Open fire, point of aim the gun.'

'Aye, aye, sir!' The message went to all guns; at the after six-inch Petty Officer Frapp, who had already laid and trained on the

174

emerging U-boat, opened fire on the instant of receiving the order. There was a flash, an ear-splitting crack and a stench of cordite.

'Bloody miss,' Frapp snarled. He brought his range down a little: the next fall of shot was short. By this time the U-boat's gun was itself in action, and a shell went close above the *Ardara*'s bridge, its wind making all the personnel duck. It whined away to port, harmlessly. Kemp saw one of the destroyers moving in at speed, her 4.7-inch guns blazing away from before her bridge. The U-boat hadn't a chance: her gun vanished in a red flash, and when the smoke cleared Kemp saw that the conning-tower, too, was shattered and lifeless. A moment later the bow's angle increased sharply, and then the submarine slid back beneath the surface, stern first.

'One gone at all events,' Kemp said.

Now the destroyer was calling by lamp. Mathias reported: The destroyer was asking if the *Ardara* was seaworthy.

Kemp said, 'Answer: Yes.'

[vi]

Dawn came up: the *Ardara* was still afloat, the engine-room was still intact and the ship was steaming at reduced speed so as not to strain the watertight sections further. There had been no further attack: apparently it had been just the one U-boat that had despatched the two torpedoes. The escort reported no less than twelve U-boats believed destroyed. It was anyone's guess how many more remained; contact had been lost. The Nazis could have gone deep to lie doggo with the intention of mounting another attack later, or they could have drawn off, preferring not to take further risks against the exceptionally strong escort. They had had an impressive enough bag as it was: Kemp believed, from reports received, that eighteen ships had gone or were severely disabled. The count would be made finally at the rendezvous. Before dawn had come up, the reports of casualties aboard the *Ardara* had been made to the Commodore: thirty-seven of the ship's company dead, forty-one wounded. The troops had been luckier, since they had almost all been on deck at their boat stations: two officers and four NCOs had died

175

whilst on their rounds below, checking that all men had cleared the troop decks. There was a corporal with a leg broken when he'd been knocked endways during a mild stampede along the embarkation deck when the torpedoes had hit.

Kemp had stayed on the bridge throughout the night; the ship had remained closed up at emergency stations. When the reports had come in from the escort that there were no more contacts, Kemp stood the men down and the galleys produced breakfast. Williams said, 'You could do with some sleep, sir.'

Kemp had been almost reeling about the bridge: because of this he had wedged himself into the corner of the wing. He said, 'I think you're right, Williams.'

'I'll call you at once if necessary, sir.'

'I'm not much use as I am.' The effect of the benzedrine had worn off and left Kemp with something like a twitch: he was dead tired physically but mentally he was racing away on a cloud though not thinking constructively: he knew he wouldn't in fact find sleep but his body cried out for rest. He went below to his cabin. His steward brought breakfast: he felt better after he had eaten, but his mind was still too active for sleep. So many things to worry about . . . things big and little. One of the lesser ones was the trouble with the second steward . . . but Pemmel had said he could sort it out on his own. Kemp hoped he could. That young nurse; Kemp felt immense sympathy for her. Not much older than his own sons – somewhere around the early twenties, he'd have said. His thoughts went homeward, ahead of the stricken ship, covering the sea miles to the London River and a small Kent village. He wondered if the dead ship's surgeon had had anyone to worry about him, wondered what the effect might be on someone at home when the news went through of a suicide. But that could be covered and if Kemp had anything to do with it, it would be. 'Lost at sea' was always a useful phrase.

[vii]

In the engine-room Burrows stood on the starting-platform feeling rather like the boy who stood on the burning deck except that in Burrows' case no one had fled. He looked down at a slop of water across the deck plates, water that rolled from side to side in

176

time to the rolling of the ship. The level had increased but only a little. The pumps were just about coping. It was a matter of time alone. They might make it and they might not: the bulkhead was shaky, and it alone stood between safety and disaster. If it went, it would go fast, very fast, one fell swoop as they said. If the rate of leak continued to rise, it would be much slower but it would end the same way: a flooded engine-room. Then they would have either to abandon or be taken in tow. The *Ardara*, in the absence of proper ocean-going rescue tugs, would be a heavy tow. Kemp, who thought of everything before anyone else did, had already asked via cs29 for such specialist tugs to be sent out from home waters – just in case. But it was still a matter of time, Burrows knew. Time and the enemy, who would be in a position to make short work of any tugs. And of the *Ardara* come to that . . .

The following day they made the rendezvous, the point where what was left of the convoy was under orders to re-assemble. Still there had been no further attack, at any rate on the *Ardara*. Something of a miracle, Burrows thought, or maybe there was a better target somewhere else – Churchill coming back across the Atlantic perhaps, or had he already made the return passage aboard the *Prince of Wales*? There was, of course, a massive security clamp-down on the battleship's movements.

One by one the ships of the HX convoy converged on the rendezvous and signals were exchanged between cs29, Captain(D) in the destroyer leader, and the Commodore. Kemp and Williams made a count as the ships appeared from their different directions under a bright blue sky: sixteen ships. The losses had been even heavier than they had feared. The HX had left Halifax with in fact more ships than the outward OB from the Clyde and other ports. Ships for home had been tagged on to them, fast ships that could maintain the speed required of a troop convoy. Two of the liners had gone: one was the *Aratapu* of the Mediterranean-Australia Line. The men aboard the *Ardara* would have lost many friends and shipmates. Kemp himself had sailed with her master, then staff captain, on many peacetime voyages through the Suez Canal to Sydney.

'A bad day for you, sir,' Williams said.

'Yes. But now we have to get the *Ardara* home. I wonder where those bloody tugs are!' Earlier a signal had come in cypher,

177

indicating that the Commodore's request was being met but giving no further information. Kemp thought about the water rising in the engine-room . . . if the engines flooded, they would wallow around the ocean, more than ever a sitting target for the Nazis. By this time their position on the chart was well eastward of Cape Farewell and every turn of the screws brought them closer to the enemy's air and U-boat bases along the coast of occupied France. Kemp paced the bridge as he had done for so many days, deep in thought. As he saw it, there were three alternatives open to him: as Commodore it was within his decision to alter the convoy's route and he could order an alteration further south, to avoid the danger zone that lay between the convoy and the approaches to the Bloody Foreland on the north-western tip of County Donegal or to the Lizard for the northward passage of the Irish Sea for the Clyde. He could drop south and then make his northing from a safer position; or he could do the opposite and go north to start with, and then drop down past Iceland and Cape Wrath for the Clyde.

But each held its own dangers.

The southerly approach would bring him too close in to the French airfields; the northerly one opened up the possibility of a German pocket-battleship or such lurking in the Denmark Strait, ready to pounce.

The third alternative was to maintain his course and chance the Luftwaffe. In this war, there was no safety anywhere at sea. All you could do was to try to peer into the minds of the enemy, of Hitler's high command or his own personal hallucinations. The Führer was well known to have those brainstorms that he called visions or premonitions sent by God to direct him aright. And only God could tell what he had put into the Führer's mind in regard to the *Ardara* and her consorts. In the meantime there were other considerations to be borne in mind: any deviation north or south would extend the time spent at sea, and the *Ardara* might not make it. Also, there could be no question of breaking wireless silence again – not now the convoy had re-assembled – to divert the ocean-going rescue tugs or the aircraft-carrier presumably now well out from her home base . . .

Kemp turned. 'Williams?'

'Sir?'

'Make to cs29 repeated Captain(D) from Commodore: Propose

178

no alteration to route. Convoy will proceed as ordered for the Clyde.'

'Yes, sir –'

'And then inform individual masters.'

'Yes, sir.' Williams stood there, pencil poised over his naval message pad. 'Sir, the engines.'

'What about them, Williams?'

'We're not maintaining the normal speed of the convoy, sir, and –'

'No. Not at this moment. But we shall. I propose to risk the bulkhead, Williams. If I dropped out, I would need to split the escort – our troops can't be left without proper protection. To split the escort would be to put the other ships at too much risk. We must proceed in company.'

'But –'

'That's all, Williams. See that my signals are made at once.'

Kemp turned away and walked to the starboard wing of the bridge. He had made his decision: like many a man before him, he could only hope it was the right one. So much, as always, depended upon luck.

SEVENTEEN

Mr Portway had had luck and he knew it: luck, plus a certain amount of personal physical push. He was sorry for the poor blokes that hadn't made it, but he preferred not to think too much about them. He thought, nevertheless, of night steward Crump, Crump had bought it, his body wouldn't be retrieved from behind the watertight section until the ship was in dockyard hands for repair. That was a bit of luck too: the principal witness for the prosecution would never give evidence now and Portway reckoned he was safe from all that. No official report had ever been made and Mr Pemmel could go and stuff himself.

Which was how Pemmel himself was seeing it. Better to let the whole thing drop: better for Jackie Ord, better for the Line. Let Portway crow if he wanted to. He certainly wouldn't broadcast anything and the crowing would be between the three of them. And Portway could sort out his matrimonial affairs all by himself and good luck to him. From what Jackie had said, it looked as though Portway's wife would be the one to sort him out. Pemmel had visions of an empurpled face and a raised umbrella and a hand deeply in the till of house ownership after the divorce.

On the bridge, Brigadier O'Halloran, much concerned by the loss of many of the troops aboard the *Aratapu*, was kept busy with signals to and from the ships of the convoy that had mounted a rescue operation to bring the survivors scrambling up the nets either from the lowered boats or from the sea direct. He was in a carping mood, hinting that the British Navy was to blame for the loss of the troopship. The army, he seemed to suggest, wouldn't have let it happen. Kemp shrugged it off; they were closing home waters and soon the brigadier would leave the ship, taking his

180

curious attitudes with him. Kemp's hopes were rising; the engine-room bulkhead was taking the extra strain of higher speed and the pumps were still just coping. The sea was clear of contacts and so far no German aircraft had appeared. It wasn't long before Kemp knew why: the coded weather reports came in on the wireless routines, bringing tidings of adverse conditions ahead. It was likely enough the Luftwaffe would be grounded – good news so far as it went.

But Kemp and Greene, and Chief Engineer Burrows, had a strained bulkhead to worry about, a bulkhead open to the sea via the hole that had proved impossible to plug effectively.

[ii]

Burrows was watching carefully; like Kemp and Greene on the bridge, Burrows hadn't left his place of duty for very many hours past. The engine-room was his kingdom and when the kingdom was threatened the king must be there. Burrows would never have it said that he'd skulked from a bulkhead that in his view might go at any moment. He could be wrong and he knew it; he wasn't Jesus Christ. And he understood the reasons given by the bridge for keeping the engine-room manned and the screws turning. A hell of a lot of troops depended for their lives . . . a lot of generals spread around an empire under threat depended on a supply of cannon-fodder. All true.

But still!

The water continued to slop from side to side, deepening almost imperceptibly, and there was the sea sound from immediately the other side of the bulkhead, a surge and slither and a curious drumming as the weather deteriorated as promised in the met reports. Bloody bad luck . . . what was good against the dive bombers was a sight less good for damaged bulkheads and Burrows didn't like the way the plates were sending up a sort of groan, a real sound of impending doom.

Burrows looked upwards, through the maze of steel ladders. It was a long way to the air-lock and the exit to the engineers' alleyway.

Kemp put down the telephone from the engine-room, his face deeply troubled. 'Where are those God-damn tugs!'

Williams decided no response was required. With the Commodore he looked out ahead. The day was darkening unseasonably early thanks to the filthy weather they were steaming into. Cold and clammy and soon the rain would come. The seas were high and the *Ardara*'s stem was butting in deep and sending back heavy spray. Some hours earlier Kemp had ordered a reduction in speed once again, had slowed the whole convoy for the sake of the *Ardara*'s engine-room. There was little risk now from the enemy: Hitler had been cheated by the weather. And the weather was the *Ardara*'s enemy as well.

Kemp was speaking again, referring to that last report from Burrows. 'Sooner them than me!'

'Sir?'

'Down below, Williams. Talk about guts! The men who choose to go to sea in engine-rooms . . . up here we're in touch with the elements, with the fresh air.'

'I see what you mean, sir.'

'Do you?' Kemp gave a harsh laugh. 'I doubt if even I do! That damned engine-room . . . it could become a coffin inside a few seconds. I've a good mind –' He broke off as an excited shout came from the signalman on watch. 'What's that?'

'Vessels ahead, sir! Fine on the port bow, sir!'

A moment later identification came from the masthead lookout who should have seen anything before the signalman lower down. The telephone whined and Kemp answered it himself. As he slammed it down again he said, 'The tugs. And the aircraft-carrier.' He took up the telephone to the engine-room, this time not waiting for Greene. 'Commodore here, Chief. Clear the engine-room. The tugs are coming up. We won't risk it any longer.'

[iv]

Burrows put down the phone and once again looked up through the network of ladders. As a precaution he had sent as many hands as possible up those ladders, just to give them a better chance of making it to the air-lock. Himself, he had remained on the starting-platform with his senior second engineer. He passed the order that had come down from the bridge.

'All hands, clear the engine spaces! Out and away!'

As he said the words, he looked again at the bulkhead. He could have sworn there was a more pronounced bulge, even that the shoring beams were starting to bend, and the run of water down the sprung seams was becoming a river. Just about in time, he thought, just about in bloody time . . . he ran for the foot of the nearest ladder, just behind his number two. The senior second went up fast while the others, already half-way up, climbed at the rush for the air-lock. As Burrows put a foot on the bottom tread of the ladder, his other foot slid on a patch of oil and he lurched sideways, his grip came off the ladder uprights and he spun along the plates just as one of the shoring beams bent and broke with a crack like gunfire, followed by the others, and the bulkhead bulged inwards. A solid wall of water suddenly released crashed into the engine-room, thunderously, devastatingly, smashing ladders and steam pipes, gauges and dials and machinery, breaking electrical circuits. The chief engineer's body was hurled away to pulp itself against the still-spinning shafts.

[v]

With the engine spaces flooded, and the ship down by the stern but held in the care of the tugs, Kemp came back once again to the Clyde with the remnant of the HX convoy steaming between the lines of the warship escort. Up the Irish Sea to the North Channel under leaden skies and a blustery wind, turn to starboard short of the great rock of Ailsa Craig to enter the Firth and move on past Turnberry and Ayr away to starboard, Arran and Inchmarnock

Water to port, through the narrows of the Cumbraes, past Toward Point at the entry to the Kyles of Bute beyond Rothesay Bay, through the boom to proceed slowly for the anchorage at the Tail o' the Bank. There was a press of troops and ship's company along the open decks as the convoy moved towards journey's end. Today Scotland looked grim and grey beneath its rain, no hint of the glories of snow-capped winter mountains and deep blue lochs, no hint of the skirl of the pipes to welcome the convoy in, the convoy that arrived as anonymously as the OB had left less than a month earlier.

Not much in terms of time elapsed. Plenty in terms of war-lost men and ships, plenty to be laid eventually at Adolf Hitler's door.

Many thoughts went out across the sullen waters off Greenock as the *Ardara* moved in towards her temporary anchorage as signalled by the King's Harbour Master. Williams looked at clouded skies and rain-slashed water and the depressing sight of Greenock on a wet day. He would get some leave before he accompanied Commodore Mason Kemp on another convoy; or he might get a new and different appointment. As to that he couldn't prophesy. But he knew that he faced an uninspiring leave in Hounslow, listening to tales of ARP and the office – that was if he went home and he saw no other prospect unless he managed to pick up a popsie in Greenock or Glasgow *en route* for the south . . . like Petty Officer Frapp, he was more or less doomed to a home leave. Not that Frapp felt quite that way, home was home and he was fond of the missus but he shrank from hearing her voice after the initial welcome to a returning hero from the sea. He knew her thoughts were of heroism or some such bunk, but she never wanted to hear the details – maybe they'd be too mundane and she didn't want her illusions shattered, but whatever it was she preferred her own moans to his. Frapp's son-in-law, if he was around, might be some solace, someone to have a pint with in the local even if he was a Brylcreem Boy. And after leave, what? Frapp knew the answer to that one: another bloody convoy, and another, and another after that, world without end. You just soldiered on, hoping for the best every trip until bloody Adolf wrote your name on a projy or a torpedo. Or you got through the war and then got chucked back on the civvy scrap-heap.

Mr Portway, like the deceased ship's doctor before him, had

184

been having trouble with his bowels for some days and was not far off wishing he'd copped it behind that watertight bulkhead. If it wasn't for the house, he'd leave his wife – transfer, like an appointment to a new ship, to Mabel. If she would have him now; in fact he knew from her letter in Halifax that she wouldn't, daft bitch.

Mr Portway had no loopholes at all. Maybe he would cut and run from the whole bang shoot and find another willing woman, up north. But there was still the house . . .

And Kemp?

Commodore Kemp had tried to keep his thoughts at bay: the death of Burrows had shaken him. If he'd given the order to clear just a few seconds before, Burrows might have lived. That was something that was due to remain with him for a lifetime. There were others too: so many ships lost, so many other lives – even that sad suicide. Perhaps he, Kemp, couldn't be blamed, but you always did blame yourself and wonder if you'd handled things right. He recalled how the doctor had rung the bridge, asking for Williams . . . the natural reaction was anger but perhaps there could have been another response, a request to someone, say the purser, to go and keep the doctor company till he'd sobered up and simmered down. As the *Ardara* crept on past Princes Pier and Albert Harbour, other painful thoughts came to Kemp: Leading Signalman Mouncey, by now presumably home to a wife dead in Devonport; Redgrave . . . but Redgrave of course was only one among so many, it was just the fact that his name had come to Kemp's attention over the desperate efforts of the *Stephen Starr* to catch up with the convoy and not be what she was, a perishing nuisance. And the people ashore? The British public at large would never know about the HX convoy. No news would be released about the losses . . .

Williams approached the Commodore, looking troubled. Kemp asked, 'What's the matter, Williams? You look thoughtful.'

'Yes, sir.'

'Out with it, then, but don't take too long.'

'It's all right, sir, thank you.'

'Very well, Williams.' Kemp stood motionless as the tugs took the ship up to her anchorage, the second offiicer watching the bearings on the azimuth circle. Any moment now the tugs would

185

be cast off, the Captain would lift his red anchor flag and when he brought it down the anchor would rattle out on its cable in clouds of rust-red dust. Just before that happened someone switched on the BBC News and Kemp heard something about air raids over England. He caught Williams' eye. 'Did you hear the start of the news, Williams?' he asked.

'Yes, sir.'

So that was it, Kemp thought. He said, 'Tell me.'

Williams said, 'Heavy air raids on London, sir. Widely dispersed.'

'I see. Anywhere else?'

'Kent, sir. They weren't specific. And Portsmouth.'

Kemp nodded, his face expressionless. Kent was a large area, so was London. Meopham, Hounslow . . . and Frapp lived in Portsmouth. You came in from a convoy, from a sea at war, to enjoy the blessings of the land for a spell, and all you could do was hope the blessings were still there and not scattered to the wind as in the case of Redgrave's wife and children. Well – they would all know soon enough. Kemp brought his mind back from Meopham to see Greene lift his anchor flag and bring it sharply down in the final unspoken order of the convoy.